BEYO

My head jerked up and ~~faced~~
me, black brows meet~~ing~~
gleam. He advanced slo~~wly~~ ~~ou?''~~ ~~b~~are
arms with a bruising gri~~p~~

My drawings fell from ~~my~~ ~~nerv~~eless fingers. All my
previous fear of him returned. Somewhere, sometime, could this man have spelled danger to me? I
was aware of our isolation . . . the silent, unfamiliar house with its winding, secret corridors . . . the
imprisoning fog . . . the mournful tolling in the
bay . . .

"Miss Blair," he demanded harshly, *"have we ever
met before today?"*

Dell Books also by Marion Clarke

THE SUMMERHOUSE

The Jade Pagoda

MARION CLARKE

A DELL BOOK

Published by
Dell Publishing
a division of
Bantam Doubleday Dell Publishing Group, Inc.
666 Fifth Avenue
New York, New York 10103

ISBN: 0-440-21182-4

Printed in the United States of America

Published simultaneously in Canada

December 1992

10 9 8 7 6 5 4 3 2 1

RAD

AUTHOR'S NOTE

Some of the characters such as Darius Ogden Mills, Count Rezanov and his Concepcíon, as well as other famous people, are as accurate as research can make them.

The streets of early San Francisco are portrayed with loving care. However, Dupont, once the main street in Chinatown, was changed much later to Grant Avenue. Morton Street, the alley of prostitutes, became an ironic "Maiden Lane."

Evil flourished in the City, but so did a wonderful feeling of adventure, tolerance, and love. Always love! Love of people, love of good food, love of fun.

In that respect, San Francisco really hasn't changed at all.

I'm proud to call it my hometown.

1

The fateful day when I encountered Drake Wynfield began the same as many others. I had no idea that I was about to meet a man who would fill me with the strangest, most inexplicable sense of fear I had ever known. I felt that somewhere, sometime, this man had brought me to the very brink of terror. But where? And when? I didn't know or I couldn't remember.

There was to be a long and turbulent passage before the answers came.

Today, as I drove my buggy along the busy streets of San Francisco, I could only think about the financial difficulty in which I found myself. Ever since my father died, I had waited and hoped that someone would request my services as an interior decorator. I was highly trained, enthusiastic, and knew the field, yet no one came to hire me. So for the past six months bills accumulated and my bank balance dwindled to an alarming figure.

Of course, I soon realized why I was ignored. My father had bequeathed his decorating business to a female who was trying to succeed in a male-dominated world.

It seemed so unfair. As I glanced around, I saw hordes of busy workers, shops filled with eager patrons, the stirring of a vibrant, prosperous city. But all these successful people, these affluent shop owners, all those offering professional services . . . were *men*.

With a deep sigh, I tethered my horse, Lady, to a post and looked wistfully at my shop. A gold-lettered sign proclaimed: "Blair and Company. Interior Decorating for the Discriminating." How proud I'd been of that "and Company" when I came back from the East. It meant that now I was a full-fledged partner. Alas, I hadn't realized that Papa's ill health had nearly drained his finances, and when he died, I had to carry on almost penniless.

However, I squared my shoulders and told myself as I did every day: Who knows? Perhaps quite soon I'll get a client. Briskly, I marched into my shop, the door bell tinkling my arrival.

Immediately, Conan Blye appeared, coming through the back door where a yard and stable separated his workplace from the shop. He was a big, good-looking Irishman who had been my father's assistant and now was mine.

"Lesley, here's a letter from Drake Wynfield!" he cried, his face flushed with excitement, almost as ruddy as his full mustache and tousled hair. "Remember? The owner of the Jade Pagoda who wanted information about redecorating his house. Bedad, I could hardly wait for you to get here."

My voice choked. "Heavens, I applied for that assignment several weeks ago. I had nearly forgotten about it. Oh, Conan, let's see what he says!"

With an arm around my shoulders, Conan read the letter with me:

Dear Sir:
Regarding your application for the redecorating of my house, I would like to discuss the matter with you on Thursday, the 16th of April at four o'clock. Please bring your portfolio and samples of your ideas to Cliffside Manor.
Yours, Drake Wynfield.

"Oh, Conan, the sixteenth—why, that's today," I cried. Wildly, I stared around the shop. "He wants to see me! I must hurry. My sketches, my notebooks, oh, do I look all right? If only I'd known sooner!"

I flew to a gilt-framed mirror, tugging at my brown form-fitting jacket, fluffing out the lace jabot at my neck. My father did not believe in going into mourning over him, so when he died, I obeyed his wishes. However, today I wished that I had worn a finer outfit, although my orange felt hat was trim and stylish with its snow-white doves and wide French ribbon trailing to the knot of hair confined tidily on the back of my neck.

"You look fine, darlin'," Conan told me heartily. "I know how much you must want this assignment. What a coup it would be if the largest art dealer in the city hired you, eh? But Lesley, there might be a wee bit of a problem."

I whirled around. "What do you mean?"

"You better take another look at this. Though the envelope is simply addressed to 'Lesley Blair,' inside the salutation is 'Dear *Sir*.'"

"What of it?" I shrugged. "He made an error,

that's all. Everyone knows the name 'Lesley' can be either masculine or feminine. When I wrote to him, I merely stated that I had studied art and decoration in the East and then worked beside my father for a year."

"But for a job of this nature, usually performed by men, naturally he must expect—"

"It will be all right. He'll soon learn that I am as qualified as any man." Swiftly, I gathered up my portfolio and all the other articles I would need.

"Drake Wynfield is a strange one," Conan muttered. "There was all that talk two years ago . . ."

"Oh, Conan, I don't have time to gossip now. I can't be late for this appointment." I swept past him out the door. "Wish me luck, my lad!"

The door closed while Conan was calling something after me, but I didn't stop. As quickly as possible, I urged Lady up the steep hills toward the residential area of Sea Cliff, where the wealthy lived. My thoughts returned to Conan's concern that Mr. Wynfield might deny me the position simply because I was a woman. Feverishly, I went over all that I would say, how I would convince Mr. Wynfield that I was the right person for the job. Even if I had never handled an assignment on my own, I knew that I could do it. I *had* to do it!

My pulses raced when I arrived in front of the imposing mansion rearing above the rocky cliffs of San Francisco Bay. Cliffside was three stories high with all the usual iron lace balconies, peaks, colonnades, and fancy fretwork that was so popular today. A graveled driveway surrounded a deep green lawn.

After tying Lady to an iron post, I directed my footsteps to the huge front door and rang the bell. A sturdy, fresh-faced maid admitted me and I was led down a marble-floored hallway where great bronze statues held unlit porcelain lamps. I was ushered into a parlor of immense size then left to wait.

Thanks to a roaring fireplace, the room felt overheated and as I glanced around, I noticed it was also overcrowded, overstuffed, and much too dark. Especially hideous in my eyes were its intricately carved furniture, olive-green velour draperies, and the many little tables covered with scarves, fringe, and bric-a-brac. The whole atmosphere was stifling and I felt I could hardly breathe.

When a deep, male voice suddenly cut through the silence, I whirled around, as nervous as an animal at bay.

"Good afternoon." The man in the doorway didn't move, just stared at me, and I thought he sounded puzzled . . . or annoyed.

"G-good afternoon," I faltered, striving to sound calm. "Are you Mr. Wynfield?"

"I am. And you?"

"Miss Lesley Blair."

He repeated my name in something like astonishment and strode into the lamplight, eyeing me up and down in a manner that at another time would have seemed insulting.

But now all I could feel was shock as I saw his face more clearly: the heavy-lidded, thick-lashed amber eyes, the wavy midnight hair. He was tall, broad-shouldered, and coldly handsome. Oddly, I had a nightmarish sense of having known this person under other circumstances in some frightening and unclear ordeal. My reaction was inexplicable, and desperately I fought to shake it off.

He looked exasperated as he examined me and ran a long-fingered hand across the denseness of his hair. "I thought you were a man. That name—Lesley . . ."

I stood up straighter and said tightly, "You erred, sir. I am a woman."

His eyes swept over me. "So I see. And are you also Roger Blair's offspring with a degree in art and interior decorating?" His firm mouth curled a little as though in disbelief.

"That all is true," I stated. "My father's shop became mine upon his death. Are you familiar with his work?"

"Yes. I've seen some of the rooms he did for Crocker, Stanford, and others on Nob Hill. They were most impressive. But I'm sorry, Miss Blair, you've had this trip for nothing. You see, I need a man, who would be harder, tougher, more able to handle workers, bargaining at ships, warehouses, and the like than a woman would be." He cleared his throat. "But at least you must take a glass of wine before you leave."

Leave? The word echoed dismayingly through my head.

He strode over to a sideboard and poured some ruby liquid into a crystal goblet. "Please sit down and drink this. You look a little faint. Are you all right?"

"Oh, yes. It's just . . . the room is rather close and warm." I sank down on a horsehair sofa with a purple velvet throw across the back. I accepted the wine as well as the delay, trying desperately to collect my thoughts.

I was reeling from his instant rejection as well as the eerie sense of déjà vu this man had given me. Slowly, I sipped the rich and fortifying liquid, telling myself I must not dwell on why Mr. Wynfield had seemed so frighteningly familiar. I was sure I never had laid eyes on him before. He was a cool, strong-looking man in his mid-thirties, dressed in fine gray serge, his satin vest crossed by a heavy gold watch chain, his cravat the color of his thick, dark hair. Perhaps it was the strangeness of his amber eyes, making me think of tawny tigers or lions in their jungles.

I looked away from him deliberately and sipped my drink. He probably had an ingrained courtesy that had kept him from ushering me out the door at once, and therefore, I now had a small chance to stall for time. But I feared it was going to be much more difficult to convince him than I had thought.

Carefully, I set my glass upon a nearby taboret, moving aside some stuffed robins on a branch and a feathered fan. "In spite of the fact that I am female, Mr. Wynfield, I don't see why it should signify—not in this case. I have often accompanied my father to shops, warehouses, and docked ships, and believe me, masculine brawn is not essential to do business with them. They are all most anxious to have buyers."

His narrowed gaze went over me and he gave a tight smile. "But isn't it an unusual occupation for a woman? A *gentlewoman*?"

Was he wondering about my morals? I drew up haughtily. "Unusual, perhaps, but don't you realize that things are changing in the world today? Just last year, two English cousins, Agnes and Rhoda Garrett, established the first interior decorating business run by women. I have read that it is quite successful in London."

He looked unimpressed and made no comment. He gave me a frowning, assessing glance. "You are very young and pretty." He made it sound like the greatest handicap.

"I am twenty-four, sir," I replied with spirit. "I have recently graduated from Vassar College and a well-known art academy in New York. I spent the past year close to my father, absorbing his teachings and then developing my own ideas."

"If you had mentioned the name of your college, I might have guessed your sex." When I opened my mouth, he stopped me with an upraised hand. "Yes, yes, most of your qualifications are above reproach. I sent for you due to the high regard I had for your father, thinking, that you were a man who wished to follow in his footsteps."

I sprang up, my hands knotted into fists. "I can't understand why a person's gender should matter in this case. There are women artists, women writers . . . Sarah Josepha Hale, editor of *Godey's Lady's Book*, constantly exhorts women to become doctors, missionaries, professors. There's a new age dawning!" I glared at him defiantly.

"Calm yourself, Miss Blair," he drawled.

I was not ready to be calm. "Can't you at least listen to my ideas? Glance through my portfolio? Try to have an open mind for a few minutes?"

"Very well."

"Don't you realize that today—" I jerked to a halt. "What did you say?"

"I will listen to your ideas and glance through your portfolio." He had acquiesced; however, his tones had not softened one iota.

I stared at his enigmatic face, then sank back to my seat, trembling a little, and placed my work upon my knees. He moved over to sit beside me on the sofa. Again I felt a flicker of alarm and again I impatiently subdued it.

"As I see it, Mr. Wynfield, San Francisco is a fairly young city, filled with new wealth and a new kind of society. After the Gold Rush in 'forty-nine, people wanted their homes to reflect everything possible to emphasize their wealth. But twenty-six years have passed since then and now another look should be considered, cleaner, fresher, more discerning. Beautiful objects that are well displayed in the Oriental manner so that nothing is overshadowed."

His voice was noncommittal. "You would suggest an Oriental look in here?"

"That would be up to you." I cleared my throat. "And your wife."

"I am a widower, and have been for the past two years, but I plan on being married again quite soon."

"Ah? Then perhaps your fiancée would care to be consulted?" Another woman might be more sympathetic, I thought, but he dashed that hope at once.

"My fiancée, Melissa Fernley, is not here yet. She will be arriving soon by train and I want the house to present a pleasant, welcoming appearance. I believe I know her tastes. She is quite amenable, gentle, sensitive, and lovely, raised in a fine old Southern home."

His thick brows drew together as he glanced around the room. "This was my first wife's taste, a trifle opulent, I fear. I was abroad so often visiting foreign ports, naturally I left the furnishing of our home to her."

My gaze traveled to chairs and sofas overburdened with plush and satin pillows, gold-swagged draperies cutting out both light and view, the walls almost obscured by oil paintings in heavy, carved gilt frames.

His oddly colored eyes surveyed me keenly as he purred, "What would you suggest, Miss Blair, just at first glance?"

If he expected me to falter, he was foiled. I answered promptly. "I have plenty of ideas. In here, I see warm tones of Chinese red and gold in draperies and upholstery, a silky beige rug or two, perhaps with a black design, inlaid lacquer tables with a few fine objects tastefully displayed. I know I could change this room and make it beautiful."

He stared at me unnervingly from beneath half-shut lids for a long moment. Perhaps my defiant manner was the wrong approach. He evidently preferred women to be "gentle, sensitive, and amenable," like his fiancée, but for the life of me, I couldn't beg and grovel.

However, I could and did make one further try for his consideration. "Mr. Wynfield, since we have talked this much, would you be willing to show me the rest of the rooms you wish redecorated and let me give you my opinions? What can you lose?"

"Time, perhaps," he grunted.

When I was about to retaliate, he rose and lifted up his hand. "Don't snap my head off again, young lady. I consider myself a broad-minded man. Therefore, let us tour the rooms, but only to get your opinions. Understand?"

"Of course." I inclined my head, hardly able to contain a swift surge of hope. Oh, heavens, was there still a chance that I might be hired?

He proceeded to lead me into several rooms along winding, dark halls and steps that twisted up into shadowed regions. We entered a musty library with bookshelves to the ceiling. I was shown a study, an ornate dining room, and a smaller breakfast room where monk's-cloth draperies covered what probably was a garden view. I made suggestions everywhere, which drew forth no response. I knew it was going to take every bit of skill and cunning I possessed to influence this hard-faced, cagey man.

We passed several maids and then met a tall Chinese man in a snowy tunic and black sateen trousers who was introduced as Li Fong, in charge of the establishment. I was used to San Francisco's large Oriental population. I had my own dear Mai Yee at home, who had taken care of me from the day my mother died when I was only five. Mai used to take me shopping in Chinatown and I met many of her friends. But this man, Li Fong, had the most closed countenance, the most inscrutable eyes, and the coldest voice I had ever encountered. He was rather like his master, both men with an air of indefinable mystery. I was glad when Li Fong glided past.

Our next encounter was with a small boy about seven or eight years old, thin and dark, who came pounding down the hallway, propelling a large hoop with a stick.

He pulled up short at sight of us and frowned. "Are you Melissa? Papa said she would be beautiful and have red hair. Are you my new stepmama?" For some reason, the prospect didn't seem to please him.

"This is not Melissa," his father told him. "This lady's hair is much more brown than red." He didn't comment on the rest of the description, but he flicked a glance at me from head to toe and smiled a little narrowly. Should I be insulted? A man would not have been subjected to such a physical appraisal. On the other hand, I probably needed all the help that I could get.

I glanced away as he continued smoothly, "She has come to see our house. Miss Blair, meet my son, Thaddeus, called Tad."

"Why has she come to see our house?" the boy demanded, going at once to the heart of the matter.

"Miss Blair's an interior decorator," his father answered. "I am thinking of having some changes made in certain rooms."

An angry flush suffused Tad's face. "B-but Papa, you promised that Mama's rooms would always stay the same." He pointed a shaking finger at the winding corridor behind him.

"I don't break my word, Tad, if I can help it. The Velvet Room will remain untouched, as always."

Tad fell silent, looking suspiciously at us both. He couldn't know the stirring of sad memories he triggered as I recalled my little brother Bobby, who had died in a boating accident. He was only seven when he sneaked off for a forbidden sail in the rough waters of the bay. He had been a lively, dark-haired boy, and until that day, my constant shadow.

"Find Prince and go outside," Tad's father told him with a sigh. "You stay indoors too much."

"It's awful foggy to play in the garden, but I guess I better bring Prince inside. When you first found him, hurt out on the road, it was a day just like this." With a worried frown, Tad trotted away in his little dark-blue sailor suit.

"Forgive my son's behavior, Miss Blair, but I am afraid he's not looking forward to living with his new stepmother." Mr. Wynfield strode to a nearby window and pushed back the floor-length panels. "Tad's right. A thick fog has come up with its usual swiftness. I fear you won't get down the cliff road until it lifts, Miss Blair."

He chewed his lip then, suddenly, seemed to arrive at a decision. "Perhaps it's just as well. We can discuss your decorating ideas after dinner."

Elation swept me. I was getting a reprieve!

"You also can meet the other members of the household although it's only my future wife's room that I wish redone on this floor. Her room is next to mine."

So Wife Number One had a far-off room while Wife Number Two was going to be next to him. Strange. I wished that I could ask him how his first wife died, but this was not the time for confidences so I stayed silent.

A little farther on, he opened a door and gestured me inside. "This will be Melissa's room. It is quite bare now and will need a lot of work."

I agreed, trying to imagine how I would decorate it for the new wife who, according to Mr. Wynfield, was both sensitive and lovely. I wished that I could have met her before starting any plans. What was she really like? What were her preferences? Did she understand Drake Wynfield in spite of his aloof reserve?

However, he must have shown her a completely different side. Observing him covertly, I had to admit that he was attractive enough to stir any woman's interest with his hard, chiseled features, strong-looking body, and his unusual tawny-colored eyes. His voice reminded me of black plush, deeply masculine and impenetrable.

"Well?" he asked, a trace impatiently, and I realized he must have spoken to me and not received an answer. "Do you think you could make something of this room?"

Hastily, I reeled in my wandering thoughts. "Of course! I can make it as beautiful as your bride, a perfect setting for her loveliness."

I looked for some softening in his face at this reminder of the beauty that would soon be his to plunder, but there was no change in his expression.

"Let us continue with the tour," he said abruptly, and catching my arm in his strong fingers, he led me briskly from the room.

2

By the time we had finished our tour of inspection, I had a general impression of a house that was an intricate maze of corridors, angles, and ells running every which way, apparently built according to an erratic plan and added on to through the years.

Finally, Mr. Wynfield led me to a guest suite comprising a bedroom, bath, and small adjoining sitting room, all in shades of brown and cream. He glanced around, adjusted a gas jet behind a wall sconce of etched glass, and said to me: "You have two hours to work on your ideas, Miss Blair. Then we gather in the drawing room for a glass of wine before dining."

"Do you dress formally for dinner?" I inquired. It was obvious that I had no other garment, and briefly, I contemplated the pleasure of a tray here in the room. "Will my costume be excused? Perhaps—"

"This isn't London or New York," he interrupted. "This is free-and-easy, anything-goes San Francisco, as you should know. People in this house dress up or down as they desire. I fear you will find me in this same cravat and coat tonight." With a slightly mocking bow, he turned to leave.

Should I make some plea for this assignment that I so urgently desired? However, pride held back the words I longed to utter and I said, as cool as he, "After dinner I'll have some sketches ready for your consideration."

He faced me slowly. "You have chosen a difficult path for a young woman. In your line of work, you may run into a lot of prejudice."

I raised my chin defiantly. "On the other hand, the women of the house might prefer another person of their own sex to confer with, someone who understands housekeeping problems, for instance."

"*On the other hand,*" he stressed, "they might fear you would be a distraction for their men while living and working closely with the family during an assignment."

I was forced to smile at the idea of myself in the role of *femme fatale*. I was a businesswoman, one of the new breed turned out by the most forward-looking women's college in America. There had been a lot of us at Vassar preparing to challenge worn-out ideas and meet the world on different terms.

"You look amused." He shrugged and spoke across his shoulder as he turned away. "You certainly are determined, but as to your ability, that remains to be seen." The door clicked shut behind him.

Difficult creature! He had told me nothing. He didn't encourage or discourage. If only my first assignment could have been with some pliable, easygoing man ready to leave all the decisions in my hands. However, once before Mr. Wynfield had left the decorating of his mansion to a woman, his first wife, and what a shambles had ensued. Now the thought of a new wife was encouraging him to make a clean sweep of the past.

Except for the Velvet Room.

As I slowly removed my hat pins and my jacket, I wondered if Drake Wynfield ever visited those quarters to dream of his first love. If he did, it had better stop before Melissa appeared. I doubted if she would like what amounted to a shrine dedicated to a former wife.

Ah, well, enough of that. Now to the more important matter facing me. Drawing back the drapes to afford more light, I gazed around and found a small desk in the corner complete with lamp, pens, and ink blotter. In the next few minutes, I had covered the top with my own paraphernalia, which included pencils, chalks, ruler, and a box of colored inks. All else faded from my mind as I set to work.

It was sometime later when a sound disturbed my concentration and I put down my pencil, turning toward the windows with a puzzled frown. I could hear the foghorns in the bay, rising and falling in their usual eerie way, but I was used to them and knew it was something else that had arrested my attention.

It sounded like the little boy, Tad, calling urgently, "Prince, Prince, where are you? Come back!"

I rose from my chair, uneasy at the anguish in Tad's voice, and pushed the window upward. Wind swirled through the grounds below so that the fog came and went in long, thick eddies. The next second, I beheld Tad in his little sailor suit, still calling to his dog.

"Tad, what's the matter?" I cried, leaning farther out.

He looked up at me as the white blanket came

between us. When it cleared, Tad had vanished, although his voice still came, muffled, calling, getting fainter as he evidently headed for the cliffs. I could hear the waves of San Francisco Bay, that terrible, rough, icy stretch of water with its fierce, unmanageable tides. The cliffs were no place for a small child and an adventurous dog.

Without a moment's pause, I whirled around, pulling on my jacket, and ran along the hall to the lower level. I remembered seeing a back door to the garden and I headed in that direction. When I found it, I emerged onto a brick walk cutting through short, rough grass beaded with moisture. Trees, bushes, and flower beds were ghostly apparitions in the mist. A vine-covered gazebo appeared and disappeared like something in a dream.

I pushed on, calling constantly, "Tad, Tad, where are you? Come back here!"

Perhaps I should have summoned his father or a servant. But at the moment, I didn't want to spare the time when at every minute the missing dog might draw Tad into greater danger. With a catch at my heart, I thought of Bobby, my younger brother, lost at sea in a sudden, deadly fog like this.

Suddenly, a parting vapor disclosed a tall, stout fence, the redwood gate ajar. From beyond, I now heard Tad's voice, his words muffled, but high-pitched with fear.

I found him kneeling at the cliff edge, looking down and sobbing. "Prince, Prince! Stay there, boy, don't move. I'll save you."

Terror flooded me as I saw the child so close to the menace down below. The waves crashed like cymbals, and high-dashing spray could be heard even through the stifling vapors.

Cautiously, I approached, steadying my voice. "Tad, be careful, lad. I've come to help you—but you must not fall. Slowly, now, come back from the edge."

He scrambled backward like a crab, then stood up, tumbling against me as our arms clutched each other convulsively.

"Oh, miss, please save Prince! He's down there on a ledge. Someone left the gate open again and he got out. I had him tied, but—but—"

"All right, now, steady. Let me look at Prince. Very carefully, we'll move closer. Tell me, is the edge safe to hold our weight?"

Still clasped, we slid our feet across the sandy soil, past wet bushes showering us with mist.

"Safe?" Tad echoed, peering fearfully. "N-not for my pup, it wasn't."

"Hold on to that branch and stay back a little way," I ordered, pointing to a tree. "Yes, I see him. Hello, Prince. Hello, boy."

The dog looked up and whined entreatingly. Never had I seen a more unlikely "Prince." His matted grayish-white coat drooped wetly, his ragged ears hung flat, and his thin tail could essay only one weak thump. A rope trailed from his leather collar.

The ledge he was on looked about two feet wide— and it was all of twelve feet from the top.

"Good Lord," I muttered.

To my horror, Prince now began to leap about, barking wildly at us, his forepaws scrabbling ineffectually at the sandy cliff.

"No, no, Prince," Tad shrieked. "Stay, Stay! Be quiet. Oh, miss, he's going to fall down on the rocks and die!"

My thought exactly. There was only one solution

as I saw it. Prince must be restrained at once while
Tad went to get help from his father.

I explained this rapidly, Tad's eyes clinging hope-
fully to my face. Too well I remembered how close a
boy and dog could be, such as Bobby and his beloved canine companions.

"I will climb down to Prince and tie his rope to
that bush there. Then you tell your father to bring
another rope to haul him up."

"All right, but . . ." Doubtfully, both of us eyed
the slope. A bush or two, a few outcroppings of
rocks, the narrow ledge—and then—the drop.

"Can you do it, miss?" He gulped. "You won't—
get killed?"

My heart swelled a little at this mark of his concern. However, I was no impulsive heroine about to
throw my life away. I surveyed the terrain carefully.
"I think that I can do it safely. But hurry!"

Tad vanished before I even started down.

First, I planned where I would place my feet. Then
I tugged on the nearest bush. Thank heaven, it was
firmly rooted. My greatest fear was that the insanely
barking pup would jostle us both off the narrow
ledge.

I leaned down, fiercely riveting Prince with my
eyes. "Hush, now! Stop that noise—quiet! Quiet!"

I held his glance and he dropped back on all fours,
his wild pleas sinking to an abashed whine. A rather
intelligent little beast, I thought, starting to descend.
He probably could be trained.

I can't pretend that I wasn't apprehensive. But if
the bushes held . . . if the rocks were not dislodged
. . . if the pup could be kept calm . . .

Too many *if*s!

However, I reached the ledge in safety. It now
looked wider and the dog was quieter, reassured by

my appearance at his side. The fog still swirled whitely between us and the crashing surf and rocky shore below. But I was glad it did. Danger not seen is not as frightening.

Now for the dog. "Here, Prince. Good boy. Let me have your rope." Speaking soothingly, I stretched out my hand.

The animal had been badly frightened and his normal world still was not restored although he must have sensed that help was now on the way. Crawling forward on his belly, tail swishing, he gave ingratiating little cries and came up to my hand.

My other fingers clutched firmly at a bush of california holly; fortunately our local variety has no thorns.

I picked up the dog's trailing rope and eyed it. It seemed rather short to hold so frolicsome a puppy. How had he gotten loose? Chewed it? Hadn't Tad said something about the gate being left open "again"? I studied the rope. Why, it looked as though it had been severed. A clean cut with a knife! That meant someone had deliberately set Prince loose.

A chill swept me that had nothing to do with the foggy atmosphere. No, I couldn't think about the cut rope now—nor the open gate. It was too puzzling and suggested something disturbing and frightening that I couldn't fathom.

My fingers were damp and icy as I tried to knot Prince's rope around the stout base of the holly. The dog and I were still in danger. Suppose—someone— came to see if his plan—whatever it was—had worked?

Just then, a shower of little pebbles rained downward and I looked up, sucking in a startled breath. A disembodied frowning face peered at me through the veils of fog.

I screamed.

And felt my foot slip into space.

3

In my panic, I grabbed wildly at the bush, almost breaking off a branch, I clutched so fiercely. I must confess that I screamed again before my scrabblings found a footing in the sandy earth.

Brushing away the pup, who was pawing at my skirt, I straightened and looked upward. A shaken cry of relief burst from my lips. There was Mr. Wynfield and his son, Tad, peering at me through the wisps of fog.

"Miss Blair, are you all right?"

That had a familiar ring. Mr. Wynfield had asked me that when I arrived. Inwardly, I groaned. What must he think of me? That I was subject to impetuous actions?

I called to him in a quavering tone that I would be distinctly better on more solid ground. However, I felt flooded with gratitude that help was here.

Mr. Wynfield then uncoiled a rope and lowered one end down to me. "Can you tie that around the dog's collar, Miss Blair? Tad can hold the other end while I help you up."

It was soon done. Mr. Wynfield stretched his hand to me as I made my way gingerly up the cliff. One false step—oh, no, it didn't bear thinking about!

At the top, I was shaking so much I could hardly stand, and before I knew it, Mr. Wynfield placed his arm around my waist and drew me against the warm, firm muscles of his chest. He had discarded his coat and wore only a white broadcloth shirt through which I could feel the strong beating of his heart.

Although I was astonished by his kindly action, I would gladly have stayed there longer, enjoying this unexpected support to my trembling frame.

But the next instant, he gripped my arms and thrust me backward. "Why did you undertake such a foolhardy stunt? Why didn't you call a man?" he rasped.

I pulled away indignantly. "There wasn't time. I handled it all right."

He gave me an exasperated glance, then concentrated on pulling up the matted, whining bundle of wet fur. I prayed the knot I had made would hold . . . and it did.

Soon boy and dog were ecstatically reunited. Then Tad flung himself on me with a hug and a most grateful look. "Oh, miss, thank you, thank you. You were splendid!"

I hugged him back. "I'm glad that I was here to help."

Tad drew back. "And thank you, Papa."

Mr. Wynfield coiled up his rope and shrugged into his coat, which had been hanging from a nearby bush. "Tad, how did Prince get out? Did you forget to lock the gate?"

"No, no, Papa! Do you think I want to lose my dearest friend? I know about the rocks. And I even tied Prince up today on one of the cypress trees. Somebody left the gate ajar and I guess Prince chewed through his rope." With that, boy and dog bounded away toward the house.

"It looked to me as though someone deliberately used a knife to cut it," I remarked to Mr. Wynfield as we started walking through the stubby grass. "Of course, I could be wrong. Perhaps some person didn't like to see a dog tied up—or—or something."

"That probably was it."

"Does Tad have a nurse or someone who looks after him? There seems to be a dangerous area around your home."

"There is. He has had a combination nurse and governess since his mother died and next year he will start to school. Miss Libby is in the hospital after having a rather severe case of food poisoning. I don't know whether she'll be returning."

"He seems to be a lively child," I ventured.

Mr. Wynfield nodded curtly. "And often lonesome. Though some of the estates at Sea Cliff have playmates for him. I hope to have a bigger family in the future."

"Indeed?" I murmured, wondering how that would set with the "sensitive and gentle" creature about to become his partner in the venture. Or didn't men think in terms of "partners"? A man's wish was still law in his home these days. My college mates and I had often discussed such matters with a frankness that would have shocked most older folk. I certainly hoped that times were changing as I so often claimed.

When we reached the lower hallway of the house, Mr. Wynfield halted. "Miss Blair, although I'm very grateful for the way you tried to rescue Tad's little pet, I must caution you that it actually was quite reckless. The cliffs near here are very dangerous, and as a rule, the gates to them are kept locked tight. I suggest you never venture there again."

"I understand," I assured him when I didn't, really. *Who, then, had left the gate so dangerously ajar?*

"Also, Miss Blair, I have another suggestion to make in view of your—um—dishevelment."

I could feel my face turn fiery. I shoved ineffectually at the locks of hair straggling about my neck and attempted to shake the sand and leaves from my skirts. What a terrible impression I must be making when I yearned so fiercely to appear mature, talented, and poised.

"Perhaps you would prefer to have a tray brought to your room tonight," he continued, "and a change of outer garments. One of the maids can bring you some things that my wife seldom wore. Later on this evening, we can discuss your decorating ideas—if you feel up to it." He looked at me doubtfully.

"Oh, I know I shall. That sounds fine. Thank you—"

"And I also must insist that you spend the night. As you can see, the fog is still a menace. The horse and buggy that you drove up here can be stabled for the night."

I was not at all averse to remaining and I responded quickly in the affirmative, trying not to sound too eager. I figured that the longer I stayed, the better my chances for being hired.

As I started up the stairs to the rooms assigned me earlier, I suddenly felt very tired. Every bone and muscle seemed to ache. It would be nice to have fresh clothes and I felt greatly relieved that I wouldn't have to face the rest of the household to-night.

When I entered my room, I was pleased to see a fire crackling in the hearth. Everything now looked warmer, brighter, and more cheerful. I drew up a chair in the little sitting room, stretching my hands out gratefully toward the blaze.

It wasn't long before a maid appeared, saying with an Irish brogue that her name was Mary. Advancing into the room, she surveyed me with bright-eyed curiosity over the top of a mound of garments carried in her arms.

"The master sent these for you to choose from, miss. Almost brand-new, they are, and hardly ever worn." She deposited the clothing on the bed and gave me a cheerful, freckle-faced grin.

While she busied herself around the room, stirring up the fire, fetching hot water for my china washbasin, brushing down my hat and jacket, I examined the three garments selected by Mr. Wynfield. They were what is known as "tea gowns" and quite informal. Someone had called them "negligees that go into the parlor." All were beautiful. One was a trailing peach satin with deep cuffs of blond lace; another was emerald velvet trimmed with fur; and the last in pale blue cashmere had the sweetest bands of swansdown around the flowing sleeves and low, round neck. I held it up to me. "I'll wear this. You may remove the others, Mary."

She had also brought me a long-sleeved muslin nightgown and a matching, lace-trimmed peignoir. If they had been worn before, I didn't care for they were clean and fresh-smelling and I would need something to wear in bed that night.

"Very good, miss. I'll take the other gowns away

and be back with your supper tray before the cat can lick its ear."

By the time Mary returned, I had washed, brushed my hair out loosely, and donned the blue tea gown. As I tied the matching ribbons in the front, I surveyed myself in the tall pier glass and was not displeased with the results.

Mary now placed a tray for me on a little nearby table and I suddenly realized that I was very hungry. Beneath the silver covers reposed a lovely slice of lemon salmon, fluffy rice, a vegetable compote touched with ginger, then sugared almonds, a preserve of quinces, and a wicker-handled pot of Chinese tea. From Mai Yee I had developed a love for the more delicate type of Oriental cooking and the meal was just like being home.

As soon as I had finished eating, however, I began to worry about my sketches. Mr. Wynfield would be looking at them with a cool appraisal, wanting only the best for his fine home. In an agony of uncertainty, I pushed away the tray and hurried to my work, examining each sketch with intense concentration, trying to visualize them through Mr. Wynfield's eyes.

Mary came in and removed the tray, and while the door was open, a heavier footfall approached. My head jerked up and I saw Mr. Wynfield staring at me, black brows meeting above a densely amber gleam. He advanced slowly, then clutched my bare arms with a bruising grip. *"Who are you?"*

My drawings fell from nerveless fingers. All my previous fear of him returned. Somewhere, sometime, could this man have spelled danger to me? I was aware of our isolation . . . the silent, unfamiliar house with its winding, secret corridors . . . the imprisoning fog . . . the mournful tolling in the bay . . .

"Miss Blair," he demanded harshly, *"have we ever met before today?"*

I swallowed hard, finding it difficult to speak. "No, no, Mr. Wynfield, I don't think so." Surely I would have remembered such an arresting face, too forbidding to be handsome yet too striking ever to be forgotten. And yet . . .

I shrank back, trying to free my arms. "What is it, Mr. Wynfield? Why do you look at me like that? You —you're hurting me."

"Oh, I'm sorry!" He released me at once, gazing at the red marks on my flesh with an expression of dismay. "Please forgive me! Something about you in that blue gown, your long hair hanging down your back . . . I thought . . ." He expelled a deep breath. "But it was just a trick of light and shadow. You reminded me of someone, that is all."

I forced myself to relax and merely nodded, wishing fervently that I had worn a different tea gown.

He bent down to retrieve my pictures, then turned the lamp wick higher and brought another chair up to the desk. "Shall we now discuss your ideas?" He was once more completely in charge of himself, his deep voice cool and steady.

Glad that things were seemingly back to normal, I eagerly began to discuss Morris wallpapers, Bigelow handmade carpets, French silk draperies, and my other ideas for decorating the various rooms.

I warmed to my topic, pleased that I had his complete attention. "With so many gray days around Sea Cliff, I think it would be more cheerful if your home were decorated in the warmer colors, crimson, buff, and gold. You have a magnificent view of the Golden Gate. Why not let that passage to the sea be part of the parlor's decoration? Windows could be draped in straw-hued silk, caught back with matching ropes of braid."

I forgot all else as my enthusiasm grew until, suddenly, I encountered Mr. Wynfield's quizzical expression and I faltered to a halt, realizing I had no idea how my views were received.

"How do you propose to accomplish all this?" he inquired, leaning back in his chair and crossing one leg over the other. "Do you intend to employ helpers?"

"Of course. My father's assistant, Conan Blye, is still with me. I also have sewers, weavers, and painters I can call upon and I know most of the wholesalers in San Francisco through their dealings with my father."

Mr. Wynfield stared at me thoughtfully. "I am acquainted with Mr. Blye. I had him paint a portrait of my wife before she died and recently he has done some artwork for my shop."

"He is very talented—" I began, but he broke in abruptly.

"If I decide to use your services, it might be a good idea for you to stay here in the house. Where do you live?"

"In the town of Millbrae. When the city became so overgrown, my father bought a house that we could reach on the train in about thirty minutes or somewhat longer by driving our own conveyance."

"That's too far from here to travel back and forth each day."

I had to agree. "It would be much more convenient to stay at Cliffside for a while." My mouth felt dry. Was he about to make a decision in my favor?

His gaze returned thoughtfully to the sketches, lingering longest on the room for his fiancée. I had suggested the French style of Louis XV that was so popular right now, but I had made the whole scheme delicate: rose velvet against pearl-gray satin walls, the carpet a thick, soft pink. Above the windows and along the baseboard I had drawn a row of seashells picked out in white and gold. On the lounge and bed were pillows of foam-green silk covered with an overlay of lace.

"Melissa should love that," Mr. Wynfield murmured. "It looks like her, delicate and beautiful."

Instantly, an unbidden vision rose before me of The Wedding Night. Melissa sitting up demurely in the bed, her red-gold hair spilling on the pillows heaped behind her. Then the bridegroom enters wearing a wine-red robe and nothing else. A single candle flickers on the dark intentness of his face, all passionate purpose in his stride. . . .

"Miss Blair. *Miss Blair!*" His brows formed a dark bar across his face.

"Oh!" I jumped. "I'm sorry, I was woolgathering. What did you say?" Flooded with my embarrassing thoughts, I couldn't look at him and nervously began shuffling my papers.

"I should think you would be hanging on my every word at this juncture," he grunted.

"Oh, I am." My eyes flew anxiously to fasten on his face.

For a long, disconcerting moment, he surveyed me arrogantly, lingering on my unbound hair, the clinging, low-necked gown. I had to stop myself from pulling up the fabric on my bosom.

However, as soon as he spoke, everything vanished from my mind except the context of his words. "Miss Blair," he drawled, "I have decided to give you a trial."

My hand flew to my throat. "A trial?" A ray of hope began to flicker.

"I would like you to decorate the room for Melissa, and if I approve the outcome, if the job goes smoothly, quickly, and professionally, then we will discuss work on the other rooms."

"Oh." I swallowed. "F-fine." With a masterful exertion of willpower, I refrained from flinging my arms around his neck or bursting into shrieks of joy. "Thank you, Mr. Wynfield. I accept." Chin up, shoulders back, I hoped to convey the image of a cool, professional, business lady in spite of my attire. "I shall do everything to the best of my ability and I am certain that you and your bride will be pleased with the results."

Standing up, he nodded curtly. "I will draw up a contract for Melissa's room that should be mutually satisfactory. And now, Miss Blair, I bid you good night. Sleep well."

Sleep? I felt more like dancing, singing, shouting. My career was taking shape at last and I felt positive that, from now on, I would have no problems.

What a blessing it is, sometimes, that we cannot see into the future.

4

I slept like a babe in the big featherbed, nestled cozily underneath a thick quilt. The day's excitement didn't disturb me anymore—or perhaps I'd just had too much and was exhausted. But oh, I felt so happy. I was to be given a chance to prove my ability. Lovely visions of the rooms I would create in silk and velvet with graceful furniture on deep, soft rugs danced through my head just before I fell asleep.

When I awoke, it was in answer to a knocking at my door. I called, "Come in," and Mary entered with a little pot of coffee and the announcement that breakfast was being served downstairs.

"Has Mr. Wynfield eaten?" I asked as I sat up and gratefully sipped the bracing brew from a gold-rimmed china cup.

"That he has, miss. And I was instructed to tell you that Himself will be waitin' in his study whenever you'll be ready."

"I'll be as quick as possible."

Washing and dressing with all speed, I noted that
someone, probably Mary, had brushed and ironed
my clothes so that I did not present too bad an appearance. Even my low, bronze-colored boots were
cleaned. Since the house felt warm, I wore just the
lacy cream-colored waist with my velvet skirt, leaving the jacket behind.

I instructed Mary to roll my hair back to its chignon and then brush out a row of curls across my
forehead, telling her it was the usual style I wore for
daytime.

She did it most efficiently. Giving my hair a final
pat, she chuckled. "Aye, neat it is in back like a
model business lady, but the curly fringe says you
are just a sprightly lass at heart, I'm thinkin'."

I eyed my image dubiously, hoping I didn't look
too frivolous. Or young. But surely, I thought cynically, an attractive appearance couldn't hurt when
dealing with a man. Actually, today I felt definitely
like a woman of the world: college graduate, art stu-
dent, and lady decorator.

Holding up my back skirt, I briskly followed
young Mary down the hall and stairs, along another
hall, and up to a door behind which could be heard
the sound of voices and the clink and rattle of silver-
ware and china.

We entered a small, dark-paneled room where Li
Fong in black trousers and starched white tunic
bowed solemnly from his place beside a buffet of hot
dishes. It was a very American breakfast set out in
the English manner so the household could eat at
any hour they desired.

Mary spoke my name to the room at large in her
lively, unabashed manner. Then she vanished toward the kitchen and I inclined my head graciously
to the two occupants of the room still seated at the

damask-covered table, which gleamed with silver-ware, crystal goblets, china, and a huge bowl of waxy artificial fruits.

I only received a vague impression of the room before my attention riveted on the man and woman staring at me.

One smiled. The other didn't.

I guessed that the haughty gray-haired woman in her sixties must be Tad's grandmother. She began to speak in an abrupt, cold voice. "I am Rachel Wynfield. Drake told us about you. I understand that you're going to tear the house to pieces. Well, of course, I have no say in the matter. The place, as well as all the money, belongs to Drake."

Without taking her inimical gaze from me, she gestured with a thin, age-spotted hand glittering with rings. "This young man is Jeremy, my own son."

My own son? Then what was Drake's relation to her?

The blond man rose, smiling with a charming display of good humor and friendliness. His looks were simply stunning and I stared frankly, loving beauty as I do in any form. With his long-lashed blue eyes, flattering mustache, and head of tight gold curls, he could have posed for a statue of a young cavalier, or at least a matinee idol of the theater.

I acknowledged the introductions, then filled my plate with Li Fong's deft, unsmiling aid. Mrs. Wynfield sat at the head of the table and I took a place nearby, across from her son. After swallowing a bite of ham and scrambled eggs, I spoke to him.

"You and Drake are brothers, then? Are there other people living in the house that I haven't seen? Besides you two, Mr. Wynfield, and his son, I have met no one else."

Before Jeremy could answer, his mother spoke up in her dry, precise tones. "You have met us all. I presume you are curious about our relationships. I was a widow with a five-year-old son when I married Thomas Wynfield. His only child was Drake, just fifteen. Thomas and I were married for twenty years until his recent death. Now Drake 'graciously' provides me with an allowance."

"As for me," Jeremy cut in, smiling, "I am employed at Drake's import shop, The Jade Pagoda. Drake hired me after I experienced some"—he paused—"financial difficulties." In a happier tone, he continued, "I have never married, but Drake is due to wed for the second time."

"Have you met the bride-to-be?" I asked, buttering a poppy-seeded roll.

"No, we've never met, but Drake brought home a miniature portrait of her and she looks exquisite. The lucky dog! His first wife, Rose, was a beauty also." He gave a little contemplative smile, staring out the curtained window where a feeble sun was struggling to perform. "Melissa is her cousin."

Hmm, I wondered if Melissa or Rose accounted for that strange expression on his face?

"I would like to see the picture of Mr. Wynfield's fiancée since he has commissioned me to decorate a bridal room for her. If he likes the result, he said he would discuss further plans for refurbishing the house."

"Rather a formidable task," Jeremy murmured. "Especially for one so young and lovely."

"Yes, indeed, a *very* odd occupation for a female," Mrs. Wynfield interposed with her own assessing glance. "Might I inquire what are your qualifications?"

I told her about my art studies and how I had

worked and studied with my father. Had she heard of him? I asked. She nodded reluctantly but still looked skeptical.

I could hardly blame her. I was almost completely devoid of practical experience. But my training was sound, I owned a reputable firm with workers I could call upon, and I believed strongly in my own ideas.

I said no more and applied myself to eating breakfast while the other two sipped their coffee. And stared at me.

I was greatly relieved when Tad bounded into the room, accompanied by his dog. This morning, Prince looked vastly improved, evidently having received a bath and brushing, and a whole new future life expectancy.

Tad saw me and gave a joyous cry. "Oh, miss, you're still here. Are you going to be staying at the house? Can you come outside with me? I've lots to show you. Inside the house, too. There are big, dark, spooky places . . ."

Mrs. Wynfield spoke with sharp authority. "Tad, where are your manners? I declare! Not a good morning or a nod for Uncle Jeremy or myself. Things have gone from bad to worse since that Libby person went to the hospital. And now there will be even more disruption." Her hooded gaze made sure that I received the import of her message.

Tad gave a funny little bow. "Good morning, Uncle Jerry. Good morning, Grandma Rachel. When is Libby coming back? I don't really care, 'cause she's no friend to Prince. But Miss here . . ." He turned a glowing pair of dark blue eyes on me, not even out of breath from running every sentence into the next one without pause. "Miss, here, is a real, true heroine. She saved my dog from certain death."

He then rattled off the story of Prince's narrow escape while I patted the shaggy white head and endured a frantic twisting in an attempt to lick my hand. Evidently I had acquired a friend for life.

Neither Jeremy nor his mother made any comment on Prince's misadventure and I thought that a little odd. Did they already know about it, or were they sorry that the little animal had been saved?

When the saga had been completed, Tad begged me again to come exploring with him, but I had to refuse. I knew the child was lonely so I promised to go some other time, saying I must have a meeting now with his father.

I rose and inclined my head to Jeremy and his mother, who still watched me guardedly. "It was nice to meet you both," I said. "I will try to disturb you as little as possible while I am working here."

Jeremy gave me his winning smile, but his mother called out in her harsh voice just before I reached the door, "Miss Blair, how long have you known my stepson?"

I glanced back in surprise. "We just met yesterday." I told them the sequence of events, adding, "Mr. Wynfield agreed to give me a trial on the bridal chamber. If he likes the result, there may be more work for me here."

I could see the slight smiles of disbelief on the two faces at the table. They seemed to be thinking: Nobody would hire *her* to do a man's job, someone so young and inexperienced. Not unless she had some hold on him.

I tilted my chin and swept out of the room. Let them speculate and wonder! My conscience was clear, and if I was hired, they soon would see that I was a well-mannered, well-trained businesswoman.

Upstairs, I washed my hands and face, saw that

my hair was tidy, then started for the meeting with Mr. Wynfield.

I turned down the deserted hallway, believing I could find a shortcut to the study, which I remembered being somewhere in the rear part of the house. But suddenly the hall angled and split in two directions. Now which way? I stopped and looked around. How silent it was! No maids appeared. No voices spoke. No doors opened.

I walked on slowly, uncertain of the right direction. I only knew that a flight of downward stairs should lead me back to the main floor.

However, I could find no stairs.

Growing quite uneasy, I leaned against the wall, berating my stupidity in not ascertaining directions before I left the dining room. Of course I knew it was because the old lady and her son had upset my hard-won equanimity and reduced me into an example of a young, foolhardy, untried person.

I had no doubt that Mr. Wynfield awaited me with growing impatience, wondering where I had gone and why I hadn't hurried to keep our appointment. If only he knew how anxious I was and how eager for that appointment!

I felt ridiculous standing undecided and I pushed away from the wall, prepared to retrace my steps if possible, when suddenly I saw the doorway at the far end of the corridor slowly open.

Catching my breath, I sped toward the aperture. "Is someone there? Hello! Please, can you help me?"

No answer came. The thick, dark silence was almost smothering, but I pushed on the door and stepped inside, calling out again to no avail.

What was this place with a door that opened silently from no human force?

Moving cautiously, I soon saw I was in a gallery of paintings, lit by a single candle on a little stand. However, the place was empty. Whoever had used the candle was no longer there. I picked it up, holding it aloft with a quickening of interest, and began to examine what were obviously the Wynfield family portraits.

I first saw an older man who looked like Drake. Oddly enough, he wore a sea captain's garb and a masted schooner had been painted in the background. The next picture was of a sweet-faced woman with a plaque below stating: REBECCA WYNFIELD, 1820–1850. Died young, poor lady.

There was no portrait of Drake, but Rachel and Jeremy already had been immortalized on canvas. Then, at the very end, I spied "Rose Wynfield" and I stopped to stare. She certainly had been a beauty, with raven hair and eyes of misty green, a dreamy, otherworld expression in their limpid depths. Her snowy bosom and shoulders rose from veils of seafoam green that revealed more than concealed her rounded flesh. And everywhere, like some romantic symbol, there were roses: deep scarlet, satiny pink, and creamy white, in her hair, on her lap, and drifting at her feet.

The background must have been the Velvet Room. It was done in shades of green with strange doll heads interspersed among the drapes and pillows on bed and floor. However, it was the living doll who had enthralled the artist and I suddenly recalled that Mr. Wynfield had said Conan Blye had done Rose's portrait.

I couldn't help wondering why such a lovely work of art was hidden away in this far-off gallery. Couldn't Drake Wynfield bear to see that lost beauty? Or did he hide the portrait out of consideration for the wife-to-be?

I turned away with a guilty start, remembering that I had pressing business with Drake Wynfield and I had tarried overlong. I hurried back the way I'd come, the shadows from my candle wavering and elongating. To my surprise, I saw that the door had silently swung shut, and when I tried the knob . . . it wouldn't turn.

5

With an acute feeling of exasperation, I shook the door handle, then banged and called loudly. All without results.

I could hardly believe my bad luck. Another outlandish escapade to be brought to Drake Wynfield's critical attention. Dear heaven, was my every act in this place going to spell disaster?

If Mai Yee had been there, she would have said there was *um ho*, "a bad spirit," after me and burned a joss stick for my protection.

But unfortunately, I was all alone and had no one to depend on except myself. I *had* to find a way to keep my appointment with Mr. Wynfield as quickly as possible. If the hour grew too late, I wouldn't put it past him to cancel our agreement. Nothing had been signed between us yet. He still was free to change his mind.

I gnashed my teeth and I'm afraid I kicked the door in a very unladylike manner. Nothing happened except that my toe began to hurt. I turned around with a deep groan, raising my candle so that I could search for another exit. The hall door had not opened by itself, of that much I was certain.

But if someone had been here, how had they escaped without my seeing them? Another exit was the only explanation and maybe it was as well hidden as the entrance had been.

Carefully, I moved along the gallery, examining every inch of wall between the pictures. I rapped and pressed, then thumped my heels, hoping to find a hidden spring. Anything was possible in this eerie place. A person could almost be convinced of ghosts.

I paused and chewed my lip. What was I going to do? How would anyone guess where I had gone? How long would I be left here? But then I gave myself a mental shake. Of course they would eventually start a search. My horse, Lady, and the trap were still lodged in the stables. They would know I hadn't gone away. I would just have to keep pounding on the door and yelling until someone heard me. I turned around and renewed my efforts vociferously.

And then somebody answered.

The echoes of my last call—"Help!"—had barely died away when I heard a grinding, creaking noise. Spinning around, my astonished gaze beheld another exit at the far end of the gallery. A panel slid into the wall and in the opening was—Tad!

A candleholder wavered in his little hand, his fearful eyes stared, mouth agape. *"Miss!* It's you! I thought you were a spook."

I could barely suppress a sob of relief. With a strong effort, I managed to say calmly, "Hello, Tad. I'm afraid I got locked in here. Where did you come from?"

"My mother's Velvet Room, back up those stairs.

Say, would you like to see it? She's got hundreds of gorgeous dolls and other things. Come on, I'll show you . . ."

I had to halt his excited jabbering. "No, thanks, not now, Tad. I'm late for a meeting with your father. Just show me how to get out of here. Some other time, though, I'd like to see the Velvet Room."

Tad skipped up to me. "I can show you anytime. Papa doesn't mind if I go in 'cause I'm very careful of my mama's things." He stopped to indicate her portrait on the wall. "That's her picture, miss. Wasn't she beautiful? I called her Princess Rose-Red like in the fairy tale."

"Yes, she certainly was lovely," I agreed, hurrying Tad along. "This is a strange gallery. The hall door seemed to open by itself."

"Not really. I guess I didn't shut it tight when I came through. This used to be a secret hiding place with a secret way to open and close the door. It was built when folks were scared of Indian attacks a long, long time ago. Spanish people had a fort here then and San Francisco was called Yerba Buena. That meant Good Herb."

The little fellow seemed to have a pretty good grasp of local history, but I had other matters on my mind and didn't breathe freely until Tad had twisted a knob hidden in the woodwork to free the door.

As we hurried down the hall, Tad looked up at me. "Miss, I didn't know it was you calling. I couldn't hear clearly in the room back there."

"I understand. Tad, perhaps I better not tell your father where I've been—unless he demands to know, of course. He might think I was nosing into places that are none of my concern. Just show me where his study is; that's where I'm to meet him now."

"All right, miss. Say, should I just keep calling you 'miss'? Libby has me call her 'Miss Libby.' Maybe we could do something like that."

"Well, you can't call me 'Miss Libby,' " I said with a straight face. "My first name is Lesley."

He laughed. "I'll call you 'Miss Lesley,' then. By this time we were in the lower hall and he pointed to one of the doors. "There's Papa's study. Now, you won't get lost again, will you?" With a grin and a wave of his hand, Tad ran off.

Before I could knock, the study door flew open and Mr. Wynfield stood before me. "Where in thunder have you been?" he exclaimed impatiently.

I swallowed hard. "I got lost." Least said, easiest mended, my father used to say.

"Never mind the explanations. I am due in town and it is getting late. Come in and glance over this agreement."

Thankful that I still had an agreement to glance over, I sank down in a chair before his desk and read the short but explicit phrases. The time allotted was not very long but I hoped would suffice, while the sum for my services was more than adequate. I wrote my name above his signature and held it out to him. "I understand you have a miniature of your fiancée. Could I see it?"

"I think Melissa will be pleased by your plans for the bridal chamber. She is very dainty." He picked up a small oval frame and handed it across the desk.

"She certainly is lovely," I murmured. However, Melissa didn't look a bit like her cousin. Rose seemed to have an aura of voluptuousness expressed in her velvet gown, roses everywhere, and almost undraped charms. There also was a kind of secretiveness in her smile while Melissa looked out of her china frame with wide-eyed innocence. I wondered if she would be able to cope with this strong-willed man whose inner thoughts were hidden behind hooded eyes. It seemed to me that he must be a very sensuous person with his obvious love of beauty—sought in women as well as his choice of a career. Would a bridegroom's passion terrify this "dainty" Southern girl? I had never been thrown with such a mature, attractive man, and to my dismay, I realized that my thoughts drifted too often on the romantic aspects of his nature. This would never do!

"When will your fiancée arrive?" I asked coolly, handing back the miniature.

"I'm not sure. She's coming from Virginia on the transcontinental train. She promised to send a telegram regarding her arrival. She will bring her maid. Naturally, she couldn't travel all that way alone."

I gave a little smile. "I did. From New York City to San Francisco."

"Of course *you* did." He leaned back in his leather chair, giving me a quizzical survey. "But Melissa is not an independent, modern girl like you. She is a sensitive Southerner, raised in what is termed 'genteel poverty' by the survivors of the War Between the States."

Living in poverty and yet she had a maid to travel with her? "Is she quite young?"

Mr. Wynfield looked down at the miniature and frowned. "Yes, she's barely twenty, and she seems very young to me as I look down from the plateau of thirty-five."

"That isn't very old for any man," I protested, thinking that he was in the prime of life.

"No flattery, please." His lip quirked slightly. "We've already signed the contract."

For just a minute, his austere containment slackened and I stared at him in wondering surmise.

Could he sometimes shout with laughter? Act young and silly while playing with his son? Be blindly overwhelmed with passion?

The next minute, he stood up briskly, signifying that the meeting was over, and the reserved mask once more settled on his face.

I rose also. "Mr. Wynfield, I promise I won't disappoint you. Thank you for giving me a chance to prove myself."

He dismissed my gratitude with a wave. "What are your plans for today, Miss Blair?"

"First, I'll visit my shop to confer with Conan Blye, then drive down to my home in Millbrae so I can pack some clothes."

He nodded thoughtfully, picked up a tall-crowned hat, and swung a short cape across his shoulders. "Until later, then." He bowed and we went our separate ways.

There was a lot for me to do, a lot to think about. I had to choose very carefully for Melissa's room. If I succeeded in pleasing Mr. Wynfield, a recommendation from him should open many doors for me.

When I reached my room, I rang for a maid and gave instructions for my equipage to be brought at once to the front door. Then I donned my jacket, pinned on my hat, and soon was on my way to the heart of that place known to all its denizens simply as "the City."

6

I always loved my expeditions into San Francisco, where I could view the mansions on Nob Hill, the constant parade of fashion along Kearny Street, the big hotels, St. Francis and the Palace, and the stores such as Ville de Paris and The White House bulging with every kind of luxury.

I loved the sounds: horses' hooves clattering on the cobbles, sea gulls on the bay, music drifting from saloons, the slap of cables running underground as they drew the dark red cable cars up and down the hills.

I loved the aromas of flowers everywhere, sold on street corners, blooming on ladies' hats and muffs, the salty air, the barrels of tar, and the fresh fish piled along the wharf.

Happily, I sniffed and gazed my fill as I guided Lady through the busy thoroughfares until I turned onto California Street. It was there I noticed Jeremy Wynfield coming from the Stock Exchange.

He now was dressed in elegant doeskin trousers topped by a darker coat and vest. At his throat he wore a purple and red cravat displaying a stickpin in which was centered a very large and brilliant stone —real or paste, I couldn't tell. Seeing me, he doffed his hat and smiled, but his face looked rather strained and he hurried off at once.

Perhaps he was late for his duties at the Jade Pagoda. I imagined that he was skilled at charming wealthy dowagers and debutantes into spending lots of money in the shop.

San Francisco was a city of quickly made, unbelievable wealth, created from both gold and silver strikes in the vicinity. Almost overnight, the rough, wild town had turned into a city of elaborate mansions, fabulous shops, sophisticated theaters, and every other kind of diversion that high spirits and ready money could invent.

However, my father had seen another way to earn his money. With a small investment and an artistic flair, he had opened a decorating service for the huge homes and new hotels and soon found himself greatly in demand. For a second, tears were close as I thought how much I owed to his training and inspiration. Now it was up to me to make it all worthwhile.

I hitched Lady near my shop and entered through the etched-glass doorway. The main room was decorated with a dark blue rug and golden fruitwood furniture. On the wide desk reposed a bouquet of fresh heliotrope and violets, perfuming all the air, the colors echoed in the cushioned seats of chairs and sofas. Against the wall hung shelves of books containing pictures of room interiors, catalogs of many kinds, and sample swatches of materials.

When the doorbell signaled my entrance, Conan

appeared almost at once from the back of the shop. "Lesley, dear," he cried, "what happened with his lordship up at Cliffside?"

Lordship? I had to smile. Yes, that was an apt description of my lordly employer though I had to admit his arrogant air of determination and self-confidence probably was instinctive.

"Great news, Conan! I overcame his slight aversion to my gender. I'm to be given a trial. Mr. Wynfield is going to let me decorate his new bride's room. If he likes the results, we probably will get a contract for some other rooms. Isn't that stupendous?"

"Aye, that's good news, *macushla*. Our first client since your father died!"

"And if all goes well, this could pave the way to other offers."

"I suppose you will be living in the house?" he asked cautiously.

"Yes, that's the plan. What are you frowning about?"

"There was an article in the *Chronicle* a while back headed 'Mysterious Death of Rose Wynfield.' "

I had been away at school so this was news to me. I sank down in a nearby chair and stared at him. "Did the paper say how she died?"

"All they knew was that she went over the cliff on her horse. The son, Tad, said he saw someone in a dark cape throw a rock toward the horse. But it was foggy and he couldn't see clearly so no one paid much attention to the lad."

I had already seen how Tad's imagination thrived on secret passageways, the Velvet Room, and "spooks." "Is that all?" I scoffed. "A small boy sees a cloaked figure in the fog? Poppycock!"

"That's what they decided at the inquest. The verdict was accidental death, but I knew Rose . . ."

To my surprise, I saw Conan's expression change. He stared beyond me at the entrance and mouthed, "We have company."

I spun around just as the doorbell tinkled and Drake Wynfield entered the shop. My face flushed with dismay before I realized there was no way he could have heard any of our discussion.

"I saw you through the window, Miss Blair, and took the opportunity to stop in and speak with you." His cool gaze swept Conan up and down. "How do you do, Mr. Blye? I believe we have some matters to discuss that concern us all."

"Of course, Mr. Wynfield," Conan answered heartily. "Won't you have a seat?"

As soon as the three of us were arranged around the desk, Mr. Wynfield spoke. "A telegram was delivered to my shop today from Melissa Fernley, my fiancée. She will be here in about four days so there must be no delay in preparing for her arrival. Can you handle that?" A hooded glance questioned each of us in turn.

Four days! That didn't give us much time. I shot a look at Conan then answered smoothly, "Of course, Mr. Wynfield. Your request shall take precedence over all our other work. We'll begin at once. Ah, will your fiancée be staying at Cliffside?"

"Naturally. And if the bridal chamber isn't ready, she can stay in a guest room. My stepmother should be an ample chaperone." His heavy eyelids narrowed.

"Indeed. Might I inquire when the wedding is scheduled?"

"No date has been set as yet. We will do so at a

large soirée after my fiancée arrives. Now, shall we get to the matters nearest at hand?"

I nodded, very much the dignified lady owner of a successful business. "Mr. Blye, please get down the sample books suitable for boudoirs and we shall see what is available in carpets, draperies, and bed and chair coverings. Tones of pink, silver, and palest green, I think, with a pearl-gray background."

We spent the next half hour making plans, discussing my sketches, and selecting our samples. Conan knew what was readily available and I knew exactly what I wanted.

We had barely finished when Mr. Wynfield turned to me. "Miss Blair, are you going to your home today? I believe you mentioned it."

"Yes, in a few minutes I'll be on my way to Millbrae so I can pick up some articles of clothing, a smock or two, things like that. I also must tell my housekeeper where I will be staying."

"Would you allow me to drive you down?" Mr. Wynfield asked. "I have an errand in that neighborhood and would enjoy your company. We can discuss further plans for my home."

Further plans? My heart began a joyous tattoo and I accepted the offer with alacrity.

"Conan, will you see to my horse? I'll leave Lady in the backyard stables."

"Of course." Conan rose at once and disappeared.

After a little further discussion, Mr. Wynfield and I prepared to depart. "Curious. I don't know what is keeping Mr. Blye," I said, peering out the window. "But I think we've finished all our plans."

Mr. Wynfield casually drew on his driving gloves. "Perhaps he was examining my new buggy. I saw him staring down the street when he went out the door."

"Well, everything is settled. We might as well leave," I replied, and with a bouncy step, I followed my employer to his two-in-hand. There was no sign of Conan so, with a snap of the reins, we were on our way.

We both were silent until we had maneuvered the busy thoroughfare of Market Street and were heading south down the peninsula on El Camino Real. Then suddenly, Mr. Wynfield spoke. "Actually, Miss Blair, I have another reason for this trip to Millbrae. A very secret reason that I didn't want bandied about."

"You deceived me, sir." I tried to speak lightly, but I was keenly disappointed that the main purpose was not further discussion about decorating Cliffside. However, in the very next moment, he shared a confidence with me, which seemed to indicate that a new threshold of friendliness had been approached between us.

He threw me a quick smile. "Allow me to explain. I am delivering a very valuable article to Mr. Darius Ogden Mills, which I couldn't entrust to an employee. Do you know the family?"

Mr. Wynfield was driving very fast and I held my purse with one hand and the seat grip with the other. "No, I'm afraid the closest my father or I ever came to millionaires was the decorating of their rooms. Of course, I've heard of all the Millses' philanthropies and the esteem in which they're held."

He threw me a quick, sidelong glance. "I imagine you are curious to see this 'valuable article.'"

I admitted that I was.

He transferred the reins to his left hand, thrust his other fingers in a pocket, and handed me a small gray velvet box. "Press that spring in the circle of Berlin crystals," he instructed me.

When the lid sprang open, I gave a gasp. I was
staring at a diamond brooch more exquisite than
any I had ever seen. Three inches across, a floral
spray of graceful proportions incorporated diamonds of the most extraordinary size and brilliance.
The leaves were emeralds, the stems were gold.
Springs called "tremblers" made the central flowers
quiver with a myriad of colored lights.

"Oh, how beautiful," I breathed. "And how extremely valuable it must be. I should have thought
you'd have an armed guard riding with you."

"That would have been a sure way to draw attention to the matter. This way—"

He didn't finish speaking because, suddenly, the
buggy listed sharply as a wheel spun out of place.
The box flew from my hand and both of us tumbled
from the seat onto the hard-packed earth.

A black cloud swept my vision, and when it
cleared, I sat up, feeling dizzy. "Wh-what . . ."

Mr. Wynfield rose and helped me to my feet, staring at me anxiously. "Miss Blair, are you all right?"

"Y-yes, I think so . . ." Then I jerked and caught
at his arm. "L-look!"

A man stood several yards away in the middle of
the road. A slouch hat covered all his hair, a full
black duster swept to his heels, and a bandanna concealed the main portion of his face.

He had a Colt revolver trained steadily in our direction.

Mr. Wynfield drew himself up like a taut steel
spring. "What do you want?" he snapped.

The answer came in a muffled, disguising
whisper. "Empty your pockets and purse. Toss your
jackets over here."

We didn't argue. However, Mr. Wynfield took his
time and I guessed why. At any minute, another

traveler might appear and cause the robber to take flight.

The disguised figure gathered up our money quickly, going through every pocket, even running his fingers down the lining. All the while, he faced us and the gun was pointed steadily.

7

"**M**ove back against those trees," the robber growled, "and stay there." The next instant, he swung into the buggy. With one eye on us, he swept his hand along the floor and turned over all the seat cushions.

What else could he be looking for? He had our money . . .

Of course! The brooch! Someone must have found out that Mr. Wynfield was taking it to Millbrae. Would the next step be to search our bodies and force us to disrobe?

I remembered the box had flown out of my hand. Darting a quick glance to right and left, I saw to my horror that beneath the bushes a brilliant ray of sunlight shone on the crystalled lid that contained the gem. In another moment, the thief would be sure to spot it. Drake was in front of me, the highwayman feverishly engaged. Quickly, I weighed my chances and decided to take action. I sprang to my feet, swept up the jewel, and shrieked, "Oh, thank God, someone's coming! Help! Help!"

The robber turned his head for just a second, the ever-present danger of more traffic making him extremely nervous.

The instant of diversion was all I needed. I ran and flung myself into the thick, concealing bushes, heedless of branches, dusty leaves, and waist-high ferns tangling in my skirts. Like a frightened animal, I plunged forward, wanting to put as much distance as possible between myself and that terrifying gun.

I could hear some distant shouts. Would the robber follow me? Could Mr. Wynfield head him off? I heard the sound of pounding hooves. Had someone really arrived to render aid? I prayed that it was so and that Mr. Wynfield would not be harmed.

All I could do now was keep on going. I had thrust the box into my bodice as I needed both hands to shove aside the barriers of leaves and branches. I had no fear of getting lost. I knew if I kept the sun on my right hand, El Camino Real would run in a straight line down to Millbrae and I could follow it behind the screening eucalyptus. An exhausting trip but not impossible. Certainly Mr. Wynfield would escape and find me before too long, and if he didn't, I would apply for aid from the Millbrae sheriff.

However, I knew I couldn't take any chances and I continued to forge on as speedily as I could. Soon my labored breaths became like red-hot knives stabbing at my lungs. Perspiration covered me and ran in rivulets beneath my clothing.

At last, I could bear the pace no longer and I dropped down on a bank of wild grasses screened from the road by juniper and sagebrush as well as the crowding trunks of trees. I fumbled with my buttons and loosened the laces of my corset so that the breeze could cool my fevered skin. For a few minutes, I shut my eyes.

It was strange about that holdup. Surely it was not just a coincidence that we had been stopped when carrying so valuable an item. Our thief had kept on searching through our jackets as well as all over the seats. His frantic, rising frustration had been quite apparent, leading to the fearful glance behind him that allowed me to escape. A true highwayman would have grabbed our money and fled. I always carried money in my purse for an emergency and Mr. Wynfield's wallet had been bulging. There should have been sufficient loot to send any robber worthy of the name quickly on his way.

Could he have been someone from Mr. Wynfield's shop who knew about the sale? A person hired to rob us of the gems?

Such men were readily available. Even though it was a long time since those first wild, lawless days, many scoundrels still dwelt in San Francisco. Scouts for white slavery roamed like deadly serpents. Tough sailors from the waterfront were constantly alert for ways to shanghai other seamen. There were streets of varied prostitutes, opium dens, and murderous Tongs living secretly in Chinatown.

In fact, the area on lower Pacific Street was known around the world as "The Barbary Coast." Side by side with all the city's wealth and beauty and high spirits dwelt this dark element of crime. Anyone familiar with San Francisco was aware of it and avoided certain streets, especially at night.

However, this was daylight and we had been stopped on a well-traveled road. Somebody must be quite desperate. Realizing this, I knew I must not dally further.

About to button up my waist, I suddenly heard

horses' hooves pounding down the road, coming closer, then slowing to a clip-clop. Darting behind a solid trunk, I peered out cautiously.

I almost fainted with relief. Mr. Wynfield, hatless and in his shirtsleeves, turned his head from side to side as he called urgently, "Miss Blair—Miss Blair! Where are you?"

Smothering a breathless sob, I stepped out of my hiding place and ran toward him. "Oh, I'm glad you found me . . ."

Changing swiftly from anxiety, his face now assumed a mask of fury. "For God's sake! So there you are!" He halted the grays and leaped down from the buggy.

"What happened?" I cried. "Did the robber get away? Who was he? I thought I heard the sound of—"

"You crazy little fool," he interrupted harshly. "What possessed you to take such a chance?"

He gripped my shoulders and shook me so hard, my clothes gaped even wider on my bare skin. Diverted, he stared down at me so that I was able to jerk away and cover up my breast. "Well, I succeeded, didn't I? What happened?"

He dragged his eyes back up to my face. "A horse and wagon with two farmers in it came careening down the road, evidently alerted by your scream. The thief immediately ran to the horse he had hidden in the nearby trees. I have no idea who he was." He ground his teeth. "I wish to God I did!"

His eyes narrowed. "Now, Miss Lesley Blair, do you have the brooch?"

"Yes, I do." Tossing my head, I turned my back on him, withdrew the jeweled pin, then rebuttoned my garments before confronting him with the box held out in my hand.

He drew a harsh breath of satisfaction as he examined the gem and placed it in his pocket. If I was disheveled, so was the formerly elegant art dealer, who was now flushed and damp-skinned, his cravat hanging loose upon a partly open shirt.

He raked back the rough locks straggling across his forehead and gave me a grim-faced survey. "Although you deserve my thanks, you took a terrible chance, which I can't condone. The highwayman easily might have fired a shot at you. Didn't you realize the danger?"

"Of course I did, but I don't think he knew I had the box. He just thought I ran because I was scared. And I was!"

He shook his head and placed a hand beneath my elbow. "You take too many chances," he said as we headed for the buggy.

What could I say?

When we were once again speeding along El Camino Real, I managed to ask rather jerkily: "I've just thought of two things. One: I've lost my jacket. Two: How did you fix the wheel?"

"One: Your jacket is underneath the seat. Two: The farmer and his son found the loosened bolt and easily put it back."

The buggy must have been tampered with before we left San Francisco. But I could speak no more. I was terribly thirsty, terribly tired, also hot and dusty.

I only roused when Mr. Wynfield drew the grays to a slower pace. "Tell me where your home is. You can pack your clothes while I deliver the brooch. I'll return for you shortly."

"Go left at the next crossroad. I live just beyond the Rojas Ranch. You'll see their sign."

"Would you care to take an early supper at my

home when you come back?" I ventured hesitantly. It seemed like such a long trip to return to San Francisco right away. We had had no lunch and the afternoon was well advanced. "My housekeeper is an excellent cook and it would be no trouble. You do enjoy Chinese cuisine?"

He stared at me, evidently mulling over the invitation. He certainly was not a man for making headlong decisions, but then I suppose a shred of pity stirred him as he noted my draggle-tailed appearance combined with the gray aftermath of fear, which must have made me look a sight.

"Thank you," he said. "I accept your offer . . . and I like Chinese food very much."

"Good, that's settled then . . . and there's my house." I pointed out the curving driveway, immediately feeling a lifting of my spirits. How nice it would be to have a long soak in hot water and one of Mai's delicious suppers followed by a tête-à-tête with Mr. Wynfield. Why the idea of an evening with him alone seemed so intriguing, I was too tired to fathom. I only knew that he was an engaged man and I must not indulge in admiring his disturbingly attractive qualities.

My employer looked around at the rambling, Spanish-style house nestled in its grove of redwood trees, the wide, colonnaded porch draped with flowering purple trumpet vine. "This is a quite delightful home," he said. "I'll leave you now and come back this evening." He put out his hand and startled me by enclosing my fingers in a hard, firm clasp. "I'm sorry to have put you through such an unpleasant experience. I never carry firearms, but if I'd had the slightest inkling that the nature of my journey had been discovered—well—I just hope that you'll forgive me for endangering you. And, er, my explosive outburst."

"Of course," I murmured, very conscious of the joining of our hands.

"At any rate," he continued. "Though I can't approve the risk you took, your calm cool-headedness in today's affair astonished me. There was no hysteria, no fainting, and now no recriminations. You are a most unusual young woman."

For a second, I couldn't speak. Then I parroted: "Calm? Cool-headed? Me? Why, I—I—" As I fumbled for the words to refute such unexpected praise, it came to me that this was the best impression I had made so far. Why not let it stand? I would be a silly goose to do otherwise.

Therefore, I inclined my head and said graciously. "Mr. Wynfield, you are too kind."

"I will tell Darius Mills how you recovered his brooch. I'm sure he will wish to convey his thanks."

I was not displeased at this new turn. Of course, it was luck that the brooch had flown from my hand to a hiding place beneath the bushes. It was luck that I had managed to run away with the box. And the final piece of luck was the arrival on the scene of the farmer and his son just in time to scare the thief away.

However, I had no intention of displaying false modesty and disclaiming any credit. It could have been quite dangerous if I'd been followed. Perhaps I was something of a heroine after all, albeit a tottering, exhausted one.

8

I told Mai Yee all about the holdup on the road, but she seemed more interested in Cliffside since that was what concerned her Little Missy's future.

We talked while she scrubbed my back and hair in our very advanced indoor bathroom. I described the mansion, its rooms, and inmates, particularly Li Fong.

"I have heard of Mr. Li," Mai stated, indicating that he used his last name first in the old Oriental manner. "Long ago he belonged to Tongs in Chinatown, which were quite famous for evil deeds. Then Li Fong disappeared. So now he's back?"

"Why would Mr. Wynfield employ such a man?" I exclaimed.

"Tongs don't bother any people now."

"But they were murderers, hatchet men—"

"Not now, Missy, not now." However, I thought she looked a little uncertain as she shook her neat black head, the carved ivory bodkins glinting in her chignon. She had been raised by a British missionary school in Shanghai and spoke English with only a slight accent. Though she was middle-aged, her skin was quite unlined. She always wore neat black trousers and a snowy tunic of starched cotton. Once a week she traveled up to Chinatown to visit the relatives of her husband, a man who had died only one year after they were married. She was well acquainted in the Chinese sector and I wondered how much she really knew about Li Fong.

"Tong associations now keep peace in Chinatown and settle disputes among their people," Mai continued as she wrapped me in a heated towel and led me to the fireplace in my bedroom.

"Of course, there may still be one or two . . ." Her voice trailed off uneasily, but when I tried to question her, she refused to talk about the Tongs and turned the talk to Cliffside.

After I told her about my contract there, she snorted delicately. "So! The master of Cliffside gives you a trial. You who need no trial."

I chuckled, warmed by her unfailing loyalty. "Oh, I can hardly blame him, Mai. Remember, I'm just a beginner." Then I added slowly, "There was one odd thing about him . . ."

"Yes?" Mai probed, polishing my long strands of hair with a bit of velvet until the curls gleamed like dark mahogany on the shoulders of my Chinese dragon robe.

"When I first saw Mr. Wynfield, it seemed to me that we had met before. I don't know where or when, but something about him frightened me. Some memory . . ." I shrugged. "Oh, it probably was just a foolish notion."

I was silent for a moment, then I added, "Later that night, he saw me with my hair down, clad in a long blue tea gown, and he seemed startled and asked me rather violently if we ever had met before."

Mai's fingers grew still on my hair. "You think perhaps . . ."

"Oh, no, I'd remember him. He's very impressive. You'll see tonight."

She smiled. "He is handsome in your eyes?"

"Well . . . not exactly. He has a very reserved expression a great deal of the time. You can't tell what he's thinking. He's . . . deep."

A chuckle came from Mai. "Sounds Chinese."

She then helped me into lace-trimmed undergarments and tied my hair in ringlets high on the back of my head. "Rest now, Little Missy. I will attend the supper cooking in the kitchen."

I yawned. "Call me in a little while." When I lay down on my bed, the recent frightening ordeal of the robbery and my precipitous flight at last took its toll and my eyes closed wearily. But just before sleep claimed me, I felt that the whole dangerous episode must have helped my image in Mr. Wynfield's eyes. Somehow, we seemed to have passed a milestone in our relationship. Even though there might have been something strange in the past between us, I pushed the faint uneasiness away. This was now and we were moving toward a new understanding. Dimly, I realized that I was smiling.

Mai woke me sometime later, saying that Mr. Wynfield had arrived earlier than expected. I sprang out of bed and dressed speedily with Mai's assistance. Keeping in mind that Mr. Wynfield would not have changed into dinner clothes, I chose a simple blue foulard with a slight train and a darker silk overskirt looped up in back, the whole thing printed with tiny rosebuds. It was the kind of day dress that would be appropriate for our return trip to Cliffside.

When I entered the parlor, I saw that Drake Wynfield was as neat and immaculate as ever, doubtless having accepted some ministrations from the staff of Mr. Mills.

With a little bow, Mr. Wynfield rose from the settee and handed me a bouquet of creamy long-stemmed roses. "These are from the hothouse of Darius Mills with his gratitude."

"Oh, thank you, they're lovely." I broke off a blossom, then handed the flowers to Mai, who vanished with them into the kitchen. I stepped up to a mirror on the wall and thrust the flower into the modest neckline of my blue silk bodice.

Mr. Wynfield eyed me when I turned around. "I see the heroine has quite recovered."

"At least I'm not hot, dusty, and disheveled now."

"At least." He gave me a leisurely inspection from my freshly washed curls to the glazed kid slippers peeping from my hem.

Our new informality made me rather flustered and I turned away. "Would you care to take some sherry or other wine on the *patio*? The evening is still quite warm outdoors."

"Sherry will be fine, and yes, I'd like to see your garden."

When I led him to the wrought iron table and chairs on the brick-floored terrace, he looked about with interest. "I see your home is built in the Spanish style around an inner court. It's very pleasant with the tiled fountain and vines and trees."

I placed the glasses and wine decanter on the table and poured out a generous libation for each of us. "I imagine Mr. Mills must have a fascinating home. There were pictures of it one time in the *Chronicle.*"

"Would you care to see it?"

"What do you mean?"

He surveyed me over the top of his wine goblet, his eyes a dusky gold, shadowed by the thick dark lashes. "We are both invited to the birthday party for his wife next week."

A thrill of pleasure swept me and I caught my breath. "Oh, that would be wonderful!"

His glance became a bit sardonic. "Yes, the party might do wonders for your career, a chance to mingle with millionaires and become known not only as the heroine who saved the brooch but as San Francisco's first female interior decorator."

I took a hasty gulp of wine and coughed. "I can't deny the idea has a strong appeal."

"You are quite an ambitious woman, aren't you?"

"Perhaps that annoys you." I almost giggled. "Oh, yes, I know that you like women to be gentle, sensitive, and amenable like your fiancée." I couldn't help wondering how the fair Melissa would have acted today during the holdup. Fainted, probably. I was pretty sure she never would have tried to carry off the brooch. I had always liked a challenge. I would not have gone away to school or followed a difficult career if I had been a timid person. In spite of my fright this afternoon, I felt exhilarated and wanted to talk about the experience.

I put down my glass. "It's hard to believe that today we were the victims of a robbery by a masked man threatening us with a gun. I think he was searching for the brooch, don't you?"

"Yes." Mr. Wynfield looked grim as he stared across the garden. "I have no idea how the news leaked out that I was delivering the gems. We took all the usual precautions. Of course, the sale was known to several people and my movements must have been watched. The thief most likely trailed me from the Jade Pagoda and tampered with the bolt while I was talking to you and Blye—"

"Then, when the accident occurred," I interrupted, "he was nearby on horseback, screened by trees, ready to spring forth."

"I guess we were lucky not to suffer physical harm," he said. "I can't tell you how I regret involving you."

Did I have regrets? Not exactly. Dangerous, it might have been, but the outcome had definitely warmed the relationship between Mr. Wynfield and myself.

Mai appeared in the doorway just then and, bowing, struck a small brass gong with a padded hammer, indicating that our supper was ready.

We did full justice to the meal, which consisted of roast suckling pig, steamed fish, white rice, rolls stuffed with chopped lichee nuts, peas and celery cooked together, all accompanied by cups of green Chinese tea. For dessert we had almond custard served with small iced wine cakes. We spoke but little until the meal was over.

At last, replete and happy, I asked Mr. Wynfield, "Shall we go into the parlor for our after-dinner coffee or do you prefer solitary splendor here at the table with your cigars and wine?"

"I will forsake solitary splendor for your company in the parlor . . . if I can walk that far," he added with a groan.

There was no mention of returning immediately to San Francisco and I was content to simply sit, relaxed, with our cups of demitasse. We avoided any further discussion of the holdup, and instead, I questioned him about his trips to foreign ports, where he sought the objects which he sold in San Francisco.

I found his descriptions of Hong Kong fascinating. Its name meant "Fragrant Harbor," but it was scarcely that as it teemed with hundreds of impoverished Chinese living year round on their boats called sampans. However, he said the crowded hilly city, now a Crown Colony of Great Britain, was a very interesting place of mixed races, poverty, and wealth. The shops on narrow, cobbled streets bulged with hundreds of different items from powdered lizard tongues and cricket cages to silk scrolls, cloisonné, and rarest jade.

"I heard there really is a Jade Pagoda in your shop," I exclaimed eagerly. "I'd love to see it."

His face clouded. "There used to be. It was stolen two years ago and never recovered."

"Oh, how terrible!" I paused, wondering whether I should go on. "What did it look like?" I asked cautiously.

"It was about nine inches high, the walls carved of spinach-green jade outlined in gold. The upturned eaves dripped with every kind of gem."

"It sounds exquisite. Where did it come from?"

"Well, my father was a trader in England before he migrated to California in search of gold. On one of his last voyages, he bought the pagoda from a wealthy merchant who had fallen on hard times in Peking. Even when my father desperately needed money before he made his silver strike, he hung on to the Jade Pagoda." He sighed deeply. "It was a great loss and a symbol of our shop."

"Do you know how it was taken?" I took a sip of coffee.

"The lock to the front door was picked open, then the glass case smashed. The doorman who usually guards the shop was found unconscious, bound and gagged in his rear headquarters."

"There certainly is an evil element in our city," I said, today's adventure rising in my memory.

Mr. Wynfield set down his coffee. "You are right, and if you don't mind, I think we should be starting back. The road is long and dark. My inlaws are often out at night and Cliffside is rather isolated from the other estates. If Miss Libby doesn't return soon, I shall have to hire someone else for Tad. I can't rely on the servants all the time."

I rose at once. "I'll get my things. It won't take a minute."

"I would like to pay my compliments to Mrs. Yee before we leave," he said. "It was one of the most delicious meals I've ever had."

I rang for Mai, then ran upstairs to don a long, warm duster and wrap a lacy wool fascinator around my head. About to leave with my bulging valise, I suddenly thought of the coming ball. Fortunately, I had a lovely gown worn only once at Vassar. It even had its own carrying case, in which I carefully folded it, then I went speeding down the stairs.

The isinglass sides had been rolled down on the buggy and we were soon traveling along El Camino Real at a fast clip. I didn't try to make conversation as Mr. Wynfield's face now looked grim and preoccupied. Was he worrying about the holdup?

I was surprised when he spoke at last, almost to himself. "Cliffside often has been a house of discord."

Did he mean his married life? Or was there something else?

"Surely Melissa's presence will change all that," I ventured.

He turned his head and seemed to study me. "Perhaps" was all he said.

9

That night, I heard the flute for the first time.

I was sleeping deeply, exhausted from the day's adventure, yet somehow the eerie notes pierced my consciousness. I sat up groggily, clutching the bedclothes, listening. Suddenly, I was filled with apprehension.

The sound came from the garden, rising and falling in a mournful cadence. My first thought was: Li Fong. But why would he be up, playing music at this hour? Moonlight flooded the room with a silvery radiance through the open window, and according to the clock above the mantel, it was half past two.

Was the music some kind of a signal? The notes were so shrill and insistent, almost as though saying: *Come to me. I command you.* The wailing sound had all the frightening elements of a nightmare. Only I was wide awake.

Unbearably curious, I crept out of bed, padded to

the open window, pushed back the lace curtain, and looked out.

The place below me was bathed in moonlight and as clear to my staring gaze as a well-lit stage: silver trees and silver grass, the white outlines of the vine-clad gazebo. Crosslegged in the center of the yard was a tiny Oriental man, skullcapped, pigtailed, and wearing a black tunic with baggy matching trousers.

In his moonlit hands he held the flute. The music held me in thrall. What did it mean? Who was that little man? Was his playing some kind of signal to Li Fong?

It was strange that no one else seemed to hear the sounds, but then I recalled that my guest room was in an ell across the rear with no other occupants nearby. Or perhaps the others did hear the sound but through familiarity paid no heed to its woeful wailing or else they slept much more soundly than I had.

Suddenly, another figure now appeared on the black and silver stage. A wide slouch hat obscured the face, a long dark cloak did equal service for the body. Man or woman, I couldn't tell. Neither could I tell where the second person had come from. House or road? Was this a tryst? Or just a curious observer?

As I watched, the small man flowed to his feet, removed the flute from his lips, and bowed. He moved into the band of trees, joined by the cloaked intruder. The next moment they had disappeared, while only the flute remained on the marble bench beside the garden path.

My hand flew to my throat. A dark, cloaked figure perhaps involved in villainy just like the highway-man!

Quick as thought, I thrust my feet in slippers, tugged on my silk robe, and sped into the hall. If there was danger from someone who should not be on the grounds, Mr. Wynfield must be aroused immediately.

I knocked on his door and urgently called his name.

"Who's there?" he answered, sounding alert and wide-awake at once.

"Lesley Blair," I whispered hoarsely. "I must speak to you."

The next minute, my employer stood before me with ruffled locks, a dark red robe open on his chest. His glinting amber gaze moved up and down my thinly covered form. "Please come in."

"No!" I drew back indignantly, tugging at my robe, suddenly aware of my late-night visitation. "I want to tell you something. Didn't you hear the flute out in the garden?"

"A flute? No, I didn't." He held the door wider and raked back his tousled hair, then beckoned me imperiously. "Step inside."

"I can't enter your bedroom dressed like this."

He gave an exasperated sigh. "Please come in so that we can talk instead of whispering in the hallway like conspirators. I assure you that your virtue will remain intact. I've never had to resort to force when seeking female companionship. Now what is this all about?"

Reluctantly, I did as he requested, then cleared my throat, trying to speak calmly. "A few minutes ago, I was awakened by a flute being played below my window. When I looked out, I saw an Oriental man in the garden. He must have been signaling someone because, the next minute, a cloaked figure appeared and they went off together through the trees."

"Was the cloaked figure man or woman?" A quick note of alarm was apparent in his voice.

"I couldn't tell, the long dark cloak concealed the figure. The Chinese man bowed, as if in recognition, and then they disappeared. The flute was left behind on one of the marble benches. I could see it shining like silver in the moonlight."

Drake Wynfield's black brows drew together. "I'll go outside and look around at once."

I didn't want to be left alone, so when he opened the door, I flung myself forward and grabbed his sleeve. "I'll show you where he left the flute."

Unfortunately, we jammed together in the doorway and Mr. Wynfield put his arm across my chest. "Look out," he barked.

In the hall, a sound caught our attention and we both stopped moving.

A few feet away, Rachel stood surveying us. She was elaborately gowned in dark maroon and had evidently just come home. She glared at us appraisingly: both in robes, emerging from Drake's room, clutching at each other in what seemed a passionate embrace.

It probably appeared that her deepest, darkest suspicions had been confirmed. The sneering words had a difficult time getting past her tightly pressed lips. "Aha! Just as I thought!"

Mr. Wynfield and I both spoke at once, unfortunately merely creating more confusion.

He said: "What the devil are you hinting, madam?"

And I said: "It's not what you think—I saw someone in the garden and—"

The lady ignored me, but her dark eyes pierced like steel at Drake. "Well, stepson, what you do is your own affair. After all, you have no wife in residence—as yet. And I suppose the girls of Morton Street have lost a customer since"—her flickering gaze swept over me contemptuously—"since you found *her*."

I caught my breath. Not for a moment did I believe that the discriminating Drake would frequent prostitutes. I was glad to see the anger flood his face and voice.

"Rachel! How dare you make such insinuations!" Mr. Wynfield thundered. "You will apologize at once to Miss Blair. Your words are outrageous and without a shred of truth."

She glanced at his dark, terrifying face, his clenched hand, white-knuckled on the door frame, and suddenly she was all innocence. "Oh, dear, just a little ill-timed humor. Pray forgive me."

With a nervous laugh, she swirled away, but she couldn't let it die so easily and twittered over her shoulder, "Of course it's no concern of mine. Whatever you do."

"In *that* you are perfectly correct, madam," Mr. Wynfield ground out between his teeth.

No sooner had Rachel vanished than Jeremy rounded the corner of the hall and strolled toward us. Like her, he was in opera-cloaked attire. He walked with a most careful gait, his handsome features flushed, his golden hair tousled on his brow. He stopped in front of us, barring the way.

"I thought I heard the sound of v-voices. G-good evening, Drake . . . Miss Lesley. Did we disturb you? The opera l-lasted rather late and then the Baldwins invited everyone to the P-Palace for a glass of pisco punch."

I jerked away from Mr. Wynfield's side and cried excitedly. "I just saw someone playing a flute in the garden. He and another person seemed to be having a rendezvous and I thought Mr. Wynfield should investigate."

"Which I was just about to do," Mr. Wynfield grunted. "Did you notice anything outside, Jeremy?"

"No, but I came from the s-stables, not through the garden. Do you want me to go down and look around since neither of you two is—er—dressed for the out-outdoors." He giggled.

I wondered just how many glasses of the potent Peruvian brandy called "pisco punch" Jeremy had consumed.

Drake Wynfield eyed him sardonically. "I think I can handle whatever is slinking around the garden. No matter how I am attired." He tightened the sash on his red robe and strode down the hall.

I started after him. "I'll show you where he left the flute."

Mr. Wynfield disappeared around a corner, but before I could take more than a few steps, Jeremy grabbed my shoulders and jerked me to a halt so that I fell back against his chest.

I gave a startled cry, feeling the spirits-tainted breath against my ear.

"Are you s-sure you weren't dreaming, Lesley?" he chuckled thickly. "An intruder playing a flute underneath your window? Really? Or was it just a p-ploy to gain Drake's attention in the night?"

Sputtering with indignation, I struggled fiercely, tugging at his seeking hands, but he held me fast.

"You're so t-tempting in that thin silk gown slipping from your shoulders. Why don't we go and have a—a—little n-nightcap?"

"What ails you? Let me go this instant!" I cried, kicking and twisting. I managed to swing around and raised my hand to strike his mottled cheek, but he caught my hand, his eyes gloating as he watched my struggles lead to more exposure.

Just then, Mr. Wynfield's authoritative tones rang out from the hall below. "Miss Blair, where are you? I don't see any flute out here . . . or any persons."

Jeremy dropped his hands and I leaped away, pulling up my robe. "Don't ever lay a hand on me again," I hissed. "Or I promise you'll regret it."

He staggered backward. "I—I'm s-sorry, Lesley. I—'pologize." He ran his hand across his face, looking suddenly abashed.

I whirled around and sped down the hallway, so upset I was shaking. My innocent wish to alert the master of the house to an intruder had turned into something resembling scenes from the infamous French boudoir novels that some of us had peeked into at college.

Mr. Wynfield was waiting in the lower hall, and when we hurried outside, I gulped the cold air gratefully.

"I've been all over," he said. "There is no one here. Are you certain you weren't dreaming, Miss Blair?"

"No," I cried indignantly. "I tell you the little man played his flute for several minutes until the other person arrived on the scene and they went off together." I looked around. "The flute was left on that marble bench."

"Well, it's not there now."

Holding up my robe from the dew-wet blades, I peered underneath the bench, along the grass, and all around the area.

"There's not a sign of anything," Mr. Wynfield said. "Perhaps the flute player returned for his instrument. Let's go in. You're shivering in that thin robe."

"You do believe me, don't you?"

"Well, certainly something happened to upset you." With a hand beneath my elbow, he steered me firmly toward the house. "No, I don't believe it was just a dream, but whatever happened, apparently no harm was done."

How could he say no harm was done? Two people had tried to tear my reputation into shreds tonight. Relations with Mrs. Wynfield and her son were going to be difficult from now on. Blast the flute player! I should simply have put my head beneath the pillow and let the music play on.

But that was not my nature. I had to go charging off to investigate and, in the process, confirmed everybody's worst suspicions. The stepmother would henceforth treat me with contempt. And as for Jeremy, he evidently now thought I was a loose-moraled wench and fair game.

"What's the matter?" Mr. Wynfield asked when we paused outside my bedroom door. "Are you still upset because you saw some stranger in the grounds? Did he frighten you that much?"

"Don't you know what has upset me?" I demanded.

He stared, thrusting his hands deep into the pockets of his robe. "I thought you were a sophisticated product of Eastern college culture. Now you are distraught because you were caught emerging from my room in the dead of night, both of us in—er—casual nightwear." His smile was cynical. "As a native of our fair and boisterous city, you should know that the motto is 'live and let live.'"

"That is not my motto," I said hotly. "Besides, where married women or widows are granted much more freedom, a single woman must guard her reputation closely. Especially working as I do in a male-dominated area. My morals will be suspect and scrutinized most closely, you can be sure. You saw how your stepmother reacted just now."

His face grew stern. "I'll have a word with Rachel in the morning."

"And Mr. Jeremy. He saw us also."

Mr. Wynfield's lips tightened, but he merely nodded.

I decided not to elaborate on Jeremy's behavior. I devoutly hoped that he would act the gentleman when he was sober. In any case, I would stay out of his way whenever possible.

"Try to sleep now, Lesley," Mr. Wynfield said. "And thank you for your concern."

Had he actually called me Lesley? I rubbed my head in an attempt to clear it, then I sighed. "It seems it was all for nothing. I'm sorry I disturbed you."

"That's all right." He raised his hand, and for a startled moment, I felt his fingers cup my chin, then trail slowly down my throat.

I gazed up at him in bewilderment, a strange warmth flooding me. Was he about to kiss me? *Did I want him to?*

I must have made some sound, for the next second, he jerked his hand away and turned. His voice grew hard. "Nothing should be left unnoticed around here if it seems odd. There could be danger in that, grave danger."

With his last words ringing in my ears and the disturbing memory of his caressing touch, it was a long time before my weariness succumbed to sleep.

10

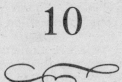

After that night Rachel and Jeremy maintained a cool politeness toward me for which I was grateful as I had a lot to do. Conan was at my side most of the time with aides who stripped the bridal chamber bare. Then the room was painted, satin wallpaper applied, while I stenciled foot-high seashells all around the baseboard. Later, Conan and I would pick out highlights with gold paint.

Sometimes Mr. Wynfield would stop in the doorway to watch us. Our eyes would meet for a brief acknowledgment, but the next time I looked up, the doorway would be empty.

I felt a little disappointed that the rapport gained from our Millbrae trip seemed to have faded. Perhaps he thought it best to keep our relationship on a business level now, and of course, he was right. I must also forget how he had touched me.

"I hope Mr. Wynfield approves of our endeavors,"

I said to Conan one afternoon. "He doesn't comment, yay or nay."

"He's an odd bloke," Conan said reflectively. "Rose made a wrong choice when she married that laddie-o."

At the moment, we were alone and I sat back on my heels, resting my paintbrush on a can. "What was Rose like? Mr. Wynfield said you painted a portrait of her a few years ago."

Conan lowered himself to the bare floor at my side and clasped his hands around his knees, leaning his bright red head back against the new, silver-embossed wallpaper. "Yes. I had just started working for Mr. Blair when Drake applied for an artist at the academy where I had graduated. They recommended me for the job and your papa, God rest his soul, told me to try for it. He was always encouraging me to continue with my painting, y'know."

"This is all news to me. I suppose Papa's heart already was failing, his letters were so brief."

"Aye, we didn't wish to worry you." Conan nodded sadly. "Well, anyway, I got the commission and moved into Cliffside at the same time that Drake left on a ship heading for the Orient. Rose said he had heard about a large estate in Shanghai with rare jewels for sale. He didn't realize that he had a rare jewel right here in his own home named Rose."

I slid him a speculative glance. "Wasn't Drake uneasy about leaving a handsome young man alone with his 'jewel'?"

"Evidently not. At any rate, both Rachel and Jeremy were here to lend respectability." A rather cynical smile curved his mouth below the full mustache. "However, if I'd been Drake, I never would have left such a beautiful wife alone for hours with someone like myself. Though as it happened . . ." Sighing, he stared down at the floor unseeingly and grew silent.

"Yes? What happened? Don't stop now." I studied my paint-smeared cotton gloves, slightly embarrassed by the trend of our conversation but too curious not to pursue it to the end.

"Nothing *happened*, as you so delicately put it," Conan grunted. "The lady wasn't interested in an *affaire*."

"But she looked so seductive in your painting," I exclaimed, recalling her half-bared bosom, the sensuous expression in her eyes, the lushness of velvet and full-blown roses everywhere.

Conan shrugged. "She had a naturally voluptuous shape and a smoldering expression in her gaze, but it was all a lie. At least, as far as I was concerned. I painted her as I wanted her to be, and before I was through, I tried all the tricks at my command to arouse her, villain that I am. However, it was all in vain. She would have none of my Irish blarney or my cajoling ways."

He grinned, quite unabashed, evidently no longer smarting from an unsuccessful seduction. I stared at him curiously. How little I actually knew this man who had been my father's assistant for ten years, although I had heard about the stream of lovelies in his life and the way he squandered money on them and always was in debt. In spite of that, my father thought highly of Conan and I sincerely hoped that he and I could work well together.

Conan's mind was still on Rose. "I think the person she loved most was her son, Tad. He was young and uncomplicated and she could take him into her world of fantasy and weave wonderful tales for him that she later wrote up in little books."

"That seems rather sad. I think you're right,

Drake left her alone too much." With a little surprise, I realized that more and more I thought of "Mr. Wynfield" as simply "Drake." When had that started? Was it when he called me "Lesley?"

"Well, Drake might have felt guilty about leaving her," Conan said. "Her portrait was commissioned to help Rose pass the time. When he returned, he brought her a chain of rare and costly yellow diamonds . . . which the lady claimed she lost."

"*Lost?* A chain of diamonds? How on earth could anyone be so careless?"

Conan shrugged. "I guess she didn't care much for such things. I only saw her once more after Drake returned. She was walking along Montgomery Street and I stepped out of the shop to speak to her. Ah, what a vision she was that day! A bonnet made entirely of blush roses, a frilled parasol, and a gown of white moiré with more pink roses at her breast.

"She nodded coolly to me when I spoke, shrugged and answered indifferently when I inquired about the diamonds: Had they been recovered? She looked uneasy, said she had lost them as the clasp was loose. I couldn't help wondering if she was telling the truth, especially as she hurried off the next minute, all excited about a sale of new French dolls at Ville de Paris."

Conan's mouth twisted cynically. "Ah, no, the lady wasn't interested in me or diamond necklaces. She was an avid collector of *dolls*! Her china ladies cost a great deal of money and she created quite gorgeous outfits for them all. You really should see her collection in the Velvet Room."

Suddenly, there was a footstep in the hall and Conan and I broke off our conversation just as Drake appeared in the doorway. My nerves gave a startled leap and a wave of guilt assailed me. Here I was caught sitting on the floor gossiping with my assistant when my employer had stressed the need for speed.

"Hard at work, I see," Mr. Wynfield remarked dryly.

I raised my head defiantly and stood up, smoothing my paint-spattered smock. My hair was bundled into a mobcap, my old work shoes plainly visible beneath a rough, ankle-length brown cotton skirt. Anyone could see that I was dressed for labor.

I waved my hand around the room. "We *have* been hard at work. The walls will be finished tomorrow and the next day the draperies will be put up—"

Mr. Wynfield interrupted. "Another telegram has just come from Melissa so I hurried home to get the enclosed carriage. She'll be here today and I must try to meet her train in Oakland." He pulled a chased gold watch from his waistcoat pocket and groaned aloud. "Gad, this couldn't have come at a more inconvenient time. A shipment of rare jade has just arrived and Jeremy is nowhere to be found. If you should encounter him before I'm back . . ."

"Would you like us to bring your fiancée here? It would not be any trouble, I assure you." Here was an opportunity to appear better in Drake Wynfield's eyes or at least negate the picture of our sitting on the floor and gossiping. I threw Conan a glance before continuing. "Mr. Blye and I have almost finished for the day and it would be a welcome change to ride across the bay and meet the train."

Conan raked back his thick red hair and grinned. "Oh, aye. Delighted to oblige, old chap."

"Well . . . that's very kind of you both and I will take advantage of your offer. It would certainly save me a great deal of trouble concerning the jade ship-

ment. It must be carefully checked before I pay for it
and only Jeremy and I are sufficiently knowledge-
able in that department."

With a few more remarks concerning the time and
place of the Chicago train's arrival, we all went our
separate ways in somewhat of a hurry.

I flew upstairs to wash, brush my hair, and don a
street dress of braid-trimmed almond serge with a
matching bonnet enlivened by a wreath of varie-
gated flowers in the facing. Gloves, purse, and a
stole of furs completed my outfit, then I tripped
downstairs where Conan waited for me. He also had
freshened in the guest room provided for his use and
looked his usual dapper self in fawn trousers and
checked coat.

Outside, a carriage had been brought to the door,
and after giving directions to the driver, Conan and
I climbed inside. He leaned back on the opposite
gray velvet seat and crossed his arms. "You're a sly
puss, lassie. You put his lordship neatly in our debt
and canceled out the picture of us dawdling on the
floor."

I admitted that had been my aim and we both
chuckled.

"I do feel curious about the bride-to-be," Conan
mused as the two matched bays trotted down the
winding hilltop road. "I wonder if she'll be like
Rose: fey, fascinating, and a disappointment romantically?"

"Well, all I know is that Melissa is Rose's cousin
from the Southern branch. Rachel told me that
Drake met her at a friend's house on one of his buy-
ing trips to Atlanta. When their paths crossed several months back, evidently Melissa wasted no time
engaging Drake's interest. He traveled to her home

and it wasn't long before he asked her to marry him and she agreed."

Conan raised his sandy eyebrows. "It sounds to me as though you and Rachel are becoming cozy gossips."

"Not really. It's just that she unbends occasionally when I evince some curiosity about the family. If she still wonders about Wynfield appointing a young and untried female decorator, she doesn't speculate about it anymore . . . at least not in my presence."

I added, almost to myself, "It still surprises me that I was hired by Mr. Wynfield without more difficulty."

"Perhaps he fell under the spell of your ravishing beauty at first glance."

I gave a trill of laughter. "Now, why didn't I think of that?"

In spite of my levity, I felt my pulses stir as I wondered what Drake really did think of me. Sometimes he seemed to look at me with amusement, sometimes with perplexity, and occasionally I imagined that I saw a glint of admiration. But all in all, he was a difficult man to fathom.

Conan, on the other hand, was all too obvious. I realized he was staring at me with a true connoisseur's appraisal. "Actually, darlin', you really have grown into a most attractive woman. Perhaps you and I should become better acquainted outside of the business hours, if you take my meaning." He gave an exaggerated leer that made me laugh.

"Not you and I! Not romantically. You knew me too well as a scrawny child with long, unraveling pigtails."

"But you aren't scrawny anymore, you've filled out nicely and your skin is fair as a white rose petal."

"There speaks the man well versed in blarney." I gave him the same assessing glance he'd given me. "You aren't so bad-looking yourself, my lad. Papa used to wonder why you never married. You certainly had enough lovely women after you."

"Perhaps I was waiting for you to grow up." His brown eyes twinkled, then he sobered. "I must admit the ladies have been very generous to me, very sweet, but I guess the ones who were not 'soiled doves' were looking for a more stable sort of fellow, not someone with a roving eye and who always was in debt. Believe me, the Tongs are bloody ruthless when you owe them money."

I threw him a startled glance. Was Conan acquainted with the Tongs? Had he borrowed money from them to finance his romantic flings? "Conan, what do you think of Li Fong? Mai Yee told me that he used to be an important member of a Chinese Tong."

Conan answered slowly. "Well, he only runs Cliffside now, doesn't he? And goes on errands for Drake in Chinatown."

I leaned forward in my seat and dropped my voice. "I didn't tell you about the night I heard a strange sound coming from the garden and saw a little Oriental man down there playing on a flute. It was almost like some sort of signal. Another person then appeared and they both left."

Conan shrugged, though it seemed to me that he looked uneasy. "Probably just one of Li's friends. The Chinese love their flutes."

That was true, of course. I probably had made too much of the affair that night, rousing Drake, getting so excited. It was just that it had come so soon after the trouble on the highway, but Drake had not found anything in the garden, not even the flute. I certainly hoped Drake believed me and didn't think I merely had been looking for attention from him. I would have to be more careful in the future before I troubled him unnecessarily.

We now were bowling along the wide thoroughfare of Market Street, which had raised such controversy at the size allotted to it when it was first built. However, in a few years it had proved to be a dire necessity. It nearly always was thronged with every kind of conveyance from carts and carriages to public horsecars.

Market Street ended at the wharves and there a ferry waited on the bay. Conan and I quickly boarded the big steamer operated by the Southern Pacific Company. We took seats inside since the day was windy as it usually was out on the water.

Conan obtained two cups of coffee for us at a counter concession, and after we had sipped for a few minutes, he turned sideways on the yellow varnished bench and said emphatically, "I'll bet you're as curious as I am to see the fair Melissa. Am I right?"

I nodded and he chuckled. "You always were a nosy little tyke. I remember you poking around in all the shops and alleys when you could get away from Mai." He regarded me with tolerant amusement. "Sometimes you ran into trouble. You often would get lost and scared."

Something flickered in my mind. Lost . . . darkness . . . airless space . . . A series of pictures flashed across my inner vision, but all were too swift for clarity. Except that there were eyes like Drake's. Tiger eyes. My heart began to race. *Was Drake going to spell danger to me in some dark, hidden place?*

Fortunately, Conan had stepped outside to watch the docking so he had no knowledge of my sudden perturbation. I forced myself to draw deep breaths. This was nonsense! Drake was no mysterious villain. How could he harm me? Why should he want to?

Mentally, I upbraided myself for giving rein to such ridiculous fears that had no slightest basis in reality. Usually I was a clear-headed, no-nonsense kind of woman. Why should Drake have this unsettling effect on me? Of course, ever since the other night when he had stroked my neck, I had found him increasingly attractive as well as occasionally alarming.

I knew I must discourage these disturbing thoughts, and when Conan called to me, I swiftly joined him on the deck, letting the fresh, cold wind blow the cobwebs from my brain.

That's all they were, I sternly told myself. Just cobwebs.

11

When we alighted at the Oakland dock, Conan headed for a flower stall beside the train depot. "I think Melissa should have a welcoming present," he said and selected a posy of spring blooms: tulips, daffodils, and violets, smelling heavenly. He had it all arranged in a cardboard holder with a frill of paper lace.

"What a nice idea," I commented, thinking it was no wonder Conan was such a success with the ladies.

The train had already arrived and people emerged from it in droves. Soon the platform and surrounding area were thronged, but still no red-haired girl appeared who looked anything like the miniature I had seen.

It was not until nearly all the travelers had dispersed that our straining eyes discerned a wilting creature borne along by the conductor of the train.

As they drew near, I noted her appearance with

dismay. Why, this girl looked ill! She had a wan white face, shadowed watery eyes, and a tiny nose reddened by the constant application of a wadded muslin handkerchief. Her hair was red, all right, but straight and lusterless beneath a crooked bonnet. One hand clutched at her thin, soft cloak beneath which her frail body shivered constantly.

"Are you—are you Melissa Fernley?" I asked incredulously, stepping forward.

The maiden nodded wanly. Speech seemed beyond her.

The conductor addressed us with an expression of relief. "This lady is Miss Melissa Fernley, all right. She has been ill with *la grippe* ever since we left Chicago."

"Oh, I'm so sorry, Miss Fernley," I exclaimed, putting out my hand.

She merely stared at it.

"I'm Miss Blair. I work for your—intended. And so does Mr. Blye. We've come to escort you to Cliffside. Mr. Wynfield was unavoidably detained."

Melissa looked too tired even to wonder at the whereabouts of her future bridegroom.

Conan bowed to her, extending the bouquet. "I'd like to welcome you to San Francisco, Miss Fernley. And I hope that you will soon be well."

She brightened slightly. "So kind." Her voice, however, was thick and hoarse.

The conductor patted her. "That's all right, then. I feared this little lady might need hospitalization, but really, she's been improving lately. A warm room, soft food, and her beloved by her side, then she'll soon recover, I've no doubt." With a kind smile, the burly, mustachioed young man removed his arm from Melissa's grasp. "I'll have a porter bring her luggage to you."

When released, Melissa promptly tottered. Conan instantly sprang forward, supporting her with an arm around her waist. "Now then, lassie, it's right as rain you'll be as soon as we get you home. Do you have no warmer cloak? You're fairly shivering."

Staring up at him, Melissa mutely shook her head.

I had nothing but my little string of martens, so I unclasped the furs and tucked them around her neck. She gave them an appreciative stroke.

"Where's your maid, Miss Fernley?" I inquired.

"Sick," she croaked. "She had to remain in Chicago, halfway through our journey. Oh, so dreadful! But I came on." She coughed. "I was afraid if I didn't, Drake . . . you know . . . so upset . . ."

I led her to a bench while Conan went to arrange for the delivery of her trunks. As soon as we were alone, Melissa began a stream of complaints about the train, interspersed with sniffs and coughs. I told her she should keep still and save her voice, but she ignored my advice, seeming to find relief in describing the woes of such a long, arduous trip. The swaying of the train had made her ill; it had been too cold for words; and when her maid was no longer with her, life became intolerable—as well as being the height of impropriety.

"Didn't you travel by private car?" I inquired, remembering some last-minute instructions from Mr. Wynfield about where to find her.

"Oh, yes. We had beds, a lavatory, and a place called a 'galley' where a cook made meals. But oh, I had no one to help me dress or undress. No one to talk with me or fetch things. I was *all alone*." Her weak voice wobbled. "I had no idea the West was so —so *wild*. When the train stopped, I saw rough men on the platforms, wearing guns and chewing tobacco. And I saw *Indians*! Oh, terrible!"

Suddenly, the tirade halted and the miserable little face before me crinkled with perplexity. "Did you tell me why my betrothed did not come to fetch me? I forget."

I repeated my explanation, elaborating on Drake Wynfield's distress at being absent. Then I told her what Conan and I were doing at Cliffside and described the room we were preparing.

Nothing cheered her. "So nice," she droned, pulling petals off the violets. "Is it far?"

"Well, of course, it's across the bay. Then you go through the City and up a hill to an area by the bay called Sea Cliff."

Tears suddenly trickled from the reddened eyes. "It's all so strange. I wish I had my Hattie here."

"Your maid? Well, don't worry, there are lots of maids at Cliffside. Nice young girls. And a skillful Chinese man runs the place."

"*Chinese!* Oh, my lord!" She shrank back, clutching at the furs around her neck. "I've never seen a Chinaman. He would scare me half to death!"

"Nonsense. Everyone will be kindness itself." I felt some exasperation intruding on my sympathy. I couldn't help feeling that there was nothing terribly wrong with her that a couple of days of being waited on in a warm bed wouldn't cure. I was sure that when her present indisposition was over, she also would display both youth and beauty. And she was on her way to a wealthy, handsome fiancé with whom she certainly must be in love. A thousand girls, nay, *more*, would gladly exchange places with her. All she needed, in my opinion, was a little backbone.

I was glad when Conan joined us and practically carried Melissa onto the ferry, where he tucked her up with a blanket obtained from the captain and supplied her with a cup of steaming coffee.

Melissa rallied a little as warmth and coffee seeped into her body. "Are you both staying at Cliffside?"

Conan answered. "Miss Blair and I have both been given rooms there until the redecorating is completed."

"I'm glad you'll be there, Mr. Blye," Melissa whispered.

Her own handkerchief was sodden so Conan handed her one of his own. The way she thanked him, you would have thought it was a priceless gift. Perhaps it was, just then.

"You're so kind, Mr. Blye." She clutched the white square to her face, adding belatedly, "Both of you, of course."

I felt guilty because I had been annoyed by her weakness and copious tears. Who was I to judge? After my mother's death due to a chest infection, I had been reared by a strong, intelligent father who encouraged my independence. He sent me away to a distant college that made my brain stretch and reach and think. I knew nothing of Melissa's background except that she came from a genteel Southern family and seemed completely dependent on her maid. Perhaps if I had been reared as she had been, I would be the same, although a corner of my mind rejected that notion.

I wondered what Drake would think of this damp, quavering creature crying for her maid?

After two cups of coffee, Melissa roused enough to ask, "How is Drake? And Tad? And please, tell me what Cliffside is like. And San Francisco."

Conan laughed. "That's a tall order, *macushla*. 'Tis better for you to see it for yourself."

"No," I said thoughtfully, looking at Melissa. "She needs to have a picture in her mind and get familiar with some things." I therefore described the crowded city, the churning bay, the steep hills, the fine shops, the busy docks with ships from all over the world. Melissa looked bewildered.

Finally, I came to the house itself. "It's a splendid mansion on a cliff. But it has too much furniture and is overcrowded with ornaments, heavy drapes, and so forth. I am a trained decorator and I want to change all that—if I can persuade Mr. Wynfield—or you—to let me."

Melissa shook her head. "Oh, no, Miss Blair, I'd never dream of changing things. And surely Mr. Wynfield likes the house the way it is."

"But we could make it so much better—"

"No, no," she whispered. Adamant.

I stared at her. What had we here? A lion in a mouse's garb? So Melissa would stand firm if she thought it was her husband's wish? Then I would just have to persuade Mr. Drake Wynfield myself.

Conan smiled at her, adding a few gentle observations of his own about the city. He didn't seem aware of the danger she could be to us if she wouldn't support our ideas for the redecorating. After all, his career was not at stake and he could always fall back on portrait painting.

Perhaps in his heart, I thought Conan was glad that Melissa was so bedraggled. It was obvious he had no liking for Drake Wynfield and had been jealous that he had possessed the beauteous Rose.

When Conan and I entered Cliffside, supporting Melissa between us, Li Fong met us in the hall. I felt Melissa jerk with fear.

"Welcome to San Francisco, Miss Fernley," he

hissed, bowing low and showing no surprise at her condition. "Master waits in parlor."

Melissa couldn't speak. It was up to me to say, "Thank you, Mr. Li," and lead the way.

Fortunately, the parlor was warm with leaping flames in the iron grates, lamps were lit, draperies drawn. When we entered, Mr. Wynfield rose and swiftly crossed the Turkey carpet. I saw his eyes grow wide.

"Melissa, you look ill! What has happened?"

He reached for her as she began to wail. "Ohhhh, I've been so sick. That train was *awful*. And Hattie had to stay behind in Chicago until she's better. I thought I'd *die*! I was *all alone*. Oh, Drake, you should have come for me on that long trip." She fell against his chest and began to sob, her bonnet more askew than ever, wisps of hair trailing into her open mouth.

Drake was not unkind. If he felt surprise, dismay, or even distaste, he didn't show it. He held Melissa gently in his arms, patting her back, and speaking words of comfort—which only made her wail louder.

His eyes sought mine. "What happened to her?"

I explained as much as I knew of the situation, then added, "Perhaps I should help her up to bed now. She needs a hot bath and some soft food and drink."

"I think I should call a doctor—" Drake began, looking down at her.

"No, no," Melissa screamed hoarsely, her little fists beating at his chest. "I won't go to a hospital! People die when they go there! Both my uncles died in Yankee hospitals during the war!"

"I was only going to have Dr. Crane come here," Drake said soothingly. "But perhaps it can wait until morning. Lesley will take you to the room next to hers and—"

"*Who's Lesley?*" Melissa demanded, rearing back.

"I meant Miss Blair."

With a narrowed glance, Melissa allowed me to take her arm. In the hall, she transferred her wet eyes to Conan, who trailed behind us. "Oh, sir, you have been so kind. I swear to goodness, I don't know how I would have survived today without you."

Conan bowed, said it had been a pleasure to serve her, and trusted she soon would be in good health.

I managed to steer Melissa up the stairs while she hung heavily on my arm. The guest room next to mine had been prepared for her and a fire burned cozily in the grate. Curtains of blue velvet were drawn tightly against the nightly chill.

Ignoring the room, Melissa shrieked, her gaze flying to the windows, "Lord above, what's that awful wailing noise?"

"Oh, you mean the foghorns? You'll often hear them. I guess a fog is coming up in the bay."

Uttering a wail of her own loud enough to drown out all other sounds, Melissa staggered to the bed. She tore off her bonnet, ripped away my furs. "Help undress me, Miss Blair. I can't wait for some old, inept maid to attend me. My shoes first, then undo my gown."

Since the girl was ill, I did as she demanded. When she was in pantalettes and camisole, she bade me take a brush from her reticule and go to work on her snarled and straggling hair. She sat on a chair in front of me and the brushing seemed to soothe her.

"Such a nice gentleman," she said in her thickened Southern drawl. "Don't you agree he's handsome, Miss Blair?"

"Mr. Wynfield? Why, yes, indeed. Extremely attractive—"

"No, no, *Mr. Blye*. Are you two sweethearts? He said he worked for you." She raised her head and gave me a hard stare.

"Mr. Blye is a free man, romantically speaking, and although he is pleasant and handsome, he is no more so than Mr. Wynfield . . . to whom you are engaged," I added rather tartly.

She gave a juicy sniff. "You don't have to remind me of that, Miss Blair. I declare, I guess I know my duty."

Duty? Was that all Drake meant to her? I was appalled. How could that be? Drake with his forceful personality that seemed to combine strength with sensuality . . . the suggestion of hidden fires that lurked in his amber-colored eyes . . . the attractive, husky voice . . . I could only suppose that Melissa appreciated him more when she was well.

When the maids entered with jugs of hot water for the bathing room, I slipped out hastily before I could be asked to scrub Melissa's back. Enough was enough. She'd have to learn I was no servant.

Outside in the hall, I encountered Drake. "Lesley, how is she?" he inquired, looking anxiously at her door. "Will she be all right?"

"She just has a head cold, I believe. A few days of bed rest, warmth, and good food should fix her up."

He sighed. "I sincerely hope so. This climate must be such a change for her after coming from the South."

"She also was upset because she had to travel alone the past few days."

He thrust his hands deep into his jacket pockets, frowning at the floor. "I arranged for a private car and paid that maid, Hattie, to accompany her."

"Oh, I'm sure you did everything in your power to ease the journey for her."

Our eyes met and I felt a wave of pity as I saw the uncertainty, the masculine dismay when faced with unexpected illness. Perhaps Melissa seemed like a stranger to him.

Impulsively, I put my hand upon his arm. It felt so strong, rock-hard, yet he was just a vulnerable human being after all. "Don't worry, Mr. Wynfield, she'll be well very soon. I'm sure of it."

He looked down at me. "Thank you for going after her, although perhaps I should have gone myself."

"We took good care of her."

"I'm sure you did. I'm very grateful to you both. But I don't think she will be in any condition to attend the ball of Darius Mills even though the invitation included any of my houseguests."

Strangely enough, I had forgotten about the ball. "I can stay home with Melissa."

"No, if the doctor says she'll be all right, I'll assign a maid to care for her. Mr. Mills insisted that I bring you and I know how much the party means to you as a business opportunity."

My spirits lifted at this unexpected mark of his consideration.

"I'm sure Melissa will want to stay in bed for the next few days," he added. "I doubt if we'll see much of the poor girl until she's feeling better."

"I think you're right," I answered.

However, we both were wrong. That very night, Melissa came screaming into my room.

12

Melissa didn't even knock. She burst open the door and flung herself upon my bed, babbling almost hysterically.

For a moment I could make no sense of what she said. "Someone called to you from the hall?" I asked, the last shreds of sleep falling away as I sat up and blinked.

"Yes, yes, first there was knocking at my door, then a voice whispering, threatening. Oh, dreadful!" She began to sob. "I want to stay in here!"

"All right." I got up and took her arm. "Climb under the covers. You're shivering." I went into the hall and peered up and down before I returned to the bedside. "There's no one out there. Perhaps you had a nightmare—"

"No, no, I swear to goodness I was awake. I'm positive!" Her voice rose shrilly.

I drew on my silk robe and lit a candle. "Do you want me to call Mr. Wynfield?"

"N-no, he'd say the same as you—he'd think— He wouldn't like to be awakened." Tears ran down her face and I handed her a handkerchief from the box upon my dresser.

"Tell me exactly what happened."

Her voice was muffled as she wiped her nose. "I took some headache powders, but I was not asleep yet when I heard a knocking on the door and then a voice. It—it said, 'Go home, go home. Stay away from the Velvet Room unless you want to die.' Oh, Miss Blair, was it a ghost? *Is Cliffside haunted?*"

"Of course not," I said emphatically. I pulled on my bed slippers, then peered once more down the hallway while Melissa watched me, trembling and sniffling. In spite of my skepticism, I felt a stirring of alarm. There had been several disturbing events recently, including the flute player. . . .

"Who could it have been?" Melissa quavered. "That Chinaman? Or—or Tad? Why don't you go and ask that boy?"

"I will tomorrow, but I doubt if Tad would—"

She slapped the covers. "No, go now! I vow I won't close my eyes all night unless I know who it was. He might come back!"

I strove for calming reason. "Miss Fernley, I think it was a dream. Ask yourself what could be gained by such a silly trick? You are a sick, inoffensive creature. Who could mean you any harm?"

She glared at me with red, wet eyes. "Don't you understand? No child likes a new stepmama, nor do servants want a new, young mistress. And right now, I am purely hideous." She let loose an angry puff of air. "I thought Drake was absolutely *frigid* for a man who hasn't seen his fiancée for at least a month."

I wanted to ask her if she suspected *Drake*!

She struggled higher on the pillow with an angry

sob. "And to think what I was down South. They used to call me 'The Jewel of Jamestown.' They really did! You have no idea of the beaux I had, flowers delivered every day, gifts, invitations—"

"Why didn't you marry someone back home, then?" I cut in bluntly.

She thrust out her lower lip, twisting my handkerchief into a rope. "We quarreled, that's why, Tom and I. He just went dashing off. It was awful! And after I'd told everyone that I expected a declaration from him any day. Then while I was visiting in Atlanta to cure my broken heart, I ran into Drake. He's rich and handsome and sometimes I used to envy Rose. She wrote one time that Drake had given her a long chain of yellow diamonds. I must ask him about that. I'd love to have them. . . ."

Her voice trailed off sleepily and she closed her eyes. "Oh, I feel so tired, my head's about to burst. You go tell that Tad his papa's going to whip him tomorrow, sure as fate."

"I can't do that," I protested. "We aren't certain he's the culprit. However, I'll look in his room. If he's asleep, we'll know it wasn't him."

I gave her another headache powder in some water, then picked up my candle and headed for the door. Melissa called after me in a drowsy, thickened voice, "I don't want to stay here alone, you hear?"

What did she think I was, some sort of upper servant? I must straighten out her thinking, but right now I had more important matters on my mind.

I slowed down in the hall, trying to collect my thoughts. Unless Melissa had been dreaming, the whisperer probably had been Tad. The little boy must have been terribly upset to sneak out in the night and disturb Melissa in that manner. I hoped

that I would find him fast asleep. But if not Tad . . .
then who?

I had almost reached the nursery, where I knew
Tad slept, when I saw something that made me halt
abruptly. A faint light shone from the portrait gallery
. . . and the door stood open!

Quickly, I blew out my candle and set it on a table.
I had no wish to be a target in case someone else
was abroad this night who had no business here.
Though in all likelihood, it was Tad up in his
mother's room, seeking solace after the arrival of
the dreaded Melissa. Poor little lad, I could swear
there was no malice in him. He was just a lonely
child who might have heard too many stories about
the wicked stepmother.

If I found him in the Velvet Room, I would try to
comfort him and put his mind at ease about Melissa,
then coax him back to bed. I must impress on him
that his father would be very upset if he knew about
his son's nocturnal mischief.

Not once did it occur to me that none of this was
any of my business.

Inside the portrait gallery, I discovered that the
light came from the rear staircase, the door of which
also stood open. I began to feel uneasy. Suppose
Conan had crept up to visit the haunt of his former
desire? Then another thought flashed in my mind.
What if the diamonds were not really lost, as Rose
had said? What if she had hidden them to sell later
so she would have money to buy more exquisite
dolls? Most likely, she hid them in her private area,
the Velvet Room. Suppose Li Fong was searching for
the chain of diamonds? Or suppose it was a strange
thief like the villain on the highway?

Until I knew, I must be very careful. A cautious
peek and that was all. If I saw an intruder, I would

fly for help, but I must be a little slower to disturb Drake than I had been the other night.

Trying to subdue my rapid breathing, I moved carefully up the staircase and edged through the door, staring apprehensively at the shadowed scene. Even in the minimal light, I could discern a lush and opulent abode. I felt thick carpets underfoot, caught the gleam of velvet drapes drawn back with golden cords, and all around on floor, tables, and shelves, I glimpsed a staggering array of staring, white-faced china dolls.

Though the room seemed empty of humanity, a faint light came from the adjoining bedchamber and someone might be in there. Inching forward, my foot struck an object which immediately tinkled: "Ma-ma!" I froze. The light went out and blackness swept the whole scene, dense and suffocating.

The next instant, I felt a rush of movement. "Don't move," a voice snarled behind my ear as an arm was flung across my chest. Then, to my horror, a hard hand clutched my bosom.

"Let me go!" I cried, twisting and struggling.

"Lesley?" came an uncertain growl. And suddenly I was free.

Light erupted and Drake, clothed in shirt and trousers, stood holding a yellow-orbed brass lantern.

I couldn't speak as we stared at each other in mutual dismay and embarrassment.

He cleared his throat. "Forgive me for—uh—manhandling you just now. I didn't expect to find a woman. What on earth are *you* doing up here?"

I jerked my wrapper tightly to my neck and swallowed hard. "I—I thought Tad might be in the Velvet Room."

"*Tad?*"

"Y-yes." I swayed a little, still trembling from the shock of being captured in the dark and the knowledge that Drake's hand had just explored my breast.

"Please sit down for a minute and tell me what this is all about." Drake put the lantern on a nearby stand, then propelled me to a sofa and lowered himself beside me, moving aside a mound of fancy velvet pillows. "Now what made you think that Tad was here?"

Nervously, I brushed back my tousled hair. "Melissa came to my room just now, very distraught. . . ."

He half rose. "Is she worse?"

"No, it's not that. She said a voice had threatened her from the hallway, telling her to go away and stay out of the Velvet Room."

"She must have had a bad dream."

"I'm not sure. She insisted that I find out who it was. She felt it might be Tad."

"He wouldn't do a thing like that." But in the flickering light, Drake's face looked disturbed.

"I didn't think so either, but little boys sometimes play tricks, especially with an unknown stepmother."

"I, too, heard footsteps in the hall," Drake said, frowning down at the hands held loosely between his knees. "When I came out of my room, I saw a light in the Velvet Room, which vanished by the time I got up here. I think some things have been disturbed, but it wasn't Tad. His mother's collection means a lot to him."

"Could it have been a burglar?" I wondered. "A servant?" Li Fong sprang to mind. "Perhaps the missing diamonds that Rose had—"

He gave an angry exclamation. "So you've heard about the blasted things? I assure you that after

Rose died I went over every inch of this place and I'm convinced she sold them, probably to a dealer in Chinatown so she could buy more dolls."

He glanced at me and then stood up. "Let's go. It's cold up here and there's nothing more to be done. I want to look in on Melissa."

The Jamestown Jewel was sound asleep when we softly entered. With the lamplight shining on her red-gold locks and her face relaxed, she looked young and beautiful.

"Let's not disturb her," I whispered. "I'll sleep in her room tonight."

"Very well." Drake nodded wearily.

He looked so sad. My heart went out to him. He had a lot to contend with right now: someone searching in the Velvet Room, Tad's antagonism toward Melissa, and a sick, complaining fiancée who must seem like a stranger. Without another word, he walked away, head bent, his hands thrust deep into his trouser pockets.

I felt certain that his inadvertent clasp upon my breast already had faded from his mind, but as for me, I still could feel that hard, warm, intimate pressure that no man had ever given me before. Had he noticed my heart fluttering like a startled bird beneath his fingers?

13

Something woke me earlier than I wished next morning. My mind seemed swathed in cotton wool. What was I doing in a different guest room? This one had shades of blue whereas mine . . .

Then I jerked upright in a spasm of alarm. Something was scratching at the door, and as I watched, slowly . . . slowly, it began to open. I stared at it, hypnotized. It seemed as though my scalp actually prickled, raising up my hair, and gooseflesh puckered the bare arms that I hugged across my body.

This had come too soon after last night's fright or I might have reacted differently. But when a black and white object appeared near the bottom of the door, I screamed and heaved a pillow at the opening.

"Miss Lesley," cried Tad. And Prince added his own dismay with a startled bark.

Boy and dog edged through the doorway, eyeing me uncertainly.

"Oh, it's you." I sank back and drew the blanket up to my chin. "Hello. Come in."

Tad picked up the pillow and cautiously advanced. "What's the matter, Miss Lesley? Did you think I was a spook?"

"Yes." I laughed. "No, I just was half-awake. I didn't expect—uh—Prince to open the door."

The aggrieved pup, quick to sense rejection, hid behind Tad's legs. He slid out only when I apologized.

"Hello there, Prince. Sorry about the pillow."

"Where's that Melissa lady?" Tad inquired, looking around the room and wrinkling his forehead. "Mary said she was in here and felt sick so I brought her some violets." He moved close to the bed and held out a ragged purple handful, still wet with morning dew, for my inspection.

I leaned forward. "Oh, they smell divine. That was very thoughtful of you, Tad, but Melissa is sleeping in my room. She came in there when something scared her in the night and then she fell asleep in my bed."

"What scared her, Miss Lesley?" Tad looked away, the violets trembling slightly.

"Somebody came to her door in the night and whispered to her not to go in the Velvet Room or she'd be in trouble." I didn't ask if he'd been the midnight prowler. Let his father question him. The boy certainly didn't seem antagonistic toward Melissa now, or at least he had repented when he heard that she was ill.

Tad dropped his eyes and muttered, "That was a funny thing to say to her."

I eyed him narrowly. "Who do you think it was, whispering like that at her door?"

"I dunno. Maybe . . . maybe it was a bad dream."

Although I didn't answer, the possibility certainly had occurred to me as well as Drake.

Tad leaned against the edge of the bed, fingering the spread. "Is she very sick?"

"No, she'll be all right in a day or two. It's just a head cold, but perhaps you better not bother her until she's better."

"What's she like?" he whispered.

"She's young, far from home, not well, and must feel very strange in this new place. So be kind to her, Tad. Give her a chance to know what a nice, good boy you are. Now, why don't you put the violets in that water glass and I'll see that she knows you sent them. Do you want to come have breakfast with me as soon as I get dressed?"

"I'll walk downstairs with you, Miss Lesley, but I always eat up in the nursery by myself."

How lonely that sounded, but I couldn't go around suggesting changes. Tad and Prince waited in the hall while I flung on my robe and then collected the necessary garments from my room (where Melissa still was wrapped in deepest slumber). When I had dressed in a warm gold-hued merino trimmed with a neat lace collar, Tad, Prince, and I went down the stairs.

Tad's small hand crept into mine. "Miss Lesley, will you let me show you around the Velvet Room this morning? We can see if everything's all right there and then I could tell you about my mother's doll collection."

"We should ask your father first," I said, but I admitted to myself that I felt an overwhelming eagerness to accept Tad's offer. My recent indistinct vision of the lovely room had whet my appetite to behold its beauties in the daylight.

Tad shook his head. "We can't ask Papa. He's gone to town already and Li Fong said he won't be back all day."

"Very well then, if you're sure it will be all right. I would love to see the doll collection. I was a rather lonely little girl and dolls were my favorite playthings."

"I'll wait for you upstairs," Tad cried joyously. "We can meet right after breakfast."

When I entered the morning room, I found it occupied by Rachel, Jeremy, and Conan, all in the midst of eating. Li Fong presided impassively at the sideboard, where dishes warmed over tiny candles and held all manner of breakfast meats and hot breads, among other things.

My eyes slid to each face and I greeted them before filling my plate with scrambled eggs, sausage, and a hot biscuit. Conan, Rachel, Jeremy, and Li Fong could all be suspect in last night's activities. Conan had hinted at his debt due to a romantic fling. Rachel and Jeremy were terribly extravagant and seemed to spend money at every turn. Perhaps what Drake was providing them with was not enough to keep them in they style they liked. And Li Fong had been involved with the infamous Tongs. I couldn't even discount Tad. He *might* have been the midnight whisperer and he *might* have been in the Velvet Room searching for something belonging to his mother. Perhaps one of her little stories?

As for the rest of the household, any of them might know where to find the lock to Rose's hideaway. They all seemed to be in want of money and some recent need could make it urgent that they find the gems . . . if they still existed.

Had one of them warned Melissa to stay out of the Velvet Room in order to clear the way for searching? Melissa was Rose's cousin and conceivably could be interested in her retreat.

Sipping my coffee, I gave an inward sigh, my eyes traveling around the table. Did I malign them unjustly? If they weren't searching for the diamonds, someone might simply seek Rose's bower to relive the time when the exquisite young woman had lived there. Conan had desired her. Drake had loved her. So had Tad. Maybe even Jeremy . . .

As my eyes rested thoughtfully on his perfect features, Jeremy smothered a yawn and then gave what amounted to an alibi for the past night.

"I guess I'll have to start curtailing my late hours in the City. I didn't get to bed until the wee hours this morning."

"Neither did I," said Rachel. "But San Francisco has such a marvelous night life: operas, concerts, plays, and parties, parties everywhere."

"To say nothing of the gambling and horse racing." Jeremy added. "Don't you find it fascinating, Miss Lesley?"

"Yes, it is a lively town. But I left for college before I was able to participate in much social life. And now I am too busy."

"You should find the time, you're so young and lovely." His narrowed eyes trailed over me like a caressing hand. "I would love to take you with me some evening. Will you give me that pleasure in the near future?"

I made some evasive answer, but in my heart, I whispered firmly: *Never!* Since our distasteful encounter several nights ago, Jeremy had been the soul of courtesy and amiability; however, the other memory of his seeking hands and wet, wine-tainted lips was still too fresh in my mind. I had shown him on that occasion that I was not the easy conquest he expected, but perhaps he was not deterred, merely biding his time for another foray. I intended to be on my guard with him at all times, even though he looked the very soul of open-faced, boyish appeal. And of course, so devastatingly handsome.

I often saw him and Rachel departing in the evening, in separate carriages or together. Both "dressed to kill," as the saying went, adorned in satin, velvet, furs, and jewels, always in long opera cloaks of some dark, rich hue. They certainly seemed to be a pleasure-loving pair, which must take quite a bit of money.

"How much longer are you staying here, Miss Blair?" Rachel's harsh tones broke in on my musings and I found her staring at me narrowly, her jeweled fingers toying with her china cup.

"I don't know exactly," I replied. "It all depends on whether Mr. Wynfield wishes me to refurbish other rooms besides Melissa's."

"Ah, yes, the bride-to-be," Jeremy drawled, leaning back in his chair. "How is the fair Melissa? Still suffering from a malaise, I hear."

"She's had a head cold," I said, "and was quite miserable when Mr. Blye and I brought her from the train. But I think she is on the mend."

Jeremy looked at Conan, who had been silent up to now. "What is she like, old man? As lovely as her portrait? By Jove, I think I'll visit her this morning. Ladies confined to bed are always . . . so . . . sweetly vulnerable." He gave a rather ribald chuckle.

"Jerry, I declare, you are an awful boy," his mother reproved fondly.

"You'll make an enemy for life if you visit Melissa

when she's ill," I told him tartly. "No woman wants to be seen by a strange man under such unflattering circumstances."

"We won't be strangers long, I promise you." Jeremy smiled, then turned his glance on Conan. "You haven't answered me, Blye. What did you think of the young maiden? She, who will not be a maiden for much longer."

Conan's glance held ill-disguised dislike and he answered stiffly, "I'm sure Melissa Fernley is a beauty when in good health. And a very sweet young lady, too." He shoved back his chair abruptly. "Lesley, I'd like a word with you before I run some errands."

I rose and met him in the hall. "Where are you going, Conan?"

"I want to check on the draperies, among other things. We'll have to speed up our work now that Melissa's here. Look, Lesley, will you try to keep that young puppy from bothering her?"

"Prince?" I gave him a bewildered glance, then I grinned. "Oh, you mean Jeremy, don't you?"

Conan ground his teeth. "Aye, the brainless spalpeen considers himself Don Juan, Romeo, and Apollo of the gods, all rolled into one."

"You can also add a goodly portion of the satyr. Don't worry, I'll ask Mary to keep an eye on Melissa. Jeremy should be going to work at The Jade Pagoda pretty soon." I thought with wry amusement that Conan certainly was susceptible to a pretty face.

"Thanks, darlin', I'll be back as soon as possible." Conan picked up a peaked tweed cap from the hall tree, threw a scarf around his neck, and vanished out the front door.

My appetite had been amply satisfied so I didn't return to the breakfast room. The complaining Rachel and the lecherous Jeremy were not my ideal companions during a meal or at any other time.

I found Tad waiting impatiently by my bedroom door. He caught me by the hand and looked up eagerly. "Are you ready to see the Velvet Room, Miss Lesley?"

I informed him that I was and we set out.

There was no dallying by the portraits this morning. Even Rose's picture was passed with no more than a brief smile from her young son. Up the short flight of stairs we went. The door was then opened by Tad and flung wide with an expansive gesture to admit me to the treasure chamber.

Now I could view it clearly, especially when Tad drew back the draperies. The Velvet Room certainly must have been worthy of Princess Rose-Red, especially in its heyday. Tad informed me that his father supervised a cleaning once a month, and although I could see dust motes dancing in the sunlight, the pink velvet draperies, filmy lace curtains, moss-green seats, and matching rugs were all beautifully kept.

Rose had favored overwhelming decorations just as she had downstairs, but up here by staying within two color schemes, pink and green, she had achieved an effect that was rich and beautiful.

Tad led me around the room, pointing out the gilt and marble tables laden with exquisite china figurines, jeweled fans, and an unusual fireplace whose green tile facing held a painted rose in every square.

Then, at last, the Dolls. On a long breath of wonder, I sank down, feeling as though I were a child again and must be in Doll Heaven. For here were fantasy creatures such as I had dreamed of, viewed in cases at the Ville de Paris, but never owned. Of course I had a lot of dolls, dearly loved, but just playthings with bodies of cloth or jointed composition. They were imitation children who could ride in carriages or be cuddled in my arms and rocked and taken to tea parties.

This divine assembly, however, was quite different.

Squatting beside me, Tad took care not to touch the highborn ladies, but he knew a lot about them, evidently learned from Rose.

"Most of these dolls were made in Germany or France," he told me in hushed tones. "The French ones were the finest. See that big one in the middle dressed in brilliants and blue gauze? She was made by Bru and her hair is lamb's wool. Isn't that funny?"

I nodded, rendered speechless. There must have been several hundred dolls, all told, on shelves, in cabinets, and just standing by the walls. Many were big creatures, nearly three feet tall with lovely faces made of translucent tinted china.

"They call it 'bisque,'" my small authority declared. "And most of their hair is human or . . ." He frowned and bit his lip. "Oh yes, mohair."

I nodded, quite impressed. The ladies' ringlets, poufs, and waves peeked out from bonnets which were strictly à la mode and elaborately trimmed with flowers, ribbons, and feathers. The gowns were similarly adorned and all had gems about their persons, even those in street attire. If the fingers were encased in little gloves, the ring was placed outside.

"My mama made all the clothes by hand," Tad told me proudly, "and I used to watch her. She would make up stories while she sewed and then write them in little books."

I wondered how much time Tad spent up here, for in spite of its romantic appeal and memories of his

mother, it was a strange playground for a sturdy
little boy. It seemed to me that he would have been
better off playing games with other children, romping, shouting, getting dirty. Well, at least now he had
Prince to gambol with outdoors and soon he would
be starting school.

Noticing how careful he was, I didn't believe he
could be the one disturbing things. But if not, then
who was it? If only the dolls could talk . . . They
looked so real with their human curls and limpid,
expressive eyes; even the parted lips looked as
though about to speak.

Especially one standing in the farthest corner. She
was a gorgeous creature, black-haired and green-
eyed, but the only one who wasn't smiling. She wore
pink velvet with an emerald satin cloak trimmed
with a design of brilliants and held a velvet rose. The
tilt of her head was haughty in the extreme as
though she scorned her simpering companions.

"What an unusual doll that is," I exclaimed, pointing her out to Tad.

"That's supposed to be Princess Rose-Red herself,
my mama." Tad chuckled. "She ordered the hair
and eyes made special and dressed the doll in a copy
of her favorite gown. Isn't she a beauty?"

"Yes, indeed." I had to drag my eyes away. The
doll gave me the strangest feeling. It seemed almost
to be imbued with some of Rose's spirit and looked
as though it knew a dark and dreadful secret.

14

In a little while, Tad and I went back downstairs. We fetched the violets, discovering that Melissa had gone to her own room next door. When Tad and I went in to see her, she seemed sunk in apathy, sipping disconsolately at a cup of tea.

Mary was in attendance, and out of Melissa's hearing, I asked her to watch the invalid closely and see that she was not disturbed.

"I will, that," Mary whispered back in my ear. "The master looked in earlier, but she was still asleep. She has had the father and mother of all colds, poor lass."

"The doctor will be here soon," I told her, "and perhaps prescribe some quinine powders and horehound drops for her sore throat. Until then, see that she has plenty of hot tea."

I then advanced to the bed, Tad hanging back, toeing the blue carpet. I turned and held my hand out to him, smiling encouragement.

"Come, say hello to your future stepmama. Melissa, this is Tad."

Melissa eyed him sourly. "What a great big fellow. I'm much too young to be your *mama*, boy. You'd best call me Melissa." She passed a hand across her brow. "I seem to have had a dream about you, boy, but I can't remember—"

"Tad brought you some violets," I said hastily.

He bowed and extended them in a trembling hand. "I hope you—you're feeling better, M-Melissa."

She turned fretfully away. "Well, I don't, I'm purely miserable. And look a caution, I'm persuaded. Maid, hand me that mirror." She looked at her reflection. "Ohhh, my heavens!"

I was relieved when Dr. Crane knocked and was admitted to the Dungeon of Despair. He was a dapper little gentleman and very unctuous, just what the patient needed. Tad and I faded from the scene with Melissa's voice whining in our ears. "Doctor, let me tell you how it all began . . ."

We made a brisk escape.

"Tad," I said, "the sun is shining. Are you going outside to play with Prince?"

"I guess so." He sighed, staring out a hall window at trees bending to the breeze with fluffy clouds skimming in an azure sky.

"I miss Mama," he said in a low voice that touched my heart. "She used to make up fairy stories for me and write them down. The last one was about her own life, but after she died, I couldn't find it. Papa looked for it, too, but it was gone. I guess a maid must have thrown it out when she cleaned the tower."

"It's too bad you're lonesome, Tad. Aren't there

any boys and girls living in Sea Cliff who can come over and play with you?"

He heaved another sigh. "Yes, but someone has to take me there, Miss Libby or Li Fong. Now she's not here and he's usually too busy going on errands for Papa. Well, I guess I'll just find Prince."

We seemed to have reached an impasse and so parted company. I put on a smock and went to complete my seashells in the bridal chamber, but my mind was still on Tad. I wondered if his father would permit me to take him into San Francisco. The new skating rink in the Plaza was becoming very popular, a big park was being built out by the beach, and Chinatown had no end of interesting little shops. I decided it wouldn't hurt to ask for permission.

Thinking about Drake, my heart gave an excited leap. Tomorrow was the Millses' party and I would be attending it in the gown I'd brought from Millbrae when Drake had told me I was invited to the ball. I had designed the style myself, then commissioned a seamstress to make it up so that I could wear it to the final soirée at Vassar.

Though my gown was lovely enough, my face and hair would not compare with Melissa's when she was in her prime. Or the fabled Rose. *They* were beauties. However, I didn't envy their personalities. I couldn't decide what Rose must actually have been like. "Fey and fascinating," Dugan called her. Had she also been selfish, childish like her cousin, or a strange recluse?

As for Melissa . . . I shook my head as I considered that young lady. Unless there was a drastic change when she was well, I didn't see how she and Drake would suit. Why had he chosen her? It seemed to me that he had a strength of will, an inner sensuality, and a high degree of intelligence that

would soon find Melissa rather shallow. How blind
men were when faced with overwhelming beauty!
But of course, Drake must have been lonesome and
wanted a sweet, amenable mother for Tad and any
other children. I smiled grimly to myself. If a head
cold could reduce Melissa to such a whining help-
lessness, how would nine months of pregnancy and
the pain of childbirth affect her? Tad would be lucky
if he acquired a single sibling.

"That Melissa is a fool."

Had someone read my thoughts? I gasped and
swung around.

Rachel stood in the doorway, arms folded on her
chest. "I visited the future mistress of Cliffside this
morning and discovered—after a few minutes' conversation—that the girl is a spineless, complaining
ninny."

"You better not let Mr. Wynfield hear you say
that." I suppressed a smile and stood up, wiping my
brush clean on a rag.

"If he doesn't find that out for himself pretty soon,
he's an idiot."

An idiot and a ninny. What a combination as Rachel had them tagged. Only Mr. Wynfield was no
idiot, I told myself indignantly.

"Perhaps he was lonesome," I said slowly, "and
certainly Melissa must be beautiful and charming
when in good health."

"Well, I can only say he didn't know her as well as
he thought he did," Rachel responded dryly. "Miss
Blair, you wouldn't believe the number of women
who descended on him like vultures, eager to capture such a handsome, wealthy widower before
Rose was even cold in her grave. That's one reason
Drake started courting supposedly 'sweet' little Melissa. A person is always vulnerable right after their

spouse's death. I should know." She gave a little smile, staring past me out the wide, uncurtained windows.

"Your stepson must have been very unhappy after Rose's unexpected accident," I remarked.

Rachel's sharp eyes traveled from the window back to me. "Accident? Was it? Perhaps not. The child declares he saw some ruffian in a cloak throw a rock at her. But who can find a shadow in the fog? At any rate, that's in the past. Melissa is the present." She gave me an odd glance. "If Drake had seen *you* sooner . . . who knows?"

My jaw dropped open while I stared at her. "What are you suggesting? Drake . . . and *I*?"

"Why not? You can stand up to him and you must have other qualities that he admires. Don't tell me there was nothing personal in his decision to hire you, such a young, inexperienced female." She looked me up and down in a calculating manner. "And now tomorrow you go with us all to the ball. He saw to that, I guess."

"You're all going?" I exclaimed.

"Why yes, Jeremy and I will be attending. There are not many social occasions in San Francisco that don't include us. It isn't bragging to say that few young men can equal my son in looks and charm. As for me, I like to dance and have a certain number of admirers." She preened a little, stroking the soft drapes of her orchid-colored morning gown, whose ruffles had a trimming of the finest handmade lace.

"It's a good thing for you that we *are* all going tomorrow," she continued. "Melissa would have had a fit if you had gone alone with Drake. As it was, she sounded suspicious. She said he called you 'Lesley,' and she wanted to know all about you. I told her what I knew—which wasn't much."

I didn't try to justify myself. What Drake called me was his business, and though it gave me a thrill of pleasure at the increased warmth of our relationship, I certainly didn't want to antagonize Melissa. I was sorry we would not be traveling alone, but perhaps, as Rachel said, it might have caused some talk.

I decided to change the subject. "Tad seems so lonely with no other playmates. Do you think that Mr. Wynfield would mind if I took him out for a drive today? I need some gold paint that is only sold near Chinatown."

Rachel shrugged indifferently. "Why should he mind? I'm sure you can have my permission, though as far as it goes, I have about as much authority here as an upstairs maid."

"Thank you," I said quickly, sidling toward the door. "I will have to go at once. I must find Tad and change my clothes." I escaped eagerly, fleet of foot, filled with anticipation of Tad's delight.

When I told him, Tad danced with glee, capering around the garden. "Can I bring Prince?"

"Well—"

"Oh, please! He has a nice, new leather leash that Papa bought for him. And he'll be good. I know he will!"

"Will you hang on to him?" I couldn't hold out against the supplication in two pairs of eyes. "All right, then. I thought we'd eat lunch by the fishing docks, then go to Chinatown. I have an errand there."

All was satisfactorily arranged. Tad and I flew to our rooms to change. I donned a gold-brown cape, waist-length, over a matching braid-trimmed serge. Tad wore knickers and a sailor coat with round-brimmed hat upon his head. Prince stood proudly in his new red harness, trembling slightly as though he sensed the coming high adventure. Boy and dog were on the *qui vive*, as the French would say.

As for me, I, too, was happy and expectant. I drove my own gig with Lady prancing spiritedly and Tad urging me constantly to let out the reins and "show what she can do." No way was I going to do that on the winding, hilltop road, but at least I was thankful that the drive occasioned no sad memories of his mother's death.

Indeed, with Prince barking enthusiastically at every sea gull glimpsed above the bay, and Tad talking almost nonstop, there was no time for memories. He knew all the residents of Sea Cliff and pointed out the homes where children dwelt, describing them at length.

It was not until we entered the City that my passengers grew silent. Blue eyes and brown eyes, human and canine, stared in awe at steep, steep hills, fabulous mansions, the clanging trolley cars, the crowds, and all the shops.

"Haven't you ever been in downtown San Francisco, Tad?" I asked, heading for the stable behind my shop on Montgomery Street.

"Yes, Miss Lesley. But it was long ago. When I was just a little boy."

"Well, let's walk around a bit. Here's my shop—if you want to take a peek inside." I opened the front door. Conan wasn't there, but Tad and Prince examined everything, and Tad, at least, expressed the most extravagant admiration.

Then we headed for the fishing pier. Boy and dog immediately inhaled the aromas and became ecstatic, dashing madly up and down the echoing planked sidewalks. Prince barked, leaped, sniffed. Tad shouted greetings and questions to the stocking-capped Italian fisherman, who grinned and waved.

Boats bobbed at anchor in a forest of masts with a constant coming and going.

A great many people strolled about and some were already eating. Huge cauldrons steamed and bubbled as green crabs were tossed inside, emerging on the waiters' plates a lovely well-done pink.

Pretty soon, we could no longer resist the appetizing aromas and ordered our own crab with melted butter, crusty French bread, and a pot of coffee. We ate at a bare wooden table by the water, enjoying every bite while Prince gulped the juicy tidbits thrown to him as though he hadn't eaten for a week.

At last, replete and happy, we sank back in our wooden seats to stare across the Golden Gate at the rough whitecaps in the bay, and the many islands. The closest one, rocky Alcatraz, a mile away, held an ugly building housing long-term military prisoners and looked bleak and grim. But there were other islands in the bay with thick stands of evergreens and scattered rooftops. Ships sailed briskly on the water; there was even a steam-powered ferry chugging and tooting across the blue expanse to Sausalito.

"I'd like to ride across the bay sometime," Tad said, dangling over the wooden railing of the pier. "I've never seen those other islands. Have you, Miss Lesley?"

"Yes, there's a big pine forest across the bay and steep hills and lovely valleys filled with wildflowers. One time the Russians lived there and nearly acquired California. That was long before it became part of the United States."

"Tell me about it," Tad demanded, bright-eyed, glancing at me over his shoulder.

So we had a little history lesson sitting by the water while Prince dozed at our feet. I told Tad the sad love story of the Russian Count Rezanov, who had dreamed of annexing California for Russia, and his courtship of the beautiful Concepcíon, daughter of the local Commandante. The enterprising count sailed away to get permission from Russia for both schemes, but he died en route and brokenhearted Concepcíon waited many years before she heard the news, then she entered a convent.

"Wouldn't it have been strange if the count had succeeded?" I mused. "We'd all have been Russians."

Tad laughed. "Tell me some more."

But I shook my head and rose, as there was my errand to accomplish, and said it was time we started walking toward Chinatown.

Tad kept on chattering about early San Francisco with many surmises about Indians, padres, and Spanish brigands. History seemed to fascinate him. He was a very intelligent little fellow with a vivid imagination. I wondered whether someday he might follow in his mother's footsteps and become a writer.

My thoughts dwelt also on Rose Wynfield, and for the first time, I felt sorry for that strange lady in her Velvet Room, her main companions a little child and a collection of dolls. Maybe Drake had been wrong to sail away so often and leave her all alone. If I were Drake's wife, I would have gone with him.

Drake's wife . . . what would it be like? For a few foolish moments, I envisioned it: the evening suppers, the quiet moments alone in our own home. We would talk, discuss so many things: his trips, my college days, the current events in San Francisco, plans for our future. . . . And then, at last, the lowering of the lamps, and the final intimacy of love-making in our own boudoir, over which scene my mind drew a swift curtain before it went too far!

I jerked myself back to reality and noted that we were surrounded by the teeming throngs of Chinatown. There were sailors swaggering along, well-dressed shoppers, Chinese men and women dressed alike in baggy trousers and padded jackets. And everywhere the familiar smells of fried fish, burning joss and incense, cats, drains, muddy gutters, pungent tea shops, lilies in water cans, and occasionally a whiff of the sickly-sweet opium from underground grates, very faint but recognizable. With a start, I realized that Tad and Prince were romping carelessly far ahead.

"Tad, wait for me," I shouted.

But on Dupont, the street that ran the length of the Chinese sector, there was a din of wailing music, singsong voices haggling over prices, clattering hooves and rolling wheels on cobbles, and here and there a drum or flute so that my voice was completely swallowed up.

Now I couldn't see Tad or Prince at all. On and on I went, knocking into people, going faster and faster. I shouted Tad's name as I peered in every small, dim shop and alley. Faces turned sometimes to regard me curiously; however most of them ignored me.

I was frantic now with fear. Drake didn't even know that I had taken Tad. He had given me no authority. Suppose I had to report to him that Tad was lost in Chinatown? A place of mystery and secrecy, of closed lips and blind eyes for the outsider. Ranks would shut tight to protect their own. I thought of shanghaiing—white slavery—kidnapping . . .

At last, panting, my hat askew, my face on fire beneath straggling strands of hair, I halted and grabbed a merchant's arm, a fat man standing in the doorway of a large apothecary shop. "Have you seen a little boy in a sailor coat? About this big?" I measured four feet from the ground. "He had a dog."

He grinned, showing gaps between spiked teeth. "No dog. Small boy go in cricket shop." He jerked a fat thumb around the corner.

"Thank you!" With a sobbing gasp, I flew into the alley.

There I saw them.

Li Fong had a small boy by the arm and they were just going through a door beneath a swinging Chinese sign displaying a big black cricket. It was a place of ebony-painted wood set in a little courtyard below the level of the street.

Before I could clear the dryness in my throat and call Tad's name, they disappeared, and a scarlet round moon-door closed behind them.

15

Where was Li Fong taking Tad?

I shouted and rushed forward. But the next second, I went sprawling on the ground, the breath knocked completely from my lungs.

Some time ago an earthquake had heaved the tiny courtyard's bricks and I had caught my toe on one. Tufts of grass grew in the cracks, but even so the impact on my knees was sharp and painful. A sturdy pine tree grew nearby in a bamboo pot and I caught a branch to help me rise.

For a second, I had to bite my lips in pain, but it soon subsided to a dull ache that was bearable. Now more important matters were at stake. Ignoring my dusty skirt and crooked hat, I picked up my purse and hobbled toward the moon-shaped, scarlet door. I found the door was locked and I pounded against it, yelling Tad's name.

When no one answered, I continued to make my presence known in the loudest manner possible. Noticing a brass gong and hammer dangling from an entry beam, I grasped the wooden mallet and swung it with all my might.

The noise was deafening, but the door flew open. Mr. Li stood before me, wincing slightly as the reverberations died away above his head.

"Where's Tad?" I demanded hotly, trying to look past him. "Why did you bring him here? I want to see him at once!"

Suddenly, the hall beyond became filled with people, all muttering and staring at me. They wore smocks or aprons and seemed to be engaged in some kind of work. They held paint brushes and strange, tiny slats of wood.

Mr. Li stared blandly at my furious, hot face, then snapped a word over his shoulder. The hall cleared instantly.

Li Fong bowed to me. "Please come in, Miss Blair. My family's shop is honored by your presence."

I had noticed before that he spoke excellent English except for the Oriental tendency to hiss on certain sounds. As usual, he was quite unruffled.

But not I. Confronting him with flashing eyes, I cried loudly, "Where's Tad? What's he doing here? I've been searching for him all over Chinatown."

"So sorry. Tad is not here."

"*Not here?* Why, I saw him enter with my own eyes, just this minute. You dragged him through the front door."

Mr. Li stepped aside and I looked around the hall. It was painted black, both floor and walls, and contained only one article: a yellow porcelain vase large enough to hide Ali Baba from the Forty Thieves. I subdued an urge to peer inside.

Voices came in a soft jabbering from the room beyond the entry, which was covered by a bamboo screen. Looking toward it, I shouted defiantly, "Tad! Tad!"

A ripple crossed Mr. Li's features as he gazed at me. In another person, it would have passed for amusement. He stepped to the archway, called several words in Chinese, and the next instant, a trouser-clad woman appeared holding the hand of a small black-haired Oriental boy in a sailor coat. They both bowed low.

I could not suppress a groan. It wasn't Tad. But it *was* the boy I had seen entering this shop.

I looked desperately at Mr. Li. "Excuse me. Tad is lost. I brought him to Chinatown, but we became separated."

"So. The child cannot be far. How was he dressed?"

"Like this little boy—and a dozen others, I suppose." When I turned my head, the woman and child had gone. "Tad is wearing a sailor coat and hat, dark blue. And he has Prince with him. Can you help me search? Perhaps someone who speaks Chinese would have better luck." I looked at him and gripped my hands together as they were shaking uncontrollably.

Li Fong nodded. "Two sons of my sisters will assist you. Please be calm, Miss Blair. The child will soon be found. Chinatown is not that large. I would go with you, but I must wait here for Mr. Wynfield so I can interpret his order."

"He's coming here?" I exclaimed. "What is this place?"

"My family makes cricket cages. Would you care to see them? Enameled, jewel-encrusted—"

"Thank you—not until Tad is found," I jerked out, straightening my hat. If only I could locate Tad before confronting Drake with the awful tidings that I had lost his son.

I should have known better. Hadn't Mai always kept my hand in hers when we came here? Even so, I had often wandered off. In seconds, a small person could be lost and become disoriented in the noisy, crowded foreign atmosphere of Chinatown.

And there would be no one who could tell you where to go. Mai, of course, when I was lost, used to question shop owners in their own tongue. I was slightly relieved that Li Fong was putting two of his nephews at my disposal.

He excused himself to go after them while I paced restlessly up and down the hall. Finally, I decided to look out in the street in case Tad should pass by.

But just as I stepped outside, who should appear but Mr. Wynfield. I checked and gulped. He was bareheaded, the wind tossing the black locks wildly about his forehead. A white wool scarf blew back from his serge-clad shoulders.

His eyes widened with astonishment, but he didn't look displeased. "Miss Blair! What on earth are you doing here?"

Imploringly, I put out my hand. "Oh, Mr. Wynfield, Tad is lost. I've been so negligent! We came to Chinatown and he got ahead of me in the crowds and—and—"

Mr. Wynfield looked past me. "Li, what is this all about?" Before Li Fong could answer, Drake's sharpened gaze returned to my trembling form. "I take it you brought Tad to the City for an outing and he ran ahead of you here in Chinatown and disappeared."

I nodded abjectly. How quickly he absorbed the situation!

"Why are you in this shop?" he asked.

I explained about the boy I had seen going in the door. "I know I'm to blame, Mr. Wynfield, but we are wasting time here talking. Tad might be hurt— have fallen in an alley . . ." I had to swallow hard. "Mr. Li has two nephews who will help us in the search."

Two stocky youths in Oriental tunics and baggy trousers stepped nimbly around their uncle and bowed.

"I speak English," one said proudly.

"All right, let's go," Drake snapped. "I'll be back later, Li."

I hurried after them out to the sidewalk.

"Do you have a description of my son?" Mr. Wynfield asked the young man who spoke English. When the reply was negative, he proceeded to supply the information. The English-speaking youth repeated it in Chinese to his cousin.

Mr. Wynfield then turned to me. "I suggest we split up. I'll take one side of the street with this fellow. You take the other. We'll meet at the end of Chinatown—Dupont and California streets."

"I'm so sorry, Mr. Wynfield . . ." I began.

"Never mind that now. Don't blame yourself." For an instant, compassion filled his face and he gripped my hand. Then, scarf flying, Drake and his assistant hurriedly crossed the street, dodging through the carts, horses, and pedestrians. They soon vanished from my sight.

"You speak no English?" I asked my Oriental aide, wishing Mai was there instead.

He answered, grinning cheerfully. "One, two word. 'Yes.' 'No.' "

"Listen, the boy's name is 'Tad.' *Tad.*" I repeated loudly, measuring from the sidewalk. "He has a dog." I bounced around and barked. He laughed out loud. So did several other people.

"Come on," I said grimly, dragging on his sleeve. We started off.

I had to admit that he was thorough. Every shop, every person he could halt was subjected to a rapid-fire exchange of words in which I heard the frequent use of Tad's name. Always the answer was *"um,"* meaning "no," or a mere shrug. A lost white child was neither uncommon nor very interesting.

Meanwhile, I continued calling loudly, asking everyone, Occidental or Chinese, if they had seen a small boy with a small white dog.

My legs were aching now and my body felt as though it had been immersed in a steam bath, alternately chilled by the wind and then swept by waves of heat. I trembled with fatigue and nerves, but I was only vaguely aware of my discomfort. All I could think was: *Where had Tad gone?* What could have become of him? Was he hurt? Frightened? Trying to find his way back to me and unable to make himself understood?

For a minute, I leaned, exhausted, against the doorway of a silk shop and shut my eyes. Then I prayed. A strong, silent cry for help.

I could hear Li's nephew questioning inside the shop and the usual negative response. Somewhere a dog barked sharply. There were lots of dogs in Chinatown.

My eyes flew open. *Prince!* Why hadn't I been calling the dog as well as *Tad*? The animal would bark if he heard his name. His hearing probably was keener than the boy's.

"Prince! Prince!" I shouted as I ran down the street. My Chinese youth ran after me and now he also called the dog. Heads turned in surprise. People in my path fell back as though afraid that I'd gone mad. I didn't care. I kept on shouting.

One more steep hill and Chinatown would be behind us. The ivy-covered walls of Old St. Mary's Church marked the meeting place with Mr. Wynfield.

I didn't see him anywhere as I staggered, gasping, up the incline to the church. With what seemed like my last breath, I shouted, "Prince—Prince!"

And heard an answering bark.

The church door opened wide and a smiling young priest, plump and blue-eyed, appeared with Prince bounding at his side, giving joyful yips. I could hardly stand upright, my relief was so great. I babbled incoherently about Tad and our search, but the priest seemed to understand me. He introduced himself as Father Patrick and led me to his study, where a small boy was lying on a leather couch.

"Oh, Tad, Tad," I cried, dropping to my knees. "Are you all right? What happened? Are you hurt? You have a bandage on your head!"

I glanced quickly at the priest, who said, "He'll be all right. Just a cut."

Tad reached up and I took him in my arms. We both tried to talk at once and neither of us made much sense. But just then, Mr. Wynfield entered.

"I saw Prince outside! Is my boy—" In two strides, he crossed the room and I released Tad to his father.

While they embraced and talked, I looked at the young clergyman. "Father Patrick, do you know what happened?"

Every face turned to him then, and he smiled at all of us. "I think so. Tad said someone kept whistling to the dog and making him run off. During the ensuing chase, Tad slipped and hurt his head. It's nothing serious, but he had reached the end of Chinatown and didn't know where to turn for help. Fortunately, the dog returned and discovered his master crying practically on St. Mary's doorstep. The animal did the only thing he knew: he barked for help."

"And you came out and helped them."

He nodded. "I attended to the cut on Tad's head and was just about to send word to the shop where he said his father would be working, the Jade Pagoda."

"I'm to blame for letting Tad get lost," I confessed. "He's never been to Chinatown before and became too excited. He ran ahead of me, and before I knew it, he disappeared in the crowds. I couldn't see him anywhere. Luckily, his father arrived on the scene and we got two Chinese boys to help us search." I glanced toward the hall. "Where have they gone?"

"Back to the Shop of Singing Happiness," Mr. Wynfield said, coming to my side. "Li's family make exquisite cricket cages there and I intended to buy some."

He turned to the young priest and said earnestly, "How can I thank you, Father, for taking care of Tad? Do you have a charity box?"

"On the desk. I will not refuse donations in the name of those less fortunate."

After some large bills were stuffed into the wooden container, we exchanged farewells and Tad, Drake, and I left the church.

"I'll take Tad with me," Drake said when we stood on the steep slope of California Street with the wind whipping at our clothes. "Do you have your own conveyance somewhere?"

"Yes, it isn't far, behind my shop in Montgomery Street. Mr. Wynfield, can you ever forgive me for losing Tad?"

Before his father could reply, Tad spoke up. "It wasn't your fault, Miss Lesley. I got too far ahead and you couldn't see me. But someone whistled to Prince and called his name. He broke away and ran down an alley with me after him. Gosh, we went all over. I got really lost and didn't know where to go. But Prince is just a pup, you know, so he thought it was a game and kept running from me to the whistler."

"Didn't you see who it was?" Drake asked, frowning.

"No, Papa, I never did. When I tripped and hurt my head, I was way down by the church and that's when Prince came back." Tad tugged at his father's sleeve. "So it wasn't her fault, Papa. Please don't be mad at Lesley!"

"Dear heaven, do you both think I'm such an ogre?" Drake looked at me with a rather unnerving warmth, his eyes lingering on every part of my face. "I'm not 'mad' at Lesley. She is a spirited, kind-hearted young lady who wanted to give a lonely little boy an outing." He reached out and took my hand, holding it with a strong, firm pressure. "Certainly no apology is necessary."

A wave of pleasure swept over me, but I felt compelled to say, looking down at our clasped hands, "I should have tried to keep Tad by my side."

"It's almost impossible when you have a lively, excited child in a crowd. He and I will have to talk. I think Tad must have some instructions and rules laid down before he ventures to the City again. Don't you agree, Lesley—er—Miss Blair?" Slowly, he released my hand.

"Yes, indeed."

But I wondered if I would ever be entrusted with Drake's son again.

"Thank you, Miss Lesley. The rest of the outing was *capital!*" Tad called over his shoulder as they started off. A subdued Prince trotted beside them, his leash firmly twined around Mr. Wynfield's fist.

I looked after them with a sigh of relief. At least it all had ended well.

Just in time, I remembered the gold paint I had wanted, and I retraced my steps for a few blocks. I couldn't help wondering, as I gazed at all the faces, Chinese and Occidental, who could have been luring Prince down alleyways. It was somebody who knew his name. A teasing playmate? Or someone with a more serious purpose?

So many odd things had happened recently: the unlocked garden gate, Prince placed on the ledge to lure Tad to the cliff, the flute playing in the garden and the mysterious caped figure, the holdup on El Camino Real.

Was it all part of some plot? I walked more rapidly. In spite of all the crowds, I suddenly felt very lonely and afraid.

16

I spoke to Drake Wynfield the next morning, being alert enough to catch him in the hallway before he departed for his shop. When I called his name, he turned around and the warm, inquiring glance he gave me only increased my sense of guilt.

"Mr. Wynfield, I had hoped to give Tad an occasional outing during my time here, but perhaps now . . ." I cleared my throat. "I certainly won't blame you if you'd rather I didn't take him out again."

At once, he stepped closer, looking down at me with a smile. "Please don't think for a moment that I hold you responsible for Tad's typical childish behavior. He is so unused to outings, he is unaware of the proper way to act. If there is any cause for blame, it is mine for not noticing how lonely he's become. I should have taken him on more excursions myself after his mother died."

Drake's softer manner puzzled me. A week ago he

might have snapped my head off for letting Tad get lost.

Now a thoughtful expression crossed his face. "However, if you do take Tad out, it would be well to avoid the Chinese sector and the docks around lower Pacific Street."

I agreed emphatically, then said slowly, "It was rather strange, wasn't it, the way someone kept whistling to Prince? Almost as though they wanted Tad to lose his way. Or lose his faithful dog."

For a moment worry darkened Drake's heavy-lidded amber eyes and he shook his head. "I fear I can't explain it. Perhaps it was just a prankster—some playmate . . ."

"Of course," I answered quickly. "That easily could have been the case. Well, then, I won't keep you. I know that you have work to do."

As I turned away, he caught my arm. "You haven't forgotten about the ball tonight, have you?"

I smiled up at him. "How could I forget? I'm looking forward to it with the greatest anticipation."

"So am I, but I'm afraid we won't be going alone. It seems that nearly everyone in the house—except Melissa—is to accompany us."

I felt an odd stab of regret that we weren't traveling à deux, but Rachel had prepared me for this eventuality so I merely nodded calmly. "It's too bad that your fiancée won't be well enough to go with us. I shall look in on her this morning and see if she needs anything."

"I'm sure that would be appreciated. As for you and me, we'll have to find another time and place to discuss further decorating plans for Cliffside. We can't talk in a crowded carriage." He gave a little smile and bowed. "Until this evening, then."

Further decorating plans? My pulses gave a leap of

hope, but as the front door closed behind him, I couldn't help a rueful sigh. That was all the ride had meant to him—a chance to hold a business conference while I had been envisioning another tête-à-tête such as we had enjoyed that night at my home. A dangerous pastime, this sudden wish to share Drake's company. I recalled Rachel's words about Melissa's suspicious nature. I must not do anything to stir up that young lady.

As for Drake, naturally he had no warm thoughts about anyone except his intended bride, who would soon be beautiful and blooming, ready to do her duty. *Duty!* If I were Drake's bride, I would feel many emotions other than that: excitement, expectancy, an eager yearning to know his lips and arms. Duty wouldn't enter into it at all.

But then, I was not to be Drake's bride.

Giving myself a mental shake, I moved briskly up the stairs, determined to get the promised visit with Melissa over quickly.

When I reached her bedroom, I found the door slightly ajar. With a soft knock, I pushed it farther open and stepped inside, hearing the low murmur of voices and laughter. No maid was in the room, but Conan was there, bending over Melissa in the bed. Evidently, they had not heard me enter.

"Good morning," I said loudly, pausing and clasping my hands in front of my waist.

The intimate conversation broke off at once and Conan spun around, his face reddening.

Melissa reared up in bed, clad thinly in a dainty wrap of lawn and lace, hardly the garment for an invalid recovering from a head cold.

"G-good morning," she stuttered, blue eyes wide and startled. "Mr. Blye was just bringing me a cup of chocolate."

I smiled benignly at the cup of liquid cooling on the nightstand.

"Those silly maids are so poky." Melissa tossed her head, recovering her poise. "I ordered a special brew since I don't drink coffee the first thing in the morning, but I swear I've had to wait a perfect age."

"I met the maid on her way upstairs," Conan informed me, "and thought I'd save her a trip and see how Miss Fernley was doing at the same time."

"Mr. Blye as always is the soul of kindness." I beamed at him as he moved back hastily to a more discreet distance from the bed.

"Are you feeling better today?" I asked the invalid and girded myself for the usual litany of ailments past, present, and soon to come.

But she surprised me and answered airily, "I am greatly improved, Miss Blair. The worst part now is that I get so bored and lonely, stuck up here by myself."

"Has Jeremy been to see you?" I asked. The Golden Satyr might help her pass the time and she didn't seem averse to a little giggling flirtation, judging by what I had just interrupted.

"Mr. Jeremy did come up to welcome me to Cliffside, and so forth. A most pleasant and personable young man. But that maid, Mary, made him leave all too soon. Said she had her orders. I declare, that creature has no idea of her proper place. When I am mistress here there will be some drastic changes made, believe me!"

Oh, I believed her. A wave of pity for the household under Melissa's reign swept over me.

She further strengthened this impression by imperiously asking me for the hairbrush reposing on the dresser. "I vow I must look a fright and I just can't do the tangles. You don't have to leave just yet, do you, Mr. Blye?" She made a pretty gesture toward him with the brush, her head tipped to one side. "Would you mind—"

It was time for a little bud-nipping. "I fear I must confer with Mr. Blye at once about the bridal chamber. Some detail of the drapes. If you will excuse us, Melissa—"

"*Miss Fernley*," the maiden reminded me haughtily, looking down her still-pink nose.

"I beg your pardon, *Miss Fernley*." I swept her an exaggerated curtsy.

Conan threw me an amused glance before he bowed to Melissa, saying in his most Irish brogue, "'Tis glad I am to see you so much better. Sure, and all the angels up in heaven will be singing when you're well."

I jerked him rather abruptly through the doorway. "Listen, my lad," I hissed as we hurried off, "you really should be more circumspect. Mr. Wynfield would not look kindly on your being in his fiancée's room when she's in bed with the door almost closed. That jacket she had on was shockingly revealing."

"Aye, I noticed." He raised a ribald reddish eyebrow.

Conan was clad in his shirtsleeves with the front open rather low down on his chest without a coat or a cravat and looked pretty rakish and devil-may-care himself. The picture of the two of them giggling together in such intimate circumstances made me quite uneasy.

"Conan, we must keep the goodwill of Mr. Wynfield, don't you realize that? Suppose he had burst in on you just now—"

"Melissa and I were only talking," he interrupted. "You sound like a little prig. I thought you had such a liberal education back East."

"Not that liberal. I know that an unmarried girl in bed can't entertain a young man alone without damaging her reputation."

He chuckled. "She is a rather entertaining young lady with cute, coy little ways."

It was all a game to him, but a dangerous one. I felt like shaking him. "Conan, for heaven's sake, this is not the time or place for any of your shenanigans. Can't you imagine what would happen if Mr. Wynfield's displeasure was aroused by your flirting with Melissa?"

"What would he do? Challenge me to a duel?" Conan bounded down the remaining stairs and struck a pose, making feints in the air as though he brandished a sword. "I say, paintbrushes at thirty paces! Here's a stroke of carmine red for you, sir! And here's burnt umber right back, you filthy cad!"

I choked back my giggles. "Listen, my boy, Melissa is not one of your San Francisco 'doves.' She is Drake Wynfield's intended, a high-born Southern lady, and undoubtedly"—I cleared my throat—"a virgin."

He finally sobered. "All right, I'll be good. But for your sake, not for Drake's. There's something about that laddie-o that brings out the devil in me. Just as his desertion of Rose used to make me want to show him what he was missing."

We paused on the threshold of the bridal chamber and Conan grunted, hands on his hips. "Can you picture Drake and Melissa in here, sharing conjugal bliss, murmuring sweet nothings? Egad, it beggars the imagination."

"Oh, I don't know," I answered slowly. "He might be a surprising lover. Still waters, and all that. I think he could be quite passionate and romantic under the right circumstances."

Immediately, I thought about our encounter in the midnight room and how his inadvertent touch had thrilled me. I could feel my face turn fiery.

Conan flashed me an oddly reflective glance. "Oh-ho, sits the wind in that direction?"

"I don't know what you mean." Hastily, I moved over to the worktable. "I just hope that you will keep your promise regarding Melissa. This job means a lot to me. Drake said something this morning about further decorating plans. You know how anxious I am about that."

"Drake wouldn't throw *you* out even if I did displease him," Conan told me soothingly.

"Why not?"

"He admires you now. At first, I grant, he probably felt suspicious and doubtful. You're a new type of woman in his experience: bright, independent, talented, and courageous."

"Why . . . why . . . thank you, Conan. But I think you are mistaken about his admiration." I suppressed a wistful sigh. I could not let Conan know how much I longed for more than Drake's professional approval. "Drake's often been annoyed by my chance taking and impulsiveness," I added.

Conan shook his head. "I've seen the way he looks at you lately. Sometimes I've observed a strange expression in those heavy-lidded eyes. I suppose you never noticed?"

"The only unusual expression I've observed on him lately has been worry."

Conan thinned his lips. "He should be worried about the trouble in this house. Something started when Rose died and it isn't finished yet."

I stared at him, but Conan wouldn't say another word.

17

That night, five of us rode down to Millbrae in the largest carriage.

Rachel and I sat facing the men, our bouffant skirts filling up the seat, the gardenias Drake had sent us perfuming all the air. My gown was seafoam green to set off the russet tones in my dark brown hair. The material was slipper satin with an over-skirt of *mousseline de soie* caught up with white rosebuds and artificial pearls. Since I considered my bust and shoulders my best features, the neck was low, the sleeves mere tiny puffs. The wrap was made of matching satin trimmed in white marabou.

Rachel's cherry velvet had panels of black lace, and a parure of diamonds adorned her head, throat, and arms. She looked like a duchess displaying the family jewels—unless they were paste, which I couldn't tell in the flickering riding lights. Part of my art course had involved the history and description of gems, which I had found fascinating. I noticed that Jeremy also wore several sparkling rings, and a large icy stone gleamed in the stiff folds of his white cravat.

Conan sat beside him, handsome and dapper but much less elegant. I felt surprise that he had been included until I recalled Drake telling me that D. O. Mills had also magnanimously invited any other guests currently at Cliffside.

All three men wore opera cloaks, silky top hats, and carried black-stitched white suede gloves, very much *à la mode*. However, the hirsute face so much in vogue was scorned by Drake, who acceded only to neat sideburns and a minimum of macassar oil to tame the thickness of his dense hair.

Since he sat directly opposite, his eyes rested on me frequently, sometimes with a little smile, and I thought to myself that he already seemed infected by the party spirit like the rest of us. He kept eying the pearl drop nestling in my cleavage with an almost bold inspection.

Somehow, tonight I didn't care. I wanted to be thought attractive and womanly. I wanted to flirt, dance, laugh, drink sparkling champagne . . . but of course in moderation.

"This is the first real ball I've ever been to," I admitted with a laugh. "The parties at Vassar were overwhelmed by women and strictly disciplined."

"Cinderella Blair." Jeremy twinkled. "Are you wearing glass slippers, I wonder?" Reaching across, he twitched up my skirts to expose the silver dancing shoes laced around my ankles.

"Stop that," I cried, and shook down my dress.

He leaned back with a chuckle, ignoring Conan's growl. "It's really funny," Jeremy drawled. "Women have a fit if men get a glimpse of ankle yet bosoms are displayed at night to a staggering degree, often just stopping short of the mammalian point." He chuckled again. "Not that I'm complaining, mind you."

Drake frowned and seemed about to speak, but Rachel forestalled him by saying playfully, "Jerry, you are a caution. Shame on you! What a subject to discuss with ladies present."

Jeremy responded with his high bray of a laugh and Rachel turned the conversation by asking Drake: "How did Melissa like the idea of the household deserting her tonight? I imagine it didn't sit too well with that young lady, did it?"

"Naturally Melissa was disappointed," Drake replied. "She's nearly recovered but needed another day of rest. It's been hard on her being ill in a strange environment and I'm sure she misses her family and the social life she enjoyed in Jamestown."

"Social life?" Rachel scoffed. "I understood the family was impoverished."

"By her standards, perhaps," Drake said. "Of course, the ending of the war affected the economic outlook of the whole South, but they slowly are recovering. Previously, Melissa's parents enjoyed a high social standing and she has been raised on tales of her family's importance."

"Speaking of importance, our host's rise to fame has made him quite a legend," Conan said. "I always have admired him."

Drake nodded. "Darius Mills went from a young bank clerk in New York to president of the Bank of California in record time. He arrived very opportunely during Gold Rush days."

"He just was lucky," Jeremy sneered. "The proverbial 'luck of D. O. Mills.' Some people have it, some don't."

"There's more to it than that," Drake said dryly. "Mills's so-called luck came from farsightedness, good judgment, and complete integrity. Instead of digging in the earth like all the others seeking a quick fortune in 'forty-nine, he brought a load of merchandise to sell out here. In no time at all, he became a legend from hard work and cleverness."

"And just think," Rachel gloated. "We're among the two hundred guests that he's invited, the cream of San Francisco. I read all about the plans in the *Morning Call*. A special train is bringing most of the people to Belmont, where carriages will convey them to the party."

"Two hundred!" I exclaimed. "It will be difficult to meet anyone in all that throng."

"Don't worry," Drake said, his lip quirking. "You'll be noticed."

I would later remember that remark—and groan.

"Lesley, darlin'," Conan said, "you should have business cards to hand out stating: Interior Homes Designed by San Francisco's First and Finest Lady Decorator."

"I'm afraid that would be too bold a maneuver at a ball." I chuckled, although I rather fancied the idea.

"I shall personally introduce you to my friends as a first-class decorator," Drake promised. "I am very impressed with the work you and Mr. Blye have done thus far."

I inclined my head and thanked him, exchanging a quick smile with Conan. Surely this augured well for more work at Cliffside. However, I felt Drake would not commit himself until my plans were approved by him.

The next minute, all conversation was interrupted by Jeremy, who let down the window and exclaimed excitedly, "We're nearly there. I can see a glow lighting up the entire sky!"

It wasn't long before we turned into the grounds of Millbrae and every eye in the carriage fastened on the twinkling avenues of trees strung with candle-lit Chinese lanterns.

"The house is aglow from top to bottom," Rachel cried. "And just look at all the carriages!"

My lips parted as I leaned forward to peer out of the window. A millionaire's ball—what would it be like? I felt this would be a night I never would forget.

We joined the stream of slowly-moving vehicles and now I could observe the acres of well-tended gardens, the huge glass-domed conservatory, and then the multitowered house with its mansard roof and white cupid faces that rimmed the windows where golden light poured forth.

When we emerged at the mansion's steps, I marveled at the display of wealth and splendor. Jewels flashed everywhere I looked. Paris gowns rustled and shimmered, decorated with lace, gold and silver gauze, intricate beadwork, and lovely flowers, both real and artificial. Egret plumes nodded from many high-coifed heads. The men in their black and white provided dramatic contrast for their more colorful companions. Only the masculine capes indulged their restricted taste, showing flashing linings of scarlet, gold, or emerald satin.

Inside, the ladies were escorted upstairs past balustrades entwined with ferns, roses, and stephanotis to retiring rooms. Here wraps were hung away by obsequious maids who also offered perfume, combs, and face powder at the mirrored stands.

At first, even Rachel seemed a little awed, but she soon began to greet acquaintances and I was left to my own devices. As I observed these chattering, poised, elaborately gowned women of such obvious wealth and distinction, I knew it would be difficult to interest them in hiring an unknown female decorator such as I.

However, at least tonight I could observe and enjoy everything. I picked up a dance card from a little pile so that future partners could inscribe their names beside the dances granted them. Slipping the attached black cord around my wrist, I made my way down the crowded stairway to the equally crowded hall. Here the walls were draped with clouds of pink mousseline and mechanical doves with maidenhair fern around their necks trilled sweetly but could scarcely be heard above the din.

A chattering, laughing line wound steadily toward a dais at the rear, where Mr. and Mrs. Mills stood to receive their guests. Just as I was wondering if I should join them, to my relief Drake appeared and placed my hand upon his arm, looking at me warmly.

He seemed like a different man tonight. As he tossed jovial greetings to the many friends who called to him, the cool, self-contained mask vanished in this environment of conviviality. He grinned, he laughed, his golden eyes gleamed appreciatively, not only at the lovely women of his acquaintance but also at me.

His fingers pressed my hand against his arm as we moved into the line. "Lesley, have I conveyed my admiration for your appearance tonight? I'm sure my eyes have told you so. I can hardly stop myself from staring."

Before I could think of a reply, he continued, "May I say now that you look enchanting and I will be very proud to present you to the Millses as the loveliest heroine who ever foiled a robber."

"You—you're too kind," I murmured, a little breathlessly.

His warm gaze traveled over my face and figure, and when his arm slipped around my waist, I decided it was time for a more impersonal approach. Things were moving just a shade too fast. "Mr. Wynfield—"

"Drake," he said deeply. "Call me Drake. Aren't we friends enough for that?"

I cleared my throat, knowing I could only call him Drake when we were alone. I remembered Melissa's flare of jealousy when he had called me Lesley in her presence. "All right—Drake. Can you tell me what to expect here tonight? What is the usual procedure at these affairs?" I took an unobtrusive step away.

With a little smile, he removed his arm. "Well, if the ball goes according to custom, the guests will promenade through the upper gallery to observe the new acquisitions from abroad in the way of statuary, paintings, and *objets d'art*. Or they may wander through the gardens and conservatory, which I assure you are well worth viewing. When the dancing starts, it will continue until the midnight supper. After that, more dancing, more champagne, more flirting until dawn, when breakfast will be served."

"Dear me," I exclaimed. "What endurance these people must have. I'm not sure if I'll be able to keep up."

"Oh, not everyone stays until the end. I never do, but you must enjoy it all you can. Let me have your dance card so that I may claim some waltzes, which I prefer to the faster numbers."

He managed to sign my card while I wielded my fan vigorously. The air was heavy with the scents of women's perfume and flowers, the men's bay rum cologne and pomades of macassar oil. The many gaslights behind etched glass wall sconces added to the heat, as did the hundreds of candles burning above in crystal chandeliers.

When we neared the dais, Drake bent his dark head to my ear. "Mr. Mills plans an announcement regarding you tonight. You'll be an object of some interest after that, I imagine."

"Oh, Drake . . ." How easily his name fell from my lips. "I don't want an announcement. It would seem too bold, too . . . publicity-seeking."

He raised his eyebrows. "I thought that's what you sought, publicity for your career. Don't worry, it will be done in the best of taste, I'm sure."

There was no time for further words as Mr. and Mrs. Mills now stood before us. Drake helped me step up on the dais and then made the introductions suavely. "Miss Lesley Blair, may I present Mr. and Mrs. Darius Ogden Mills."

"By George, Drake," boomed the millionaire with complete informality. "You didn't say she was a raving beauty. May I claim the first polka, little lady?"

I nodded and smiled. "I'd be delighted."

Mrs. Mills, a queenly woman in elaborate robes of rosy silk festooned with crystal bugle beads, extended her hand to me with a warm smile. "I'm so delighted that you could come tonight. See, my dear, I'm wearing the diamond pin you so bravely saved. I can't tell you how much I enjoy wearing it and how very grateful we both are."

"I'm glad I helped." I wished I could step down now away from the sea of curious faces focused on me. Though I had wanted some attention for my business, this publicity was overwhelming and my aplomb suddenly had deserted me. When would the announcement take place, for heaven's sake?

I didn't have to wait a minute longer.

"Now, Sam Fat." Mr. Mills flung out his arm and a tall Chinese man dressed in golden silks swung a padded mallet against a brass gong, which reverberated through the hall.

The voices stilled while Mr. Mills related the brave (and exaggerated) actions of "this incredible young lady, Lesley Blair, San Francisco's newest interior decorator," he explained. "She was assisted in the recovery of the diamond brooch by my good friend, whom many of you know, Drake Wynfield, owner of The Jade Pagoda."

Everyone applauded and I prepared to step down, but he wasn't finished yet.

"Now, if anybody wants to use this pretty lady's talents—which I am assured she has just demonstrated in a Cliffside boudoir—just tell her and make an appointment."

There was a moment's silence while Mr. Mills beamed, all unaware of his faux pas. Someone coughed. Another snickered. Then there was more clapping while I stumbled down the step in an agony of embarrassment. I couldn't see Drake so I pushed through the crowd, noticing a few grins here and there and fans covering smothered laughs.

Dear heaven! What kind of propositions would I receive before this night was over? I was sure they would have little to do with my decorating talents. Here, I had hoped to interest a few customers in my professional ability, but now I simply longed to hide away somewhere until the crowd forgot Mr. Mills's unfortunate and unwitting remark about my services in boudoirs.

I knew I had to collect my shattered poise, and

since there was no sign of Drake, I headed for the nearest exit, where I cornered a footman in green and silver livery. "The conservatory—is it open?"

"Yes, miss. Just go through this door and down the path. It's lit and open for the guests."

Picking up my skirts, I sped off into the night.

18

It wasn't long before the cool night air and the calmness of the scented gardens brought me to my senses.

Why was I running off like a silly goose? I was not some green schoolgirl to be shocked by an inadvertent double entendre. Why mind because some people laughed? They probably considered it a good joke. As the humor of it struck me, I had to chuckle, albeit weakly. Actually, I felt awed by this gorgeous assembly of wealth and importance and I only wanted to make a good impression.

To bolster my morale, I sturdily began to recount my assets: a college degree, a talent to be proud of, my own business . . . On the physical side, my gown was stylish and becoming and I know many people had admired my appearance. Though it bore no couturier label nor any jewels, still Drake had complimented me most warmly. I felt a pleasant glow as I recalled the friendlier, more admiring manner he now showed toward me.

At the same time, I wondered where he had gone. There was no sign of anyone from Cliffside, but they scarcely could be expected to stick beside me when they must have dozens of friends here waiting to be greeted. However, I didn't want to return to the mansion yet and I felt at loose ends until the dancing started.

People now streamed down the walkways, exclaiming at the beautifully kept lawns and the lantern-hung trees whose soft light shone on beds of early blooming bulbs and bushes laden with flowering branches.

I walked around a curve, where the crystal-paned conservatory rose like a little palace in a fairy tale and I joined the throngs pushing through its doors. In the warm, moist interior, cement walks wound between the most exotic flowers I had ever seen: giant red and orange lilies, orchids ranging from white through lavender to brown, begonias in hanging baskets with thick-fleshed petals, pink, cream, and yellow. Palms brushed the high-domed ceiling in the center as did the twining vines and jagged-leaved banana trees.

After I had strolled through several areas, I noticed that the humidity had become most enervating. Spying a vacated redwood bench, I sank down, plying my ivory fan before my heated face. For a while I idly watched the streams of richly clad guests, but when the crowd had thinned somewhat, I became aware of voices whispering nearby behind a wall of screening plants. The word "Cliffside" had arrested my attention. I looked around but couldn't see who spoke, and though I listened shamelessly, the rest of the dialogue was indistinguishable until one voice hissed clearly: ". . . the Tongs. You have been warned before."

I rose to my feet, an urgent wish to investigate consuming me. There had been so many strange events connected with Cliffside lately. However, before I could take a step, my fan clattered to the stone path and an elderly gentleman handed it to me with a courtly bow. "Ah, you are the beautiful lady decorator. May I wish you all success?"

I was forced to exchange a few words with him, but as soon as I was alone, I quickly circled the screening plants behind the bench. I was scarcely surprised that no one stood there now. The words I'd heard, muffled and secretive, had sounded threatening, but perhaps I gave them an erroneous interpretation. Later, I would mention it to Drake, but right now I was feeling very thirsty. From the heat of the conservatory, my throat was parched, and I pushed my way outdoors.

Somewhere I would be sure to find a drink. And I did. Almost immediately, Jeremy came up behind me with a glass of bubbling champagne in each hand. He called out merrily, "Lesley, darling, I've been searching for a lovely lady to share a drink with me. Come, sit down on this bench."

I accepted gratefully, finding the iced beverage most delicious. Waiters now strolled along the garden paths with silver trays and it wasn't long before we had our glasses filled again.

"Where have you been?" Jeremy asked. "I wanted to claim some dances."

"I've been in the lovely conservatory. Have you seen it?"

"Just a peek. I'm more interested in the lovelies on the outside." When I handed him my dance card, he put his name down only once, probably wanting plenty of dances with other ladies. "Why did you run off?" he asked. "Drake was looking for you."

"Was he?" I brightened. "Well, I became foolishly upset by a rather risqué—though innocent—remark made about me by Mr. Mills. Didn't you hear it?"

Jeremy looked puzzled, then he laughed. "Oh, yes. I doubt if many people even heard him. No one mentioned it to me. What did he mean about your being a heroine?"

I repeated the story briefly about the highwayman, feeling heartily weary of the subject.

Jeremy grunted. "You were foolish to risk your life. Lord, Mills can afford a dozen diamond brooches." He waved his glass. "Look at this mansion, the magnificent estate. This is the way I'd like to live. Endless wealth, a rich wife, a Midas touch on all my enterprises."

Before I could reply, Conan came along from the direction of the conservatory, a glass of spirits in his hand and a buxom beauty on his arm. He slowed down only slightly and called to me: "Save a dance or two for your darlin' partner, *macushla*." Then he and his companion pranced off into the trees. I expected this would be a busy night for Conan.

Jeremy was no better. Two damsels came cooing up to him, batting lashes, flirting fans, calling him "Dearest Jerry."

He sprang up eagerly. "Come here, my little angels. I'll get us all some champagne. You also, Lesley?" He glanced at me somewhat indifferently.

"No more for me, thanks." I rose briskly and started toward the mansion, deciding to view the gallery now, even if I was on my own.

However, just inside the door, I almost collided with Drake and felt a stab of pleasure when he caught my arm and exclaimed, "Lesley! Where on earth did you go? I left the dais area for a minute because someone called to me, and when I returned, there was no sign of you. I've been searching everywhere."

"I felt the need for some cool air so I strolled down to the conservatory when I didn't see you." Since Drake did not seem aware of Mr. Mills's blunder, I decided not to mention it. However, the voices in the conservatory were another matter.

Trying to sound offhand as we strolled outside, I asked Drake if Li Fong was still a member of the Tongs.

He threw me a sharp glance. "I've never inquired into his past. He performs his duties admirably and that's all I am concerned with. Why do you ask?"

"Mai Yee said he used to belong to one of the Tongs years ago and just now in the conservatory I overheard someone mention Cliffside and the Tongs."

"That's all?"

"Yes. It's not important?"

"No, it isn't. The Tongs exist mainly in their own community. They would have no interest in Cliffside." He drew in his breath. "What a balmy night though I thought I saw some storm clouds earlier. At least it's held off for a while. Are you enjoying the gardens, Lesley?" When I nodded, he continued, "Mills brought botanical specimens here from all over the world. He also has a magnificent dairy herd and three big lakes. There won't be time to see it all, the dancing will start soon. Ah, wait, here's a couple you should meet."

A young fair-haired man escorting a sweet-faced girl stopped before us. Drake greeted them and the ensuing introductions disclosed that they were newlyweds who wished to build a large home in the fashionable Rincon section. They expressed delight at finding a recommended decorator and promised to call at my establishment.

After that, Drake introduced me to a number of people. Several of the men signed my dance card, and while Drake always stressed my profession, no sign of amusement crossed any face. They asked polite and interested questions, perhaps masking any surprise they felt to find a woman in commerce.

When strains of music drifted from the mansion, Drake and I headed for the ballroom. Inside, I was glad to see that an attempt to achieve coolness had been made by opening all the long French doors, as well as fountains in each corner spraying jets of colored water. I knew my eyes were nearly popping from my head as I observed the many famous personages streaming onto the floor. I recognized actresses, singers, and famous writers from their pictures. I saw the flamboyant heiress, Lillie Hitchcock Coit, who never missed going to a fire because she was so grateful to the firemen who had once saved her life. William Ralston passed me. He was called the "Silver King," because of his successful strikes of ore, and also had achieved fame as the builder of the brand-new Palace Hotel on Market Street. I even spied the Hearst family: George the senator and Phoebe the heiress. Their son, little blue-eyed William Randolph, was undoubtedly home in bed.

I could have been happy just staring from the sidelines, but the "Swedish polka" started, Drake moved off, and Mr. Mills arrived to claim his dance. I wondered if anyone had mentioned his earlier slip of the tongue. Probably no one had dared and it was just as well. The matter seemed forgotten or ignored by everyone I'd met so far.

Just before we started dancing, Mr. Mills withdrew a jewel box from his inner pocket. "Didn't get a chance to give you this before, little lady. You ran off too fast. Shy, I guess."

When I raised the lid, I gave an astonished exclamation and gaped at him. "Oh, Mr. Mills!"

Of course, D. O. Mills immediately became the focus of everyone nearby and none had any compunction about sidling closer while I held up the beautiful gold-linked bracelet from which swung a little crystal ball. When I examined it closely, I could see it was filled with sealed-in fluid containing several golden fish with ruby eyes and emerald fins. They all moved gently when I swung the ball.

"It's wonderful," I gasped.

"Aw, it's nothing." He chuckled. "Just a little thank-you."

Everyone around us wanted to inspect it. "Chinese antique?" guessed one old gentleman, peering through a monocle.

"Well, it could be," Mr. Mills replied. "Drake Wynfield picked it out for me at his shop, The Jade Pagoda, which specializes in foreign jewelry."

"It's too much—you shouldn't have . . ." I protested.

Mr. Mills dismissed my breathless thanks with a wave of his hand, then snapped the links around my wrist, and whirled me onto the dance floor. "It's nothing compared to the fact that you risked your life to save that brooch. Now, let's talk about something else. This business of yours, do you have a lot of people coming to you that used to know your father?"

"None," I said succinctly. "Frankly, I don't think the majority trust a female in the working world, but tonight Drake, er, Mr. Wynfield, introduced me to a young couple who might be interested."

"I'll mention your services to anyone I can. Drake gave your work unstinting praise."

"He did?" Suddenly, my heart felt as light as my feet.

Later on, when Drake escorted me out for the "Blue Danube" waltz, I showed him the gift from Mr. Mills. "He said you picked it out."

"Yes." He swung me onto the dance floor, holding me the required discreet distance away. "It had just come in from Peking, part of an old family estate. Mills said he wanted to show his gratitude by giving you a gift, and since the bracelet intrigued me, I took a chance that you would like it, too."

"Oh, I love it. I'll wear it all the time, it's so exquisite and unusual. One of a kind, I should imagine."

He drew me closer for a second and I felt his breath stir in my hair. "So are you, Lesley Blair. One of a kind. I mean that as a compliment."

"I'm glad you made that clear." I managed a breathless laugh to cover my swift pleasure.

We moved apart then and focused on the dance. Drake was very competent, a tall, strong dancer who made me feel as light as thistledown in his arms as he whirled me around and around. I had removed my long gloves earlier because of the warm atmosphere and Drake wore none, holding a folded handkerchief against my back as was often customary. Thus when we swung into reverse, the pressure of his bare hand tightened on my palm. For a moment, I felt his body, warm and muscular, and I wondered, shamelessly, how mine felt as I leaned into him.

He glanced down, tawny eyes glimmering beneath the heavy lids, his lips curved in a little smile. I looked away, aware of the accelerated beating of my heart. "This evening is so—so exciting," I said breathlessly.

"Indeed it is." He pulled me hard against him, but when I gave a little gasp, he moved back at once to the proper distance and remained that way until the dance ended when he bowed and thanked me, once more suave and cool. It seemed there was a suggestive gleam beneath his lids, and I quickly fanned myself.

In the time before supper, I danced twice with Conan, once with Jeremy, and with many others, but each partner seemed to be no more than shadows as I relived in my mind that waltz with Drake. I felt both excited and uneasy by my response to his potent masculine appeal and his new opinion of me as an attractive woman. This could indeed be dangerous, I warned myself, but surely it would not continue past these enchanted moments. Tonight I would enjoy his attention to the utmost.

Drake's name was on my card as dinner partner, and when it was announced, he came at once, bowed, and offered me his arm, pleasant and correct. If I felt disappointed by his manner, I had no time to ponder.

We paused on the threshold of the dining area so we could drink in the fabulous scene before us. Several rooms had evidently been thrown open to accommodate the crowd. All was pink, which surely must be Mrs. Mill's favorite color. Pink shades on lamps, rose-trimmed tulle swaths on walls, satin cloths at each round table, which had space for a dozen diners. Corsages of pink and white sweet peas reposed at every lady's place in holders of silver filigree. In the center of the tables on a sparkling mirror ringed with rosebuds stood a fairytale creation made of spun sugar. Each one was unique. Our centerpiece depicted a little castle complete with towers, banners, and drawbridge, truly a work of art. I could scarcely tear my eyes away.

Speechless, I sank into the chair Drake held for me. Soon introductions followed and such immediate chattering arose from every table that the strains of music from an electrical Swiss Orchestrion in the gallery scarcely could be heard.

A real waxed rose decorated the menus of white satin at each place and inside the cover was a list of viands to tempt the most jaded palate. Suffice to say that oysters on the half-shell, frog legs, dove pie, terrapin soup, ham, turkey, and numerous *salades* were among the items offered for our delectation with different wines for every course, including French champagne.

We ate, we drank, we laughed and talked. The other people from Cliffside were not at our table, but I didn't miss them at all, everyone was so friendly. Drake, extremely jovial and talkative, still saw that I lacked for nothing and had a part in all his conversations.

"This is the most wonderful night of my life," I told him. Emboldened by three glasses of champagne, I leaned against his arm and touched his hand.

He caught my fingers with his own. "And it isn't over yet," he whispered in my ear.

19

As soon as the main courses had been cleared away, a huge birthday cake was wheeled in for Jane Cunningham Mills. It was a replica of the Millbrae mansion right down to the cupid decorations on the windows, but instead of candles, it had blazing sparklers all around it. After wild applause, speeches, and toasts, the cake was cut and slices were placed in gilded souvenir boxes for the guests who wished them. I decided to give mine to Tad and added some of the sugared violets, Jordan almonds, and other sweetmeats from the table.

After that, the dancing started up again, my scheduled partner came to claim me, and Drake disappeared. For a long time, I caught only a glimpse of him. The tireless dancers, the blasting orchestra, and upraised voices seemed to have grown more shrill and excited as the night went on and the champagne consumption merrily advanced unchecked.

At last, I sank down on a couch beside the dance

floor. My head was spinning from too much champagne, my feet ached, and I felt ready to go home. It was with great relief that I saw Drake coming toward me through the crowd. In order to be heard, he had to bend down to my ear. "Would you like to leave now? We can say good-bye to Mr. and Mrs. Mills."

I nodded emphatically and rose quickly to accompany him.

We found our host and hostess in the gallery and there ensued a round of "thank-you's" that threatened to get out of hand. I thanked them for inviting me and praised everything with the most heartfelt sincerity. They thanked me again for saving the brooch. Then I enthused about the antique bracelet, claiming I would seldom remove it from my wrist. After that, Drake and I left them to claim our outerwear.

In the retiring room, I took an apprehensive peek into the mirror, expecting to see a haggard image, but except for the wilted gardenias in my hair, I merely looked flushed and a little shiny about the nose. I removed the flowers, tucked up a few stray ends of hair, and applied some of the contents of a puff box extended to me by a maid. Then, donning my cloak, I collected the cake for Tad, and wended my way to the entrance, where other couples awaited their conveyances.

Raindrops now were blowing from the bay and I could hear a distant roll of thunder. I looked around but saw no sign of Conan, Rachel, or Jeremy. The only familiar figure was Drake, pushing his way toward me, his crimson-lined opera cloak billowing in the wind.

"The rest of our party have chosen to stay on and ride back with friends from the Sea Cliff area," he told me. "But I think it's a good thing for us to start now before the storm gets any worse. Do you mind?"

Of course I didn't mind. When our carriage was announced, Drake took my arm and we ran down the steps. The rain was heavier now, but we got only slightly wet as we fell breathlessly into our vehicle. We removed our damp cloaks at once, placing them on the opposite seat, then sat side by side.

Drake leaned back and smiled at me. "Did you enjoy the evening, Leslie?"

"It was wonderful! Thank you so much for bringing me."

"I loved having you there."

Tonight he seemed so much younger, more relaxed and approachable. Hadn't he spoken about "further plans" for Cliffside? Here we were alone, no interruptions, at ease with one another. This was a perfect opportunity.

I slid a little closer, drew a deep breath, and leaned toward him. His gaze lowered to my décolletage. "Lovely," he murmured.

I drew back, flushing. He mustn't get the wrong idea. "Wouldn't this be a good time for us to discuss further decorating plans for Cliffside?"

"I can think of other things I'd rather do." He laughed. "Don't turn into a businesswoman now. All evening you've been so warm, so carefree, so . . . enticing." He reached out and clasped my arm, drawing me close beside him. "Just let yourself be a . . . woman for a while."

"Mr. Wynfield!" I caught my breath and attempted to break his hold, but it was useless. His strong fingers stroked downward to my wrist and captured it. "What are you doing?" I gasped.

"Perhaps I'm trying to make love to you." He

chuckled richly and pressed against me so that my head went back against the seat.

When I whispered "Don't!" he didn't seem to hear me. I could feel the strength of his body, the wine-tinged breath, the heady aromas of cologne, pomade, and warm male skin. A strange lethargy invaded me, and suddenly I couldn't move or speak.

His gaze went slowly across my hair, my eyes, and lingered on my parted lips. He traced them lazily, then trailed his fingers down my throat to the pearl in the hollow of my breasts. He lifted the jewel, his knuckles resting on the rise and fall of my rapid heartbeats.

"You are so exciting tonight, Leslie," he murmured huskily. "I've always thought you were unusually attractive, but tonight you overwhelm me."

Making a great effort, I attempted to change his mood. "What . . . about . . . your . . . house?"

"I want you to remain at Cliffside and decorate everything. Take as long as you like. I enjoy seeing you around." His hand moved upward to caress the bare skin of my shoulder and his face came closer.

I couldn't drag my eyes from his, and though I knew I should be elated at his words, a terrible kind of thrall held me. In another second, I knew that he would kiss me and then . . . what? We would have crossed the barrier between employer and employee. What would he expect then? Favors? Melissa seemed far away and, dear heaven, I was not myself tonight. He attracted me to an alarming degree. The tingling awareness that our lips might join and flood me with a desire such as I had never known filled me with excitement. I only had to turn my head to meet the consummation of his kiss.

"Lesley, you are so adorable," he breathed, and closed his eyes.

"So is Melissa."

Had I said that? Where had that speck of common sense come from? I hadn't meant to speak. . . .

However, it broke the spell. His eyes flew open, and for a long moment we stared at each other without speaking. Then he gave a short, harsh laugh and leaned back in his corner. "Oh, Lesley, you only dare up to a certain point, don't you? So brave, so indomitable, so spirited, and yet—"

"So straightlaced," I interposed. "Shall I consider myself out of a job?"

Immediately, he stiffened. "Of course not. What do you take me for? A lecher demanding favors because I hired you?"

My voice trembled. "Well, you've never acted like this before with me—"

"And I won't again. I beg your forgiveness." He cleared his throat. "I want you to stay on at Cliffside and complete the decorating. Things got out of hand tonight, that's all. Too much wine, excitement, and you—so lovely . . ." His voice dropped deeply. "But I swear to you that I am not a cad."

"I never thought you were. I understand."

"You'll stay?"

"Yes." I knew that I must struggle to ignore what had just been between us. Thank goodness, my voice now sounded cool and calm. "Perhaps we should discuss Melissa's preferences regarding the other rooms. Her favorite color schemes? A certain style that she might favor in her future home?"

"I'm sure your choice will be perfection. You decide," he answered wearily.

"You don't think Melissa will wish to be consulted?"

"I doubt it. I imagine she's not used to decorating anything except her person."

He sounded cynical and depressed. I thought about the Gold Rush days when mail-order brides had been sent for, sight unseen. What disappointments, what misrepresentations on both sides must have occurred. Yet promises were binding, then as now. A broken engagement was a catastrophe. Drake would never ask Melissa to release him in spite of the fact that she might seem entirely different out here on the Coast . . . and quite unsuitable.

Silence fell and we both stared out at the wild, dark, stormy night as we bowled along the deserted roads. However, the atmosphere was not strained between us. Perhaps it was closer than before. How could it not be? For a moment, we'd been on the heady brink of emotions that could have escalated easily to passion. His touch, his obvious desire for me, had kindled a response such as I had never felt before, frightening in its intensity.

Was this the danger I'd first sensed in Drake? His ability to arouse dark passions and strange yearnings in me that I had no right to feel? I drew a deep, smothered breath, thankful that I'd had the strength to pull away . . . but would I always be that strong?

I sat up straighter. Yes, I had to be. From now on, I would concentrate on my career . . . and nothing else.

That night I fell asleep at once, but suddenly I heard someone knocking at my door. My eyes flew wide, and scarcely knowing what was happening, I rose and crossed the room, answering the summons.

Drake stood in the doorway, his whole stance rigid with some consuming emotion barely held in check. "There is an unfinished matter between us," he whispered hoarsely.

My heart began to pound as our gaze locked, and I found I couldn't move or speak. With a swift stride he caught me to him and the next instant I felt his mouth on mine, fierce, hot, and somehow . . . despairing.

Heedlessly, I clung to his hard shoulders while every nerve responded with a whirl of feelings I never had experienced before.

But then he pulled away, and as I trembled in the aftermath of shock, he left the room without another word.

Slowly, as the light grew in the room, I realized what had transpired . . . a dream, just a dream! Breathlessly, I wondered . . . *was it perhaps the essence of something that I secretly desired?*

20

When I was more fully awake, I worried how I could restrain my wayward fancies. Was I falling in love with Drake? Since we first met, I'd had many different emotions regarding him. First, an odd sense of fear and awe, then admiration, pleasure in his company, sympathy for his problems, and now . . . what? I wasn't sure. I only knew that more and more I felt a strong feeling of attraction for him and that was dangerous. I must stop this consuming interest in him. I had to concentrate on other, more important matters. Flinging off the covers, I donned my Chinese robe and rang for coffee.

I was sipping it in my chair by the window when Melissa knocked and entered abruptly. "So! You're awake at last." Her voice was strong and she appeared to be recovered, with clear rosy skin and bright blue eyes. Her hair had been arranged in red-gold ringlets caught up by a blue silk ribbon that exactly matched her dress and eyes.

Surveying me with an inimical stare, she put her hands upon her hips. "Well, Miss Lady Decorator, how was the party? What time did you-all get in? I declare, I never heard of such a thing, taking an *employee* to a grand ball." Her eyes bored into me, hard and icy.

"I'm sorry you couldn't go," I said placatingly, wishing she would leave me in peace. Her baleful attitude was triggering a headache. "Is your cold better?"

With a curt nod, Melissa flung herself into a nearby chair. "Today I could have gone to the party. It just makes me furious! Well, Miss Blair, I asked a question. Why were you so honored above all the other servants?"

"Why didn't you ask Mr. Wynfield?" I tried to control my rising ire, telling myself that she was merely venting her disappointment on the nearest one at hand.

"I asked *you*, Miss Blair," she snapped. "Let's hear your version. Why did you accompany the family to the biggest ball of the year, as the newspapers described it? You, a mere servant, and a temporary one at that."

Carefully, I set my cup down in its saucer. "Mr. Mills requested my appearance so that he might thank me for helping to restore an item to his wife." As briefly as possible, I told her the oft-repeated story of the highwayman and the brooch.

She was not impressed. "Ridiculous! I still don't see why you should have been personally escorted by my fiancé. It was not your place—"

The time had come to make my status clear. "Miss Fernley, I am not one of the servants. I have degrees in art and interior design from Vassar College. I am a professional woman with my own shop. Mr. Wynfield hired me at extremely high wages to redecorate his house.''

"Indeed?" She sneered. "Are there no men in San Francisco to perform this . . . service? Why would he hire you—a woman?"

I answered evenly, "Mr. Wynfield knew my father, who did similar work, and he was impressed by my training and background. Perhaps Mr. Wynfield is a forward-looking man who thinks the world of industry will profit by the addition of some females.''

"Rubbish," Melissa cut in rudely. "Women were born to function purely in the boudoir, drawing room, or nursery. Unless, of course, they're servants, in which case, you can add the kitchen. But if the hiring of you is up to me, Miss Blair . . .''

"Yes?" This I had to challenge. The rest of Melissa's statement was too ridiculous to answer. I had known from the beginning that she was a narrow-minded bigot. "Since Mr. Wynfield hired me, perhaps we should discuss this with him. If you will leave me for a moment, I will dress and we can face him together.''

An ugly flush swept the beauty from her face. She looked down angrily, pleating her silk ruffles. "Oh, well, fiddle! I guess that won't be necessary. Whatever Mr. Wynfield wishes, that is my wish, too.''

"Very commendable, my dear," Drake drawled from the open doorway. "If you will always be so tractable, what a harmonious life we will have. How pleased I am to see that you've recovered. And you, Miss Blair, how are you on this bright and sunny day?"

"F-fine, thank you," I stuttered. Memory of my recent dream as well as his seductive actions in the carriage made my face flame, but he didn't seem to notice.

His glance slid over me, bland and impersonal. Last night never might have happened. He showed no signs of weariness, either from the ball or our emotional encounter.

"Since everyone appears to be in good health and the storm is past, I thought you two might like to go into the City with me to select some fabrics for the parlor. Are you both agreeable?"

"Why, yes," I answered promptly. "That sounds like an excellent idea."

"And you, Melissa?" Drake asked. "Will you join us or do you wish to leave the decisions up to Miss Blair and myself?"

"No, indeed. I certainly think I should go with you since I am to be the mistress of this place." She sidled up to him. "I just bet you are simply perishing for the wedding to take place, aren't you?"

"Indeed." He gave her a slight smile, then took her arm and walked her toward the door. "We'll meet downstairs, Miss Blair, as soon as you are ready."

I immediately summoned a maid to bring me juice and rolls while I swiftly washed and brushed my hair. I dressed in a neat, dark green alpaca, its only trimming rows of velvet bows around the skirt. Over this, I put a matching sacque and my marten furs, and on my head, a small felt hat adorned with shiny black cherries and a light-green ribbon hanging down the back. I couldn't help admiring the overall effect. I had to have something to bolster my morale when traveling with Melissa.

Picking up my portfolio and purse, I stepped into the hall, where I found my small friends, Tad and Prince, awaiting me.

"That Melissa got out of bed today," the little boy said gloomily. "I guess she's well now, huh?"

"Yes, she is." I smoothed my kidskin gloves. "We're going into town with your papa this morning to select some materials for the parlor."

"Then you're going to stay on? Hooray!" He flung his arms around me and Prince gave what might have been a joyous bark.

I hugged Tad back while Prince wriggled from ear to tail and tried to lick my shoe. Perhaps he hoped that I would take him on another romp through Chinatown.

"Oh, Miss Lesley, let me go with you this morning," Tad implored. "I promise I'll be good. I'll never leave your side for a single second. I swear I've learned my lesson."

"Oh, Tad, I don't think so." I hesitated, torn between two pairs of beseeching eyes, then softening I added: "Well, we'd have to ask your papa."

I could see Drake and Melissa talking in the hall below. He, all polite attention. She, a simpering darling. I had to admit, however, that she looked lovely in her azure silk and tiny cape, with a becoming bonnet of white straw trimmed with pink rosebuds. But her garments looked more suitable to the mild weather of a Virginia spring than to the erratic chills and fogs of San Francisco.

When I reached her side, I eyed her doubtfully. "Do you think that you'll be warm enough, Miss Fernley?"

"Why, the sun is shining, can't you see it?" she asked airily while her eyes examined every fragment of my outfit. She twirled a fragile lacy parasol tied with a big blue bow, and I hoped the San Francisco winds wouldn't blow it inside out. Well, I'd warned her.

"Miss Lesley," Tad asked, tugging at my jacket.

"Oh. Mr. Wynfield, Tad wants to know if he can accompany us today."

"Of course not," Melissa shrilled. "Heavens to Betsy, this won't be a social occasion. We aren't going out for any larks. We must devote all our energies to the business at hand. There will be no time to watch a little boy."

"Yesterday you said I was a great *big* boy," Tad muttered, sending her a glowering look.

My lips twitched, but I knew Tad's plea to go along was doomed.

His father sighed. "Melissa's right, son. This would not be a good day for you. We have important business at Miss Lesley's shop."

"Please, Papa, let me go. I won't be a bit of trouble. Please!"

"Don't whine and beg," Melissa snapped, sounding like a stepmother already and not a very pleasant one at that. "You heard your father. Drake, let's go."

"Listen, Tad, I'll take you to town the next time I go in," I promised. "Perhaps we could drive out and see the big new park they're planting by the ocean."

"That would be much better." Drake sent me a grateful glance. "We don't want Melissa to become fatigued by any added matters today." His eyes swept her costume. "My dear, don't you think you should wear a warmer wrap as Miss Blair suggested?"

"No, indeed. I'll just be inside the carriage and then the shops." Melissa tossed an irritated glance at me. "Isn't your place of business heated, Miss Blair?"

"Of course. Probably Mr. Blye is already there."

Drake shook his head. "He isn't up yet. The rest of

the party returned home in the early morning hours."

"Oh, you-all must have had such fun," Melissa wailed. "Drake, I want you to make this up to me. Promise that we'll go to lots and lots of balls and socials after we are married."

"Whatever we have time for. Remember, I'm a working man." He headed for the door. "There's the carriage, shall we go?"

I turned back to the downcast little figure in his white serge blouse and pantaloons, watching us depart. Even Prince looked disappointed, his ragged tail flat upon the floor.

"Listen, Tad, I brought you some cake and candy from the party. I put it in the dining room last night. You can have it with your lunch."

"Thank you, Miss Lesley."

Melissa's shrill voice reached us from the porch. "For pity's sake, Miss Blair, can't you talk to the boy when we return?" She stepped back in the hall and hissed, "Are you trying to impress your employer with how sweet you can be to his son? Much good that will do you."

She shook her parasol at Tad. "When I'm in charge of you, little boy, you'll spend all your days at school instead of whining underfoot. You may even spend your nights there, too."

Tad and Prince both turned and fled.

An angry statement trembled on my lips and I had to clamp them tight. If I antagonized the Maiden Fair, who knew how far she'd go with Drake to get me dismissed? I couldn't take a chance.

As we rolled down Sea Cliff's winding lanes, Melissa chattered and bubbled as if everything were rosy and she had never been sick a day in her life.

The resilience of youth, I thought, or else she had not been as ill as she had pretended.

When she finally paused for breath, Drake addressed us. "Perhaps you both might like to see my shop, The Jade Pagoda, before we undertake the other business matters."

Melissa clapped her little, lace-covered hands. "Oooh, yes. What a charming name, The Jade Pagoda! Is there a lot of jewelry there? Perhaps I could find something for this?" She wiggled her fingers underneath Drake's nose and tittered.

"Indeed. Whatever you desire, my dear."

Melissa leaned toward me. "You see, Miss Blair, I don't have an engagement ring yet. Drake brought his mother's ring down to Virginia, but it was far too old-fashioned and heavy for my tiny hand."

She clasped Drake's arm possessively, looking across at me like a complacent pussycat. "Why aren't you engaged, Miss Blair? You better not wait too long, you know."

"You're right. I'm aging fast."

"How old are you?" she inquired rudely. "Twenty-nine or more?"

I bared my teeth. "Much older. They call me the Grandma Decorator."

"Oh, surely you jest," she said uncertainly.

"I try to."

Drake laughed outright. "Miss Blair is only twenty-four. Do you think she looks over the hill? I certainly don't."

Melissa shot us each a narrowed glance, then drew Drake's attention by crying prettily, "Oooh, I do declare I see the famous City! Tell me all about it, dearest."

"Very well. This is the heart of San Francisco we

now are entering. It is the most colorful, lusty, and exciting city on the globe and I have seen them all."

Melissa looked obediently out the window, making appropriate comments.

When the carriage stopped, we alighted in front of The Jade Pagoda. A Chinese man stood at the door dressed in red and gold satin with a thin mustache that drooped below his chin. He opened the door for us with a low bow and much polite hissing. Melissa edged past quickly. Drake greeted his doorman and I murmured good morning in Cantonese as Mai had taught me: "*Jo sun.*"

I received a gap-toothed grin and the same reply before he resumed his dignified pose to greet some approaching patrons.

Oblivious to all else, Melissa flew to a large case of modern jewelry in the center of the store. Drake left her after a moment and said to me, "Why don't I show you around while Melissa is occupied?"

"I'd like that. This certainly is a beautiful store." Raptly, I gazed at walls hung with embroidered scrolls, glass shelves containing curios of jade, ivory, carnelian, and cinnebar. There were intricately carved vases, some of them jewel-encrusted, and many snuff bottles made of porcelain, crystal, or enamel. Cloisonné jars had lovely flowers outlined in threads of gold.

Directly beside the entrance hung a painting of what could only be the "Jade Pagoda." It was drawn much larger than its original size, which Drake had described to me, but it displayed the carved walls of "spinach green" as certain jade was called, as well as the upturned eaves of goldleaf dripping with gems and pearls. It reposed on a table covered with black velvet.

Drake followed the direction of my gaze and sighed. "Yes, that's what it looked like."

I knew it represented more than a unique and valuable art object. It was the trademark of the shop and had been treasured by Drake's father for many years.

"A tragic loss," I said.

"Yes, but that's history now." Deliberately, he turned his back on the painting. "Come over here. I want to show you something else."

He led me to a small alcove at the rear where walls and floor were a black background for cabinets of clear glass containing women's Chinese robes. I had never seen such exquisite things. Drake held up each robe for my inspection. One had great sprays of chrysanthemums in cream and gold on a soft blue background. Another had pink lotuses embroidered on a snow-white silk. Silver dragons flashed across a robe of lustrous black satin.

Then Drake slid a pale green and white garment from its padded hanger. "These are your colors. Why don't you try it on?"

However, just as I reached for it, a soft voice spoke behind us. "Excuse, please. Miss Fernley would like to see you now."

Drake replaced the robe and both of us silently returned to the main room. Drake seemed more elegant and important than ever in his beautiful shop and I regretted the curtailment of his warm attention. I smothered a sigh as we rejoined Melissa.

The Jamestown Jewel was all delight and pretty eagerness. "Oh, Drake, honey, I do declare I'm in such a quandary. Shall I take this great blue sapphire with the pearls around it? Or"—her voice sank low with awe—"this absolutely fantastic diamond solitaire?"

"Well, you could save on lighting bills if you take the diamond," I said.

Drake laughed. "Take whichever one you want, Melissa. It is up to you."

While Melissa pondered, someone asked to speak with Drake and I drifted over to the shelves of dinnerware made in China to which King George III had given his patronage in 1773 so that it was thereafter called "Crown Derby." Later, when Queen Victoria also chose it, the word "Royal" was added. Perhaps I could give a piece to Melissa and Drake for a wedding present. The idea of their marriage sent a stab of pain through me, yet today the purchase of the engagement ring certainly had solidified the coming event.

Staring blindly at the case, I suddenly heard a voice call Melissa's name, and when I glanced across the room, I saw a young man hurrying toward her.

He looked quite young, but he had a full mustache, curly brown hair, and an erect, forceful carriage. When he called Melissa's name again, his voice sounded hoarse and urgent.

Melissa whirled around. She grew pale, then her color flamed. "You! What—what . . ." For the first time since I'd known her, she seemed completely overcome and speechless.

"They told me at the house where you had gone," he said, attempting to take her arm. "Melissa, I have to talk to you . . ."

"Why—why have you f-followed me here?" I could see her struggling for composure. "There— there is nothing for us to discuss. I'm going to be married. Oh—here he is. Drake Wynfield, Tom Warren, who is—*was* a family friend."

Both men bowed curtly. Then the young man grimly eyed the ring she held and, turning on his heel, left the shop without another word.

21

Half expecting Melissa to begin a fluttering explanation about the young man, I was surprised to find that she made no further mention of him. Neither did Drake.

Melissa's chatter extended only to the diamond ring now firmly established on the third finger of her left hand for all the world to admire. She glanced in my direction to see if jealousy appeared on the face of such a poor working woman, so dangerously close to being "on the shelf." I schooled myself to express only the most fulsome admiration.

We left The Jade Pagoda soon after that and drove the few blocks to my shop. Conan was there now and talk became brisk as I set forth my ideas for Cliffside's rejuvenation. I displayed samples of drapery, upholstery, and carpeting for consideration.

Melissa looked to Drake for all decisions with a pretty show of deference, while he agreed to every one of my ideas with a rather forced attempt at interest.

My heart went out to him, though I knew that I was on dangerous ground here: pity mixed with attraction. I couldn't help the pity. Drake just didn't strike me as a man in love. He seemed more like someone now caught in a trap. I imagined that the girl he had known down South had displayed a charming facade concealing the person who had finally showed up in San Francisco irritably complaining when faced with any slight unpleasantness. Not that Melissa was weak or soft. Oh, no. Unless I was very much mistaken, her will was ironclad, selfish, and quite ruthless. She always would try to get what she wanted, either with beguiling ways or subterfuge. I wondered what would happen when she clashed with Drake's equally strong will.

I didn't like the outlook for poor Tad, either. Melissa showed no sympathy or even any liking for him. Tad's doom, as well as Drake's, was more certain with every passing moment. And now I had to decorate the house for her. But no matter what I felt, I must do my best so that the outcome would be a credit to my training.

At last, the main items were decided on, the color schemes selected, and back in the carriage Drake invited Melissa and me to a late lunch at William Ralston's "Palace." We both accepted with alacrity, though Melissa frowned at me. I didn't care. I was very curious to see San Francisco's most-talked-about new hotel.

We found it to be a resplendent mass of curved windows and white paint, seven stories high, said to contain one thousand rooms. Carriages used the center court to unload their passengers in a large, skylit well surrounded by balconies. Stamping hooves, jangling harnesses, creaking wheels, and upraised voices all created quite a din, and I wondered how the hotel patrons up above could stand it.

However, the dining room presented a different picture. Here the portals led to a place of crystal chandeliers, potted palms, and beautifully carved and gilded walls. An army of waiters swarmed around the tables, which boasted centerpieces of carnations, heliotrope, and roses, as well as glittering cut-glass and heavy, gleaming silver.

Society had discovered this new attraction and were out in full force garbed in their best attire—tall silk hats or feathered bonnets; broadcloth, serge, or silk and satin according to their sex. Lorgnettes or monocles were raised constantly to observe friends and celebrities as they arrived.

While we ate, Melissa's delighted gaze darted everywhere. At the same time, she managed to consume large portions of jellied consommé, boned quail, salmon mousse, and so on, to the final selection of desserts wheeled in on a cart. These included almond cake, citron macaroons, and English trifle, as well as numerous tarts, ices, and hothouse fruits.

I dined quite heartily myself, and it was a good thing, for that evening my appetite was banished by a new catastrophe.

When we pulled into the driveway at Cliffside, Drake jumped out and we all stared at a black gig tethered by the door.

"The doctor's here," Drake exclaimed. "What on earth can be the matter?"

Instantly, my heartbeat quickened and I hurried up the stairs after Drake, dreading what we might find. The hallway and adjoining parlor were filled with nervously milling members of the staff and household. My anxious gaze swept them all, but I did not see Tad.

Li Fong entered and even his face had lost its usual impassivity. "Master Tad became ill, Mr. Wynfield, but he will recover. Doctor is with young person now."

Drake turned without a word and bounded up the stairs.

I started to follow him, but Rachel put out a hand and stopped me. "Miss Blair, there is nothing you can do right now. You'd just be in the way."

"What happened?" I gasped.

"Well, at lunchtime, Tad began to eat that cake you'd brought him. He took a mouthful and, seconds later, gave a cry of pain and doubled over. He became so ill, I sent for Dr. Crane. Fortunately, Tad threw up and the doctor said that saved his life."

"Dear heaven!" I gripped my hands together. "I can't understand how it could have happened. We all ate a slice of that cake."

"Perhaps something fell into it," Rachel muttered. "The box was in the dining room all morning."

"Poison!" Melissa shrieked. "We all may die! Maid, help me to my room. So horrible—I must lie down at once."

"Don't be silly. No one else is sick," Rachel called after her, but Melissa continued moaning up the stairs.

I let her go and turned to Li Fong. "Did the doctor offer any explanation?"

He shrugged. "Possibly lead poison from paint on box."

Lead in paints. Li had access to such things in his family's business. So did I. So did Conan. A queer chill crawled over me, and wheeling around, I hur-

ried to my room. After dropping my outer garments
on the bed, I went in search of Tad.

The nursery door stood open on a large schoolroom with bedrooms on either side. Evidently this
was where the absent Miss Libby had slept. Had she,
too, been the victim of a malignant substance?

I heard low voices coming from one of the bedrooms, and tiptoeing to the door, I spied Dr. Crane
conversing with Drake. Tad seemed to be asleep, but
Prince, nearby on the rug, kept both eyes alertly on
his little master. Perhaps the dog sensed, as pets
often do, that all was not well with him.

I shrank back in the schoolroom as the doctor
picked up his hat and satchel. When he came
through the door, I approached him. "How is he,
doctor?"

The physician recognized me from his visit to Melissa and gave a short nod, still moving toward the
hall. "The boy should be all right tomorrow. He is
young and strong and vomited up most of the
adulterated food at once."

"Doctor, I gave the cake to him. I feel so guilty.
How could it have happened? We all ate some of the
same cake . . ." My voice faltered, thick with un-
shed tears.

The doctor paused and gave me a kindly glance.
"Don't blame yourself, Miss Blair. This was an accident. Perhaps paint from a nearby decoration or
even on the box. I'll send word to Mr. Mills to be on
guard."

He turned away. "I have an urgent childbirth to
attend so I must hurry. I'll return tomorrow, but I'm
sure the boy will be all right. I gave him a few drops
of laudanum to soothe his stomach and make him
sleep."

"Thank you, doctor." When I peeped in the door

of Tad's room, I saw Drake still sitting beside the bed with its deeply sleeping patient.

I cleared my throat and Drake looked up. "Thank heaven the doctor says that Tad will be all right."

Drake nodded wearily.

"I'm so sorry—it's all my fault."

"What do you mean? Oh, because you gave the cake to Tad? No, no. Dr. Crane says some noxious substance probably fell accidentally onto that slice. Dyes used in decorations often are poisonous if ingested. Tad may have licked something on the box."

Drake looked worriedly at his sleeping son. "He should have a governess or nurse to oversee him. He's too little to be left alone so much. Miss Libby won't be back, and besides, Tad needs someone reliable and more understanding."

After a moment, I suddenly exclaimed, "I know just the person to look after Tad—Mai Yee."

Drake's eyebrows rose. "Your housekeeper?"

"She's much more than that. Mai Yee was my childhood nurse. She made me obey when necessary, learn good manners, be honest and loyal, and keep reverence for my parents. Now she is my loving friend as well and would do anything for me, I'm sure. The Chinese enjoy children. It is part of their belief in the continuance of life."

"But would she be willing to leave her peaceful, ordered existence down in Millbrae?"

"It would just be during my stay here, perhaps a month or less. After that, I'm sure you can find someone else. It will give you a little time to look around."

Drake drew a deep breath. "Lesley, it sounds like a wonderful solution." His eyes turned to the ragged aristocrat lying on the rug. "Does Mai Yee like dogs?"

"Yes, indeed. My brother and I always had pets when I was small. As you know, the Chinese often keep canines statues for good luck, such as the ones called Foo Dogs used to guard their temples."

Aware of our eyes on him, Prince acknowledged us with one thump of his tail, then resumed guard duty.

"I can go tomorrow and ask Mai if you wish," I ventured.

"Thank you, Lesley. I would appreciate that."

Before he could continue, a maid knocked on the open door and bobbed a quick curtsy. "Begging your pardon, Mr. Wynfield, but Miss Fernley is upset and wants to speak with you or—or . . ." The maid looked uncertainly from one of us to the other.

Drake rose from his chair.

"Wait." I pressed his arm. "You stay here. I'll go see if I can help Melissa. If she really needs you, I'll let you know."

"Very well. She probably wants to hear about Tad. I'd like to remain with him a little longer." With a weary smile for me, Drake sat down, his eyes returning to the small figure in the bed.

I hurried from the room, wondering what new whimsy irked the Maiden Fair. I soon discovered that I was an inadequate substitute.

"Where's Drake?" Melissa shrilled. "I distinctly told that stupid maid—"

"Mr. Wynfield is concerned with Tad at the moment so I offered to see if I could help. What's troubling you?"

"It's *Mr. Wynfield* who must see this, but since you're here . . ." She stalked into her bedroom and I followed.

Melissa flung a hand dramatically toward her bed. A doll with midnight hair sat there, gazing at us with sea-green eyes. It was the one dressed like Melissa's predecessor in rose and moss-green satin with gems sparkling on throat and wrist. A note was pinned to the small bodice. I bent down and read it:

Go home or Rose herself will hant you.

The poor spelling was a giveaway and inwardly I groaned. Tad had paid no heed to my advice.

Melissa's voice shook with rage. "I found this—this—*thing* underneath the bedspread when I turned it down to take a nap. Did you ever see such a monstrous insult?"

I cleared my throat and sought equivocation's artful aid. "Miss Fernley, evidently you are not used to childish pranks."

"Pranks? Pranks?" she screeched. "How dare you call it that? It's been one malicious trick after another ever since I came. I've just recalled the whispers in the night. Why wasn't Tad punished for that? And his insolence when he couldn't go with us today. What do you suggest I do? Wait until the little monster knocks my brains out with a heavy toy? Or tells that mangy hound to sink his teeth into my jugular some night while I'm asleep?"

At this exaggerated picture, I had to bite my lips to keep from laughing, but I knew Melissa was not at all amused.

"Please, Miss Fernley, calm yourself," I said soothingly. "You aren't hurt, are you? Tad would never actually harm you. He's just upset and uneasy about a strange stepmama. Give him time to get used to the idea. And—"

"*I—want—Drake—to—see—this!*" With gnashing teeth and dilated eyes, Melissa grabbed up the doll and shook it as viciously as though it had attacked her. The china head wobbled and swung toward her, looking up with an almost evil expression in the staring eyes and tiny red-lipped mouth.

The pink velvet skirt flapped wildly as Melissa shook the doll, and the next thing we knew, the head broke off and rolled upon the floor!

We both caught our breath and stared.

"Hooray! You killed her!" I shouted. Then against all reason, as a sort of insane release from the recent fears and tensions, I began to laugh with unbridled mirth.

Melissa didn't even smile.

"Is it . . . very valuable?" she asked when she could be heard. Her former anger had vanished to be replaced with deep dismay. She bent and picked up the delicate hollow head and gave a cry. "It's cracked! Oh, good heavens, will Drake have a fit?" She looked at me wildly, her lips shaking.

Instantly, a solution burst upon me. Assembling my features in a grave, censorious expression, I replied, "Yes, Miss Fernley, the dolls in Rose's collection are priceless. They were imported from France and designed by master craftsmen. Note the human hair, the delicate features, the soft coloring of the bisque, the pierced ears—"

"What can I do?" Melissa cried, and beat her hands together feverishly. "Miss Blair, take the thing away—hide it. I'll pretend I've never seen it. Put it someplace . . ." Terrified, she placed the doll upon the bed.

I nodded. "Don't worry. I know where to put it—back in the Velvet Room. I may even be able to mend the crack and replace the head. Neither of us will say a word. Just set a lucifer to that note."

"Yes, yes!"

"Remember, it was just a childish prank and of

course Tad never would admit to it anyway, so what's the use of mentioning it now?"

"None, none!"

"If Mr. Wynfield wants to know why you wished to see him just now, I'll say it was concern about Tad's condition. That would only be logical, wouldn't it?" Actually, the future stepmama had not asked a single word about her future stepson's condition.

"I would suggest you take your nap and put the matter from your mind, Miss Fernley. I'll take care of everything."

Melissa nodded eagerly. "I'm greatly indebted to you, Miss Blair, indeed I am. Go quickly now and remember—not a word to anyone about the doll."

I put a finger to my lips. Moving to the door with exaggerated caution, I peered into the hall, nodded to Melissa, and stole swiftly on my errand.

22

When I reached the gallery, there was no trouble about finding the secret carving that unlocked the door. I imagined that everyone in the house knew about it, too. At any rate, I was glad Tad had shown me how to enter the doors and stairs leading to his mother's quarters since my errand involved the utmost secrecy.

After placing the doll carefully on a nearby taboret, I stopped at the doorway to the Velvet Room and gazed around. I detected a strange atmosphere up here compounded of Rose's perfume, mustiness from thick, stifling velvet, and an unaired, overcrowded environment.

Since night was falling I soon found a lamp and lit it. Holding it aloft, I took a moment to look around the beautiful apartment. When I saw the opening to Rose's bedroom, I stepped inside. Dominating the area was a large bed, its pink and silver hangings slightly tarnished, the lace-edged pillows becoming dingy. Had Drake shared nights in here with Rose? Of course he had. I jerked my eyes away from the romantic bed and gazed at a mirrored clothes press, a flounced and ribboned dressing table, a velvet padded chair.

There were dolls in here as well. All were dressed in robes and negligees as befitting a bedroom, the silken garments edged in lace or swansdown with miniature buttons, tiny bows, and ribbons. On their feet they wore perfect boudoir slippers, some embroidered in seed pearls or the smallest sequins. Whatever else she was, Rose had been an artist when it came to clothing her astonishing collection.

I wished I could observe them longer, but I was anxious to see if I could repair Rose-Red. Back in the sitting room, I discovered that the broken head just had a small crack, which could be concealed by drawing some black curls lower on the brow. The eyes had been dislodged a little so I peered inside the hollow head and set the weights in place. To my surprise, I saw a scrap of paper caught upon the inner wires, and when I drew it out, handwritten words were sharp and clear: "After that, Princess Rose-Red was in the direst danger."

What was this? It seemed to have been torn from a paper that preceded it. On an impulse, I thrust my fingers deeper in the hollow shoulder cavity and felt paper crackling. Carefully, I extracted several sheets sewn together like a little book, covered with extremely small handwriting. Was this the last fairy tale that Rose had written for Tad? The one that never had been found?

Why were the pages hidden in the doll?

Eager as I was to peruse the booklet, right now I must repair the doll and leave the tower as quickly as possible. Picking up the china head, which was molded in one piece with the shoulder plate, I noticed that there were four tapes, one at each corner to fasten in the matching openings of the kidskin body. Since the tapes were worn through in parts, it was no wonder the head had left its moorings after such rough shaking.

Rose's sewing basket stood nearby and in it I found a roll of cotton strips and a pair of scissors. In no time at all, I had attached the shoulder plate firmly to the body, smoothed out the velvet robes, adjusted the wig, and returned the doll to its former niche. Rose's effigy again peered haughtily at her companions as if she knew she always would be triumphant.

As for me, I could wait no longer and thrust the booklet in my pocket. Flying back to my room, I sank down in a chair, turned up the lamp and began to read the tightly written sheets:

Once upon a time, a lovely princess named Rose-Red dwelt in a distant, lonely place. Her aged parents gave her every luxury and all the clothes and jewels that anyone could want, but Rose-Red was not a happy person. She had no brothers, sisters, or friends. Not a soul to entertain her.

Because she had no flesh and blood companions, Rose-Red began a doll collection, endowing each one with a personality and sewing beautiful wardrobes for them all. She also wove stories about her dolls and wrote them down in little books until her china friends became more real than anyone around her.

The years passed, and suddenly, Rose-Red found herself grown up with suitors begging for her hand in marriage. Lords and princes came, summoned by her dying father, who insisted she must choose one to protect her when he was gone. Their kingdom had become poverty-stricken due to a recent, terrible war and all their money had been lost.

Reluctantly, Rose-Red knew she must obey her father so she chose a handsome, wealthy prince and they were married. The prince took her to live in his tower by the sea, and in due course, a child was born to them. The little boy was nicknamed "Tadpole" because he was thin and dark and lively. At first, the princess was disappointed because she had wanted a little girl to share her love of dolls, but soon Tadpole began visiting her room so she could read aloud the fairy tales she had written and instruct him about the history of the dolls. However, Tadpole was after all just a little boy and liked to romp and play outdoors so he was not a true companion. Rose-Red wanted her husband to amuse her, but he often sailed away to foreign shores so the princess was alone for months on end.

The last time he returned, the princess knew he had become a stranger to her heart and she grew cold. To win back her love, the prince gave her a valuable chain of yellow diamonds, but Rose-Red didn't care for jewels. She only wanted dolls, so one day she took some of the stones to a Chinese man who discreetly bought such things. With the money, she planned to add to her collection. However, on the day she entered the merchant's secret room, the princess beheld a startling sight. Someone she knew quite well was selling an article of rare value belonging to the prince! Something

that had been stolen! The villain turned and saw
her and she fled in panic. After that, the Princess
Rose-Red was in the direst danger.

That was all. Blindly, I stared at the pages on my
lap. Was the person Rose recognized trying to sell
the Jade Pagoda? If only she had written down the
name! She must have returned home with all speed
to write the ending, then hidden it as a safeguard for
herself. Perhaps when she took her horse back down
the hill, she was racing off to Drake's shop or going
for the police. Had Tad been right that someone
threw a rock at Rose and killed her? *Was it the thief
himself?* I pondered for a long time, then I placed
the booklet in my pocket, determined to show it to
Drake at the first opportunity.

At dinner, Drake informed us that Tad had improved and enjoyed a light repast before he slept.
The haggard lines had left Drake's face, but he
seemed preoccupied. Even when the meal ended
and I asked to have a word with him, he agreed
absently, and putting down his napkin, led the way
into his study.

Before I could speak, Drake strode to the fire
burning in the grate, and clasping his hands behind
him, stared down soberly. "Tad told me everything a
little while ago. He confessed that he had whispered
outside Melissa's door one night, telling her to go
away. Then he put one of the dolls on her bed with a
message that Rose would come back to haunt her
unless she left. In his weakened condition, I couldn't
chastise him too much, but he knows how he must
behave in the future toward Melissa. I don't understand why he dislikes her."

"He may have gleaned some wrong ideas about

wicked stepmothers from fairy tales," I ventured, "such as 'Snow White' and 'Hansel and Gretel.' He's a little boy with images of evil stepmothers . . ."

"Perhaps. I guess Melissa didn't tell me about the doll because she didn't want to make trouble for the lad."

Balderdash, I thought.

"I knew about the doll, Drake. Melissa asked me to return it, but the head came loose and I discovered something rather odd inside it. Here, take a look at this." I pulled the little booklet from my pocket.

Drake took it with a puzzled frown, thumbing through the pages. "This looks like one of Rose's little fairy tales. You say it was inside the doll?"

"Yes, and I must confess that I read it, thinking it was just a little story, but . . . perhaps you better read it, too."

Drake opened the book at the beginning and seated himself at his desk while I sank into a nearby chair and watched him. His lips thinned and his face changed color as he recognized himself and Rose depicted in her book. However, he made no comment and I didn't know what he was thinking.

When he finished reading, he leaned back. "Tad said his mother had come home that day, very excited, but after a short time in her room, she rode off down the hill again without a word to anyone. Tad watched her go and always maintained that something spooked the horse, but it was foggy then . . ."

"She mentions an Oriental merchant who bought things in confidence. Do you know of such a place?"

"There are many in Chinatown. I wonder if she sold him all the diamonds." His face looked grim and sad. The whole story must have brought back bitter regrets, but I had one more thing I had to ask him.

"After reading her account, don't you think it's possible that someone might have killed your wife to ensure her silence because she saw him selling the Jade Pagoda?"

Drake looked thoughtful, then he answered slowly. "Perhaps. Perhaps not. You would have to understand Rose. She dwelt in a world of unreality. Who can say whether this account is truth or fantasy? Even placing it inside the doll might have been part of some game."

"I guess that's possible," I said uncertainly.

"Please don't mention this matter to Tad, Lesley," Drake said wearily, and thrust the booklet deep inside a drawer. "He's just getting over his mother's death. There's no use resurrecting all the pain."

"Of course. I understand." I rose and he moved around the desk in front of me. "I just thought you should see it."

"You are always so concerned and caring," he said softly.

There was something so miserable, almost heartsick, in his face, that I couldn't help myself. My hand went out to touch his sleeve, and the next instant, he caught me close, his face pressed to my hair. It was so swift, so unexpected, and yes, so thrilling, I could only cling to him with pounding heart, trembling as I felt the hardness of his body touching me from thigh to chest.

It didn't last more than a flash in time. He put me from him and crossed the room to grasp the doorknob. "Please don't hold that lapse against me, Lesley," he muttered huskily, and vanished out the door.

That night I cried myself to sleep, a thing I very

seldom do, but I just couldn't help it. My heart had
realized its secret when Drake embraced me. Now I
knew without a doubt that I had fallen deep in love.
It was a flame of bitter joy, a sweet, sad pain. And
absolutely hopeless.

23

Worn out at last, I slept soundly the rest of the night, and if I dreamed of Drake, I didn't know it. I awoke with a strong determination to control myself in future. No mooning glances, no seeking out his company, no encouraging my thoughts to dwell on him. I would perform my duties as swiftly as possible, then leave and get on with my life. Perhaps someday there'd be another man, but right now I couldn't bear to think about it. I knew that I would carry the burden of my secret love for a very long and painful time. Perhaps forever.

I had things to do today and the main one was going down to Millbrae, but first I had to discuss it all with Tad. I donned a tweed skirt and cape in tones of heather and pinned a gray silk turban trimmed with violets on my head. Then, carrying my purse and gloves, I made my way up to the nursery.

I found Tad pale but otherwise looking like himself as he sat at a low table and consumed a bowl of hot milk toast with every evidence of enjoyment. I told him what the doctor had thought about some poison from a painted decoration falling on the slice of cake, but Tad shrugged it off, not being of a mind to dwell on his past discomfort.

Next, I mentioned the distinct possibility of Mai Yee becoming his *amah* for a little while. This idea filled him with the greatest interest and he wanted to know all about her, tasting the strange word *amah* over and over.

"Do you think my new *amah* will like Prince? Miss Libby sure didn't."

"Mai Yee is quite partial to small white dogs. We had one when I was little."

"I can hardly wait to meet her. What is she like?"

Taking a seat beside him, I described her to the best of my ability. "But remember, Tad, she will only be your temporary *amah*. You father will have to find a permanent replacement for Miss Libby."

"That's all right. Miss Libby taught me to read and write a little, but I'll start regular school this fall. Some of my playmates go to St. Ignatius and they like it fine."

In a few moments, I rose. "I'm going down to Millbrae now."

"Wait, Miss Lesley, I have a con-con—"

"Confession?" I sank back down, giving him a smile of encouragement. He then admitted in a difficult whisper that he had threatened Melissa, once from the hall, the second time with the doll.

"So you didn't take my advice about dealing with Melissa," I told him sadly.

He hung his head. "I'm sorry, but—but she doesn't like me, you know, and I'm afraid she might send me away to boarding school, day *and* night."

Indeed she might. I had to harden my heart

against the sad little face. All I really wanted to do was take him in my arms and comfort him with hugs and kisses.

Instead, I told him gravely, "Melissa was very upset. She showed me the doll and the note you put upon her bed. So right now, Tad, I want to give you some more advice and I pray this time you'll heed it."

"All right, Miss Lesley," Tad whispered.

"For your own sake, as well as hers, and your papa's peace of mind, you should treat Melissa with the utmost kindness and politeness. Soon she will be used to her new home and things will improve, I'm sure." I didn't quite believe it, but continued, "I know you are too smart and nice a boy to actually hurt people. Just remember, it hurts your papa, too, when you do those things."

Tad was concentrating on picking at his toast, and for a moment he didn't answer. Then he looked at me and said wistfully, "I wish Papa was marrying someone like you. Couldn't . . . don't you . . . like him? He's rich and handsome and awf'lly nice."

My face flushed, and for a moment I couldn't speak. "That's all true and I do like him, but he's engaged to marry Melissa." I bent and gave him a quick hug, then rose and hurried from the room, feeling very close to tears for what could never be.

In a few minutes, I was urging Lady briskly down the winding lanes of Sea Cliff and then slowly through the teeming city until I reached El Camino Real. As I traveled down the eucalyptus-bordered road, I considered my present errand. Would Mai take kindly to the idea of caring for lively little Tad? I would tell her exactly what was going on at Cliffside, but I couldn't pressure her in the slightest; it would have to be her own decision.

When I arrived at my home among the redwoods, I found Mai in the kitchen making rice cakes. As soon as she saw me, she exclaimed joyfully and we embraced with our usual deep affection.

"Little Missy, what happiness to see you!" Hands on my shoulders, she examined my face more keenly. "But what is this? Has a moon of sadness risen in your life? I know you so well and I think your mind is not at ease."

"Yes, dear, I—I am a little troubled." Hesitating, biting my lower lip, I glanced down at the floor, the boards so freshly waxed, the blowing curtains of starched gingham, the row of herbs thriving in glazed Oriental pots above the sink. Anywhere but into Mai's discerning eyes.

She knew that it was hard for me to speak. She clapped her hands together. "Aiee! What a miserable, mannerless old woman I've become. First we'll have *deem sum*, then we talk."

I took a deep breath. "Good. I'll run upstairs, then come right back for *deem sum* and a talk."

Mai nodded, her face alight with satisfaction that I was there, no matter what the reason.

Upstairs, I washed, removed my cape and hat, then went back down to the *patio* and sat at a table in the sun. Though the peninsula was much warmer here than the northern tip where San Francisco rested on its many hills, still the breeze blew brisk and fresh across the springtime garden, wafting fragrance from a bed of purple hyacinths and stirring the leaves of the pines and redwood trees. I could hear the cheerful whinny of Lady from the stables, where I knew Alonzo Ruiz, our young gardener, was watering the mare and giving her some freedom from the gig. I felt myself relaxing in the quiet, undemanding atmosphere.

It wasn't long before Mai appeared, so neat, so starched in her high-necked tunic and black sateen trousers. She placed a lacquered tray before me with a steaming pot of tea, two handleless cups, and the components of a fine *deem sum:* buns stuffed with citron, plates of sweet and salty tidbits, strips of candied ginger, and of course Mai's special rice cakes.

"So much," I said, laughing. "I won't want lunch."

"You'll stay to lunch?" Mai gave a joyous chuckle. "The gods are truly smiling on this unworthy person."

I had to laugh. "You know you don't believe in that 'unworthy person' business."

Mai drew up proudly. "I believe in manners—Old China style. As well as missionary manners—English style."

"Yes, you raised me well," I told her fondly as I poured our cups of tea. "And now there is another child who needs your care."

"Indeed?" She looked surprised. "Tell me. I am here to listen, Little Missy."

While we ate, I told Mai about Tad and his mishaps: the dog let loose to fall from a dangerous cliff, the former nurse who would not be returning, and the time in Chinatown when an unseen person lured the dog away until Tad became hopelessly lost. I didn't mention the mystery of Rose's death or the booklet I had discovered in the doll's head. I could tell her all that later. Right now, I wanted to concentrate on how much Tad needed someone to look after him. I ended with his recent bout with poison.

By that time, I realized how bleak a picture I was painting and I began to have second thoughts. "I know that Mr. Wynfield intends to pay you well if

you take care of Tad, but it won't be worth it if anything should happen to you." I chewed my lower lip.
"Perhaps this isn't such a good idea."

"It has been lonely here without you," Mai murmured. "I would welcome the opportunity of seeing
you each day."

I shook my head. "My dear, I didn't think about
the possible danger to you. No, I'm asking too much.
Mr. Wynfield will just have to find another nurse-
companion for the boy."

"Why, when I'll be there?"

"Now, Mai, we better think this over . . ."

"You ask. I come. All is settled."

The rest of my arguments fell on closed ears, and
finally, I gave in with relief. To have Mai at Cliffside
in any capacity would help my spirits immeasur-
ably. Perhaps there would be no further trouble. We
could all be on our guard.

I had previously told Mai about Melissa so now
she turned the conversation in that direction. "Tell
me about this coming marriage of Drake Wynfield.
He is happy? What is your opinion of the bride?"

I looked away uncomfortably, wondering what I
could say without sounding like a jealous shrew—or
a woman deeply in love.

"Speak of that which troubles you, Little Missy,"
Mai said softly. "Only the trees and I will ever hear
your words."

That broke down my defenses. For long years, Mai
had been my confidant, even more than my father,
who always was so busy in the City. No, it was Mai I
turned to first, the one who listened.

Impetuously, I blurted out, my face on fire, "I've
done a crazy thing. I—I've fallen in love with my
employer." I couldn't meet her eyes and looked
down, fingering the teacloth blindly.

Mai didn't move or speak, but I heard her breath expelled in a soft hiss.

I swallowed hard, and when I continued, my voice was husky. "I don't know how it happened—but it did. At first, I was grateful that he hired me. Then we were thrown together quite a lot and—well—you've seen how attractive he is, how charming and considerate . . ." I broke off, seeing in my mind's eye the square-planed features, so controlled and intelligent, and then the other time when his face had flamed with desire—for me.

"Does he know about your feeling for him?" Mai asked, eyes on her teacup.

"No, and he never will. He intends to marry very soon. Even though I sense he is disappointed in his fiancée, he is a man of honor."

Mai nodded, deeply thoughtful. "I understand. He has made a contract with the woman."

"Yes."

"My heart is heavy for you, Little Missy."

I forced myself to say, "Don't worry. It will pass. Especially after I leave Cliffside." That hardly was a consolation, and besides, I didn't believe it.

Mai sighed. Neither of us spoke for a while. We ate and drank our tea in silence while, gradually, I grew calmer, relieved that I had shared my burden with my dearest friend who always sympathized.

At last, Mai rose. "I must pack some clothes now and then prepare food for our lunch."

"I will also need some extra clothing and, Mai . . . thank you for accepting this new responsibility."

"To see you every day will give me the greatest joy." She eyed me tenderly, then departed.

Glad of the diversion, I went upstairs to fold frocks and jackets, tuck bonnets into bandboxes, and fill a valise with fresh undergarments and nightwear.

We left soon after lunch, and as we rode along, I found myself wondering about the coming confrontations. How would Mai and Li Fong get along? The strictly raised missionary orphan steeped in Christianity who still burned joss sticks? And the enigmatic former Tong member who was now in charge of running Cliffside?

Then there was Melissa with her silly prejudices, her irritating tempers, and her selfish ways. And Tad . . . lively, mischievous, who must be encouraged to submit to Mai's edicts until a permanent nurse was found. When we reached Cliffside, I felt distinctly apprehensive.

My anxiety wasn't helped when we drew rein before the mansion in time to behold a new disturbance.

The young man I had seen at The Jade Pagoda stood by the open doorway. His hands gripped Melissa's arms and his voice was fierce and loud: "Don't be a fool! It's the only way we can face the future. You must not fail in this, you hear?"

His handsome face was red and contorted with emotion and Melissa was not in much better shape. Her ringlets dangled in dishevelment, her lace collar unbuttoned, and when she spoke, I hardly recognized her strained and anxious tones. "I can't! I just *can't*, Tom. Try to understand. It would be awful . . ."

Tom shook her and spoke through gritted teeth. "You must! I'll make you do it!" He flung away and she staggered backward. The next instant, he leaped on his horse, completely unaware of his audience—or at least not caring—and shouted over his shoulder in a white-hot passion, "Don't think that I'll give up, because I won't. I'm coming back!"

Melissa stood staring after him as Mai and I hurried up the steps. "What's wrong?" I exclaimed. "What did that man want?"

She drew herself up, gradually resuming her usual haughty expression. Even in her extremely emotional state, the Jamestown Jewel was mindful of her superiority. "Really, Miss Blair, you do have a most unfortunate tendency to ignore your station. None of this is any of your concern, can't you understand that? Now, pray forget what you have just seen and speak no more about it."

She turned to go, then noticed Mai. "And who is this? Another foreign servant?"

"Mrs. Yee is going to take care of Tad while I'm staying here. She is my former nurse."

Melissa glared at her and snapped, "Just see that you keep that tiresome child away from me." With that, she vanished into the house.

I glanced at Mai, wondering what she thought of Melissa's rudeness, but Mai only looked back at me, calm as ever, and we continued on our way.

When we were inside the hallway, Mai and I saw Tad running swiftly toward us, calling eagerly, "Hallo! Is this—is this—"

"Yes." I nodded to him with a smile. "Mai Yee, may I present Thaddeus Wynfield, better known as Tad."

Mai bowed, hands clasped. "I am honored to meet you, young master."

She looked so small, so quaint, her dear ivory face so kind and loving. Tad surveyed her with sparkling eyes, clearly enchanted with his new *amah*.

He bowed in imitation and clasped his hands. "I, too, am honored, Mrs.—er—Miss—"

"Just 'Mai' will do, Master Tad."

Drake came down the stairs just then and advanced to meet us. If he had spoken to Melissa or been privy to her meeting with the excitable Tom, I had no idea. His features were schooled to harsh restraint, his amber eyes so shadowed they looked dark brown. However, when our glances met, he gave me a strained half smile. I introduced him to Mai Yee, and to my surprise, he greeted her in Cantonese. Then I realized that he must know many foreign languages from his travels.

Mai's face shone with pleasure as she bowed and answered him, but almost at once they switched to English in deference to me.

"We have a compatriot of yours here," Drake said. "Our household chief, Li Fong."

Mai bowed again. "I have heard the name, but it was—"

She never finished her sentence because in the next split second it happened.

A terrifying noise began beneath our feet sounding like a mammoth train hurtling through space. The ominous roar held us all immobile as it advanced, gained speed, drew closer, grew louder, became deafening. The walls vibrated and the windowpanes rattled with a sharp, unmistakable warning so familiar to every dweller in San Francisco.

I flung my arms around the nearest object, a swaying marble statue. Dizzy, sick, and gasping, I felt my feet slide back and forth. Dimly, I heard cries, shouts, the screams of "Earthquake!" But then the world became a deep black pit and I fell in.

24

When I regained consciousness, Drake was bending over me, his face white and anxious as he felt my pulse. I had been placed on the settee in the parlor and the place seemed to swarm with people all talking in loud voices. Pictures hung awry, tables lay on their sides with bric-a-brac strewn everywhere, some vases shattered on the rug. Clustered in the doorway, maids howled to the saints for protection while Prince added wildly to the din. Mai and Tad sat on the floor, clinging together, white with fright.

I sat up dizzily, catching at Drake's jacket. "That was an earthquake! Did something hit me? My head hurts . . ."

"It was a quake, all right, and quite strong," Drake replied, smoothing back my hair. "The statue in the hall grazed your head. You have quite a lump in back."

"Little Missy," Mai gasped, struggling to her feet. "you need my care?"

"No, no, thanks, I'll be all right." Gingerly, I touched my head and winced. Mai and Tad came close as I fell back on the cushions with a groan. "I'm glad nobody else was hurt."

"Don't crowd her," Drake warned. "She needs air."

"I can feel air—cold air." Carefully, I turned my head and noticed that a windowpane had shattered, littering the rug with shards of glass.

"Shall I send for the doctor to look at you?" Drake asked.

"No. I'm just a little dizzy. The pain is subsiding."

"Lean on me, Lesley," Drake said deeply. He sat down and gently put his arm around my shoulders.

It felt so good to rest against his warmth and strength that I told myself it wouldn't hurt to let him hold me for just a minute.

A minute was all it lasted, for suddenly a shrill voice cut through the other babbling, causing Drake and me to jerk apart.

"So here you are," Melissa stormed, marching up to us. "Drake Wynfield, why didn't you come to see how I was? Why are you just sitting here *hugging her*?"

Drake leaped up. "Melissa, forgive me! I was coming right away, but Miss Blair was injured and—"

"Where? She looks all right to me."

"She received a blow on the head and fainted," Drake explained. "Are you all right, Melissa?"

Instead of answering, she merely glared at us.

Drake expelled a short, hard breath. "Well, that's good." He turned to the door and addressed the servants hovering in the entry. "Now, calm down everyone. At once!"

Immediately, there was silence.

"I want each room checked for damages and then cleaned up. After that, report back to me. Li, send for a glazier to repair the windows."

Li Fong bowed and clapped his hands forcefully several times so that the other servants scuttled in all directions. I observed Mai looking at him curiously, but they did not exchange greetings.

The front door slammed and two other members of the household made their way into the room.

"Grandma Rachel! Uncle Jerry!" Tad shrieked, bounding forward. "What happened in the City? Did buildings fall? Were people swallowed up in cracks?"

Jeremy unbuttoned his jacket and tossed his hat onto a chair with an excited laugh. "It wasn't that bad. We haven't had that 'Big Quake' yet."

"Were you at the shop when it struck?" Drake asked sharply.

"No, old man. We were already on the road up here. I picked my mother up at the Palace after her tea party and we were rolling along in the carriage when the ground began to shake. Egad, but it gave the grays a scare! Thought for a minute I'd have some runaways."

Melissa uttered a shriek, hands flying to her cheeks. "Oooh, horrible! I think I'm going to faint!" When no one paid her any heed, I noticed she seemed to change her mind.

Rachel dropped into a chair, flinging back her sealskin cape. "Well, I can tell you I was scared. I hate these quakes, the awful noise, the ground rocking, people running out of their houses screaming. Of course, as soon as it ends, they always go back in, laughing sheepishly."

Drake shook his head. "As long as I can remember, people have been predicting that a quake will cause San Francisco to break off from the mainland and slide into the bay. I guess this one wasn't too severe."

"Not too severe?" Melissa cried. "Lord-a-mercy, whatever does it take to be called severe? The city leveled? Thousands killed?"

"Melissa," Drake said, "not many people have been killed so far in earthquakes. You just have to get out of the way when things start falling. That's the biggest danger—like Lesley getting hit by a statue in the hall just now."

Everyone looked at me and Mai started forward. Rachel stared at her. "Who's that?"

"Mai Yee, my former nurse. She's here to take care of Tad for a little while." Suddenly, Mai tottered and I sprang to her side. "My dear, have you been hurt?"

"No, just dizzy from a slight fall in hallway. So sorry."

"Sit here for a few minutes." Carefully, I led her to a chair and eyed her anxiously.

Melissa gave a little smirk. "It's a good thing nobody was up in that place the maids call the Velvet Room."

"What do you mean?" Drake demanded.

"Well, I could hear stones falling from that side of the house. Rose's bower may be completely destroyed."

"I'll go and check on it." Drake swung around, then halted and looked from me to Mai. "Are you both going to be all right?"

I answered briskly. "Certainly."

Tad's lip trembled as he stared after his father. "My mother's dolls—oh, golly—they may be smashed!'' Suddenly, he tore out of the room, followed by a frantically barking Prince.

"Be careful," I called.

"What good is it to be careful?" Melissa moaned. "The house is caving in about our ears. The whole place may be unsafe and collapse at any minute."

"Oh, pshaw," Rachel said sturdily. "You'll get used to lots of fires and earthquakes if you stick around San Francisco, young lady."

Melissa gave a little scream. "Quakes—fires—*lots* of them?"

Rachel nodded vigorously, shoving at the pansies on her velvet toque. When she spoke, her voice held a distinct note of pride. "Seven big fires have all but leveled the City so far. You see, we build mostly with wood because of quakes, though Cliffside has some stone walls from the old days before sawmills."

Melissa's chest heaved. "Fires, earthquakes, malicious children creeping about to threaten me, h-horrible hounds. And"—her wild eyes stabbed me— "*and* my betrothed languishing over a fancy, forward, flirty . . ." She floundered for another alliterative appellation.

"Floozie?" I supplied brightly.

Jeremy and Rachel both laughed, but I saw an odd glance flicker between mother and son. Had they noticed Drake's increasing warmth toward me?

Melissa wavered toward the hall. "Ohhh, why did I ever leave my dear, safe home down South to follow my foolish, trusting heart into the wilderness?"

The doorbell must have rung sometime during Melissa's melodrama because the next thing she cried was, "Someone for me? Oh . . . I'll come." and she ran out behind the maid.

Perhaps Tom had returned to see if she was all right. I really couldn't care. My mind veered to the bridal suite and I knew I must check on it as soon as possible. I glanced at Mai and she looked sick and white. I took her arm. "Come with me now, dear. There's a bed for you beside the nursery. I'll order you some tea."

Though she protested, I soon had Mai established beneath a quilt with a pot of tea beside her. "I'll be back soon," I promised her.

I found Melissa's future boudoir virtually untouched, inasmuch as there were no pictures or ornaments to be dislodged. When I closed the door, I met Conan coming down the hall toward me, his jacket streaked with plaster. He stopped and groaned, drawing a hand across his grimy brow. "Well, Rose's room is a mess. I fear the Velvet Room will soon be no more." He looked both sad and bitter and I knew he must have memories that he never would forget.

"Was Tad up there?"

"Yes, but his father took him away at once. It was too upsetting for the lad."

"Oh, what a shame. I suppose the dolls were damaged?"

"Some of them, yes. After Drake and Tad left, I took a look around. I thought the quake might have unearthed the diamonds, but I couldn't find them anywhere. I always suspected Rose might have used some of the stones to buy those expensive dolls of hers, but that would still have left a lot hidden somewhere in her room."

I wondered if Conan would have kept the jewels if he had found them.

He seemed to read my mind and shrugged. "Drake once said he never wished to see the chain again after Rose rejected it . . . and him. Perhaps she really sold them, after all."

I had no intention of telling him of Rose's last words about the diamonds so I didn't speak. He started down the hall. "As soon as I've cleaned up a bit, I'm going into town to see about your shop. I should have thought that would be your first concern, but you're more involved with Cliffside and its master these days, aren't you?"

"No, that's not true," I called after his retreating figure. "But the shop's survived a lot of quakes."

Wearily, I continued toward my room, where I found little damage, an overturned chair, a picture or two on the floor. I straightened things, then shook some headache powder into a glass of water as my head now pounded miserably and the lump behind my ear was painful to the touch. I sank down on the counterpane and, before I knew it, fell asleep.

"Missy, are you all right?"

My eyes flew open. I stared up at Drake. Was this another dream or did I really feel Drake brush his lips across my cheek? " 'Missy!' You called me that once before. I think there was an earthquake then and that you frightened me somehow. I was about seven or eight . . ." My voice trailed off.

He sat down on the bed, smiled, and took my hand in both of his. "You've remembered."

"Y-yes. How strange! Was that really you?"

He nodded. "I was in my late teens. You came into The Jade Pagoda all alone, staring around until, suddenly, the earthquake hit."

"Oh, Drake, I remember that! I started crying, told you that my name was Missy—and I was lost."

"That's right. Everything began falling and shaking so I put you in a closet to be safe while I went looking for my father, who'd just left."

"That's what frightened me—that closet. I thought

you were going to keep me there, locked in the dark."

"My father had fallen, and when I got back to the shop with him, you were gone. I guess Mai came by looking for you and heard you crying."

Drake's eyes searched my face with a little anxious frown. "I never would have hurt you. I just thought you'd be safer in the closet."

"I know that now. Drake . . . when did you remember?"

"Oh, a while back. I think it started when you wore that blue tea gown with the little bands of swansdown. You must have had a blue coat on that day." I saw you a couple of times on the street after that, but we never spoke and I knew you didn't remember me. And then Mai Yee always calls you 'Missy.' "

"Why didn't you tell me all this sooner?"

"Darling, I was afraid you might resent me when you recalled that I'd put you in the closet and then left."

"Not anymore. I know now that you were only trying to help me." I couldn't stop myself. I reached out and touched his cheek. He had called me "darling"!

Our eyes clung wordlessly. Then he gave a smothered groan and pulled me up into his arms, pressing his mouth to mine with a fierce, pent-up hunger that demanded a response. I clutched him just as eagerly, all promises to myself forgotten, returning kiss for kiss.

I felt as though a blinding light engulfed me and I knew at last that I had found the wild joy poets wrote about, the thing that people died for, lived for . . . Drake loved me. And I loved him.

My fingers threaded through the thick waves of

his tousled hair, and when he raised his head to gasp for air, I dragged his mouth back to my own to be invaded deeper with hot probing that searched for ever more possession. He lay practically across me and I could feel the heavy thunder of his heart against my breast where his fingers were caressing me.

"Drake, Drake, love me!" I cried, hardly conscious that I was yearning, entreating with a reckless abandonment that had completely claimed me.

However, Drake was more aware than I of the encroaching danger, more experienced with love and passion and their consequences. He drove his lips on mine with a last fierce, shuddering breath, then jerked away and rose to his feet.

"I can't trust myself to be close to you a minute longer," he said hoarsely. "But darling, now you know. You are my life and always will be."

I sat up, clutching my unbuttoned gown, emotion still pulsating hotly throughout all my being. Where did he get the strength to walk away?

"I love you, Drake," I cried brokenly. "What can we do?"

"Marry," he answered tersely.

"But—how—"

"I'll not let three lives be ruined by the silly convention about not breaking an engagement," he ground out furiously.

"Melissa may not agree," I faltered, suddenly frightened by the savage expression on his face.

His eyes ran over me with hot possession. "I intend to have you for my wife. Believe me, I'll find a way to get rid of Melissa." He swung away and slammed the door behind him.

The next day Melissa disappeared.

25

The first alarm came shortly after luncheon the next day. Conan and I were in the bridal chamber crossing off the final arrangements on our worksheet.

All the earthquake debris had been cleared away and the glaziers even now were replacing the broken glass in other windows on this floor. Fortunately, this room's windows had been spared. Conan reported to me that no harm had come to my shop except for books and bolts of cloth that had been shaken from the shelves. His bitterness of the day before had vanished, or else he kept it hidden. I was sure he had sad memories of the Velvet Room, where he had painted Rose and fallen in love with her, but he and I were both professional people and must concentrate now on the work at hand.

Goodness knows, I had enough of my own distracting emotions to contend with. A bittersweet joy flooded me because Drake returned my love, but a

future with him seemed so hopeless, I couldn't bear
to think about it.

I hadn't seen Drake since the day before when he
had gone to check on his shop, and worry gnawed at
me. No matter what he said, I was certain Melissa
would not give him up without a struggle. I felt sure
Tom was the former sweetheart she had mentioned
to me and she had said they'd quarreled. What was
he doing confronting her in San Francisco if not to
patch things up? But would they? How could the
young, wild Tom measure up to mature, important
Drake, who had both money and social position?
And if Drake tried to force the issue, there might
even be laws to safeguard Melissa, broken promises
on the part of her betrothed that harmed her health
and mind, or something of the sort.

So deeply was I immersed in these troubling ru-
minations that it was a few moments before I realized that Li Fong stood in the doorway, tapping dis-
cretely on the frame. When I glanced at him
inquiringly, he bowed.

"So sorry for intrusion," he hissed, "but must ask
important question. Is Miss Fernley seen today by
honorable decorators?"

"Why, no. She wasn't at breakfast or lunch." I
exchanged a puzzled glance with Conan. "Could she
be indisposed?"

"Why do you ask, Li?" Conan said.

"Maids report Miss Fernley's bed not slept in last
night and she has not been seen today." Li Fong
paused. "And clothes are gone."

I repeated stupidly, "Her clothes are gone?"
Somehow, a chill seemed to seep into the room.

Had Drake sent Melissa away? Oh, surely not that
precipitously. He never would be so inconsiderate.

Conan rose slowly, a frown upon his face. "What

are you getting at, Li? Do you mean to say that overnight Miss Fernley—"

"Is gone." Li folded his hands inside his sleeves,
looking at us implacably.

It was too easy. Melissa, the unwanted, simply
. . . going?

"Didn't she leave a note? Or speak to anyone?" I
asked.

Li shook his head.

"It's inconceivable that no one would see her go."
Conan fumed. "Is there a horse or buggy or any
other conveyance missing?"

Again a negative head-shaking.

Conan threw me a disturbed glance, gnawing at
his red mustache. "What do you make of this, Lesley?"

I had no answers, but my thoughts were churning.
I turned to Li Fong. "Have you told Mr. Wynfield?"

He nodded. "Messenger was sent to Jade Pagoda."

"Perhaps Miss Fernley went somewhere with Rachel or Jeremy," I suggested.

"Master Jeremy just left for shop and Miss Rachel
knows nothing."

"You've checked all the other rooms?" I inquired.
"As well as outdoors?"

"All searched, Miss Blair."

My eyes went from Li's impassive countenance to
Conan's puzzled face. "I'm sure there is a simple
explanation."

"Perhaps." Li bowed politely, then added, lifting
his opaque black gaze to mine. "Perhaps not."

I wished I knew what lay hidden behind those
blank, cold eyes. Did he suspect that Drake and I
had reason to wish Melissa hence? Did he wonder if

one of us had hustled her away in the dark hours of the night? *Or did he know more than he was telling?*

I gave myself a mental shake. This was melodrama! I said briskly, "Mr. Wynfield probably knows where Miss Fernley went. Perhaps she decided to leave for some reason and sent for a public hack."

"I will ask . . . again." Li bowed and glided off into the hall.

After a few fruitless conjectures, Conan and I tried to return to our lists, but it was impossible to concentrate on decorating.

Finally, Conan shoved back his chair and rose. "I'm going to take a look in Melissa's room. Maybe there's a note somewhere or a clue that was overlooked."

"I'll come with you." I followed at his heels, glad for any action that might quell the uneasy thoughts tumbling through my brain. I couldn't help remembering Drake's desperate words and the desire for me that now might drive him into recklessness. How far would he go to enforce his wish for freedom from Melissa?

My hands felt damp as I climbed the stairs, and when I rubbed them on my smock, I noticed they were trembling.

However, our search of Melissa's room yielded nothing except evidence of a hasty departure. A few cosmetic jars had been left behind; a large straw hat still rested on a shelf; and a pair of white kid slippers apparently had been forgotten underneath the bed. But there was no note, no message to servants or family.

Conan and I even peered out of the window, eying the thick ivy vine clinging on the wall. I shook my head. "I can't imagine Melissa climbing down two stories in the dead of night."

Suddenly, another idea occurred to me and I pounced upon it with relief. "Conan, she might have run away with her former sweetheart. We met this Tom Warren in town the other day and then I saw him again here at the house. Both times he seemed extremely agitated, furious actually, demanding that she comply with some demand of his."

Dugan stared at me. "A sweetheart, you say? Where did that boyo come from?"

"Melissa told me once that she and her beau, Tom, had quarreled in Virginia. After that, she accepted Drake, perhaps to heal hurt pride."

"But if she's broken her engagement, why not tell Drake where she was going? Why sneak off? But of course," he added uncertainly, "we aren't certain that Drake doesn't know . . ."

I shook my head. "He would have made some mention to the household. What I think is . . . Drake and Melissa may have had a fight."

Conan's eyes narrowed. "Oh, aye? Wasn't that rather sudden? Here she was flaunting her ring all over and the house about to be decorated just for her. How could she give that up so easily?"

I couldn't meet the suspicion in his gaze as he muttered, "Is there something more you're knowing about all this?"

"I—I can't discuss it, Conan."

"Perhaps you should," he grated. "Drake has the devil's own temper. I saw evidence of it when I stayed here to paint Rose's portrait and they argued about his many trips. He may be responsible for Melissa's mysterious removal. Just as he may have removed the other one, Rose, when he no longer wanted her."

"*Removed?*" I cried. "Never! What are you saying? Drake is a man of honor. You better watch your words, Conan Blye.''

He grunted, eying me up and down. "Especially around you, eh?''

I didn't answer and Conan left, slamming the door behind him. I couldn't follow him just yet. I went next door to bathe my heated face and try to calm my turbulent thoughts. Drake was a man of great integrity with hidden, surprising passion, but did I really know *all* of him, this man I loved so desperately?

I stayed in my room for quite a while, achieving very little calmness, until finally Drake came home, knocked at my door, and entered.

I checked my eager steps toward him. This was not my lover of the night before. He looked grim and angry with deep grooves beside his mouth.

"Drake, do you know where Melissa has gone? She vanished in the night and took her clothes."

"So I heard." He strode across the room to stand beside the window, hands clasped behind his back. "I don't know where Melissa went. Perhaps the earthquake upset her."

"That much?" Bewildered, I shook my head. None of it made any sense. Not even my idea that she might have gone off with Tom Warren. I felt sure that material possessions weighed heavily with Melissa and I imagined that she loved herself better than anyone else on earth.

At any rate, when I mentioned what I knew about Tom Warren, Drake brushed the idea aside. "That was all over long ago."

Another idea occurred to me, and preposterous as it was, I had to voice it. "Do you think Melissa could have been . . . kidnapped?" By Tom Warren, was my unspoken thought.

Drake grunted. "Pretty accommodating kidnappers to allow their victim to pack all her clothes."

He paced restlessly back and forth, his face a mask of granite. "For the second time, a woman in my life has raised the question of foul play. What a field day the newspapers will have when this leaks out!"

"Is that what you're worried about—newspapers?" I exclaimed. "Aren't you going to alert the police?"

"I have already done so," he replied impatiently. "However, they can't do anything until the person has been missing for twenty-four hours."

He turned his narrowed gaze on me and gave a crack of bitter laughter. "Do you think I may have done away with Melissa as well as Rose?"

I caught my breath and choked out, "No—no . . ."

He didn't seem to hear me and his voice grew savage. "Dear God, didn't I have enough suspicion to last me a lifetime when Rose died? For weeks, the tabloids hinted that I might have had reason to instigate her death since she and I were never seen together anymore. And then a servant I'd dismissed gave out a lurid tale of terrible scenes and fights between us." His lips thinned. "However, there were not sufficient grounds to charge me with a crime."

His eyes focused on my face and he suddenly gripped my arms so hard, I cried out with the pain, but the pain was stronger in his glinting eyes. *"Don't you trust me either?"*

"Yes, of—of course I do." I tried to speak forcefully, but I knew Drake had a temper and was possessed of an indomitable will. Could he have frightened Melissa into leaving secretly? Something of my uncertainty must have shown in my face, for his eyes flamed with reproach. He flung me aside and the door slammed shut behind him.

I tried to catch my breath. "Drake—wait," I cried, but when I stumbled into the hall, he was out of sight.

I decided not to follow him. It would be better to wait until his anger had cooled down.

Feeling drained and sick at heart, I sank down on my bed. Not for a moment did I truly think that Drake could be a murderer. All his actions spoke of honorableness and responsibility: caring for his son, putting up with his in-laws, refusing to take advantage of my love. Only perhaps in seeking the right way out of his dilemma, his anger might have frightened Melissa into running away. As for Rose, her death had been either an accident, or else the man she'd seen selling the Jade Pagoda had come after her. Who could that have been? Someone in this house? An employee in Drake's shop? A person she believed to be a friend?

At last, spent and weary, I closed my eyes and dozed. When I sat up later, the room was deep in shadows and I felt stiff and chilled. Rising, I lit a lamp and the first thing that my eyes fell on was a folded paper underneath my door. I tore it open, saw it was from Drake, and feverishly began to read:

My Darling:
I have never felt so wretched in my life. Without your love and trust, I face a dismal future. If it weren't for Tad, I would go far away. However, I must now look for Melissa, if only to determine that she has not met with any misfortune from which I can extricate her. I hadn't spoken to her yet about releasing me from our engagement, she

was still too upset after the earthquake. I owed her a little longer time. I swear to you I don't know how or why she left. Perhaps she soon will get in touch with me. I pray that this is so; until then, I will stay in the rooms above The Jade Pagoda so that I can conduct a constant search for her.

As for Rose, my gravest error was in neglecting her, but the truth is, both of us had ceased to care. I've never loved anyone as I love you, I know that now. Please believe me, I am yours forever, Drake.

Tears ran down my face when I had finished reading. How I must have hurt him. Could I now make him realize that I loved and trusted him completely? Tomorrow I would go to his shop and ask him to believe me, since it was too late for traveling tonight. I decided to ask for a supper tray in my room, but I couldn't sit here brooding until then. To fill the interim, it might be a good idea to visit the Velvet Room and see what had happened to the dolls.

Carrying a lighted lamp, I made my way down the corridors, through the gallery, and soon stepped into Rose's once lush and opulent abode.

A sorry sight met my eyes. Stones had fallen from part of one wall, wind blew through a shattered window, plaster was scattered everywhere, chairs and tables had overturned, and small objects were toppled on the rugs.

Raising my lamp on high, I began to inspect the dolls, and gave a gasp of horror. Poor creatures! Nearly all were tumbled and sprawled in ruined finery: limp feathers, torn bonnets, cracked china heads and hands, jewels and bangles scattered everywhere. I could hardly keep from weeping like a child.

Rose's effigy had fared the worst. Its head was snapped in two, the hands smashed, the lovely clothes crushed by debris fallen from the ceiling. Sadly, I lifted the doll, trying to brush plaster from the strings of beads around her neck. Amazingly, some of the stones were quite unharmed while others had turned to powder. Puzzled, I held them closer to the light.

Was it possible? I picked up a chunk of stone and brought it down with all my might on the necklace. Some beads broke into dust. Some didn't. Rubbing them fiercely with my handkerchief, I knew what I had found.

Real diamonds, the hardest substance known to man.

For a long moment, I stared down at them in awe. Rose had placed her diamonds among the fake stones on her dolls. Perhaps she thought placing them in plain sight was a clever way of hiding them so they wouldn't seem any different from the paste jewelry. Or perhaps she was indifferent to their value and merely wanted to use them as decoration. Were there more on other dolls? Or had she sold the bulk? It was impossible to tell without a more thorough search and I decided to return in daylight when I would have more time. Until then, I would study the ones I had discovered.

Back in my room, elation swept me as I gloated over the lovely stones. I washed the dust off them and polished each one carefully, watching the fire flash in their heart like nothing else on earth. I really had to congratulate my keen eyes and the course I'd taken in gemology, which had helped me to uncover Rose's secret. Other people probably had searched unsuccessfully for the past two years. Even Conan hadn't found them.

Tomorrow I would seek Drake at his shop and show him what I had discovered. How surprised he'd be! But that would not be as important as the words from me to let him know that I loved and trusted him implicitly.

This wonderful euphoria lasted until midnight, when I heard the flute once more.

As the eerie wailing notes crept into the room, I started up in bed, my pulses hammering. What did the flutist want tonight? Who was it? After a few minutes, I crept to the window and peered outside. However, I saw no one. The flute had sent its message and departed.

26

Next morning, a loud pounding on my door aroused me from the depths of a druglike sleep. "Wh-what is it?" I mumbled, shoving back the covers. Alarm streaked through me as I realized that no maid would ever knock so loudly.

Before I could get off the bed, Rachel burst into the room, her gray hair still bunched in curl papers beneath a lacy nightcap, her purple wrapper billowing out over a voluminous nightgown. I knew she never would have appeared in such public dishabille unless a dire emergency existed.

She could hardly speak, and when she did, her words made no sense whatsoever. Panting, she flew across the room and jerked me to my feet. "Come quick—it's Tad! The Chinese woman can't be understood—but Tad's *gone*! The dog was doped . . ."

"Rachel, what are you saying?" I gasped, reaching for my robe.

"Tad's gone—someone took him in the night.

That's all I know. Servants are searching the house and grounds. Come! You must find out what that Chinese woman knows. She was supposed to take care of him, wasn't she?"

Rachel gave me no time to do more than put one arm into my robe and shove my feet in slippers, then we tore along the hallway to the nursery. Before we reached it, I could hear servants babbling excitedly, doors slamming, footsteps running.

The nursery door stood open and I followed Rachel into Tad's bedroom. I coughed. "What's that sickening, sweet smell?"

"Chloroform," Rachel bit off the word. "It's a kidnapping. Tad's been taken and you can see the dog's been doped as well. Drake's a wealthy man, he'll pay anything to get Tad back."

"My God," I whispered, clutching my silk wrapper with a shaking hand. Dazed and almost uncomprehending, I stared around. Tad's bed was empty. The ever-vigilant Prince lay quite still on the rug, his sides almost imperceptibly moving in and out.

"How did it happen? How did they get in?" I gasped.

"I don't know."

"Where's Drake?"

"He's staying at his shop. I've sent Li after him."

As though it had happened long ago, I remembered that scene with Drake, his letter stating that he would stay at The Jade Pagoda while he searched for Melissa.

"Why don't you speak to the Chinese woman?" Rachel demanded. "She was hit over the head, but she must know something."

At once, I ran into the adjoining room, where Mai was swaying on her cot, a wet compress at her nape, and tears running down her twisted face.

"Mai, what happened?" I cried. "Have you been hurt? Who did this?"

At first, she could only sob and mutter in her native tongue.

"You must get hold of yourself," Rachel told her harshly. "And tell us exactly what happened. Tad's life may depend on it."

"Yes, Mai, she's right." I sat down beside her. "Please, dear, start at the beginning, calmly now." I knew an Oriental person never could be hurried and rushed into speech on an important matter.

"I . . . will try, Little Missy." Mai gulped painfully and wiped her eyes on the sleeve of her white tunic. "Last night we all were worried about Miss Fernley. Small Boy seemed to feel much guilt. He said he had shown dislike to her, and feared it was his fault she went away."

"I'm sure that he was wrong," I murmured. Suddenly, I wondered: Could the two disappearances be connected? Could Melissa and Tom Warren have planned Tad's abduction? It seemed inconceivable . . . and yet I had heard those frantic words between them.

I took Mai's shaking hands in mine. "Go on, now. Tell us just what happened."

"I told Small Boy happy stories about Old China to calm his spirits and after that we both went to our beds. While I waited for sleep, suddenly, it came: the message of the flute."

I caught my breath, hand flying to my lips. Oh, why hadn't I investigated the strange notes in the night? "I heard the flute, too, but I took too long and no one was there when I looked out. What did it mean?"

Mai's voice sank to a frightened thread. "I think it

was demand for a meeting, but why, I do not know. I ran to the window and saw . . . someone."

"A small Chinese man?"

She nodded. "The music stopped and then the door gave a small click, but before I turned around, someone hit me." She bowed her head, voice muffled. "And while I lay in blackness on the floor, Master Tad was taken!"

She rocked back and forth, hugging herself, as tears slid, unchecked, down her cheeks. "Oh, Little Missy, what shall we do? How can we tell the father? What will happen to Small Boy?"

I had no false words of comfort. I felt cold and sick. I could only put my arm around her and pat her shoulder, murmuring that she mustn't blame herself.

My eyes sought Rachel's anxious face. "You've searched the house?"

"Yes, yes! I sent servants into every nook and cranny when the first word came that Tad could not be found. He hasn't just run off—you can smell the chloroform."

"Yes." I locked my hands together. "How I wish that Drake would come!"

"Poor Drake," Rachel moaned. "First, he has to look for that fool Melissa, now he has to face this, too. If only we knew what to do . . ."

I felt completely helpless, but I managed to suggest, "I think we should contact the police."

Before Rachel could reply, one of the gardeners appeared at the open door. He held a small object in his hands and held it out to us. "Miss Rachel, we found this on the path in back."

Mai gave a stifled scream and staggered to her feet. "*A boo-how-doy was here!*"

A hatchet man! It seemed as though my heart

stopped beating at the ominous words, then started
up at a frantic, rapid pace that left me breathless. To
murder enemies I had heard the Tongs used men
who could cleave a skull with one swift throw of just
such a small weapon.

"What does this mean?" Rachel shrank back, eying with repugnance the little two-headed ax with its
handle wrapped in red and yellow cord.

"It is a message," Mai whispered hoarsely. *"Boo-
how-doy* is saying they were here. They must have
Tad! *Aiee!"* She put her hands across her face.

"You're certain of this?" Rachel demanded, and
Mai could only nod.

"Get the police after them!" I cried. "Send for
men to go at once to Chinatown."

"The kidnappers might kill Tad if they saw police," Rachel protested.

Mai clutched my sleeve. "She speaks truth. That is
not the way."

"What then?"

Mutely, Mai shook her head, lips trembling.

Rachel moaned. "If only Drake would come to
advise us. That silly female would have to run off at a
time like this. He's probably out searching everywhere for her. Why didn't he just let her go?"

"He feels responsible," I said. "Melissa may be in
trouble."

In spite of my preoccupation with the missing
child, again my mind went back to that scene on the
front steps. Tom furiously trying to convince Melissa
to act—on what? She, trembling, frightened, and refusing. He had seemed more angry than loving.
Could it possibly be connected with Tad's kidnapping? Perhaps Tom and Melissa needed money if
they planned to run away. It was odd that both
events had happened at almost the same time.

However, there was the Tong hatchet . . . and the flute.

I turned to Rachel. "Are you aware that Li Fong is an ex-Tong member? Perhaps he knows more than he's telling."

"You mean he's shielding someone? A relative, perhaps?" Rachel glanced sidelong at the malignant little weapon. "It's possible, I suppose. He's very secretive and hasn't been here very long."

It suddenly occurred to me that all the events of the past few weeks smacked of an insider, someone who knew all our movements. The dog put over the cliff, the holdup on the highway, the chase in China-town, the person who searched the Velvet Room, and then Tad's poisoning. Finally, his being kid-napped by someone who knew that Tad and Mai were still weak from the earthquake, and who also knew his way around the house. What did it all mean? Someone who needed money, probably. Per-haps when the villains couldn't steal the brooch or find Rose's diamonds, they decided on the most des-perate plan of all: Tad's kidnapping.

Certainly Melissa and Tom were not the only ones at Cliffside who might want money. It could be Ra-chel, an extravagant woman who was always com-plaining she wasn't given enough money by Drake. Or the high-living Jeremy, whom I'd seen coming from the Stock Exchange, where an investment of his might have failed. Then there was Conan, who had admitted he always was in debt and said: "The Tongs are bloody ruthless when you owe them money." Even the mysterious Li Fong might have incurred a dangerous gambling debt playing mah-jongg in Chinatown.

Thinking of Jeremy and Conan made me wonder

where they were this morning. When I asked Rachel, she said both had left quite early for the City.

"Perhaps Drake summoned them to help him look for Melissa," Rachel said, shoving back a gray curl beneath her cap.

I didn't answer. Pacing back and forth, I longed for action. "Are you certain we can't send for the police? Mai, you know something of these Tongs. Have you any suggestions?"

Mai shook her head helplessly, winced at the pain, then shrank back in fear, her eyes darting to the hatchet, which Rachel had placed upon the bedside table. I couldn't blame Mai for her terror. No one cared to confront a member of the Six Companies, as the Tongs were called, but if Mai was right, one of them had taken Tad.

We had stood here moaning long enough. I whirled around and headed for the hall. "Rachel, I suggest we put on our clothes and be ready . . . just in case. Mai, go to bed. I'll have a tray sent up for you."

"That's a good idea," Rachel said and followed me eagerly, evidently also glad for something positive to do. "I'll meet you downstairs for breakfast. We must all keep up our strength. I'll tell the servants to continue searching for—for anything."

I could hardly think coherently as I dragged on my clothes, fingers fumbling with side hooks, buttons, belts. All I could see was Tad's little white face filled with fear and bewilderment. Probably alone in a dark room . . . not knowing what would happen next. I knew I must get hold of myself and not give way to fanciful pictures. Perhaps even now Li and Drake were on their way to some Chinatown headquarters where they would negotiate a ransom payment.

Downstairs in the breakfast room, I told Rachel my idea while we consumed stewed apples, toast, and coffee, eating feverishly and tasting nothing.

After she had finished Rachel became calmer, gaining back a little of her usual poise. "As you say, I'm sure Drake will soon take care of everything." She slanted a glance at me over the top of her coffee cup. "This business of Melissa running off—I wonder if it could be a ploy to bring Drake back to heel. I'd say his interest had begun to stray in another direction, which I am sure Melissa noticed. Not that I blame him."

Flushing, I looked down at my plate and didn't answer. Had we been that obvious, Drake and I? Could Rachel be correct about Melissa? I knew she was given to excessive jealousy, but I thought she would have been more likely to confront Drake and demand that I be sent away. There must be another reason for her disappearance.

I told Rachel about Tom Warren just to get her reaction. "At first, I wondered if he and Melissa could be responsible for Tad's disappearance, but since the Tong hatchet appeared, I've changed my mind. I doubt if they would know how to contact a *boo-how-doy*."

"I don't know." Rachel frowned thoughtfully. "It could have been arranged by them. The young man might have connections here."

"That's true, but I've also suspected Li Fong, as I told you before. There was the flute giving some kind of signal . . . and I heard that before Melissa arrived."

"Oh, yes, I remember that. Jeremy and I had been out and we arrived home to find you and Drake about to investigate the matter."

I thought she looked slightly embarrassed as she

cleared her throat. "I was very unpleasant to you that time and I'd like to apologize. Now that I know you better, I realize you are a decent and hard-working woman. But all I saw then was a young beauty performing a very strange service for a female. I believed Drake had brought you here for his own pleasure and I didn't like it."

My face flushed, but I managed to say calmly, "I'm glad you've changed your mind about me."

Ah, but look what did happen, an inner voice jeered at me. Drake and I fell desperately in love.

As though she read my mind, Rachel bent a keen eye on me. "I've noticed the infatuation growing between you and Drake, almost from the moment you arrived. Not that you have ever been indiscreet . . . and I have no idea what Drake intends to do about his engagement to Melissa."

She looked at me inquiringly, but I merely shook my head. Something stopped me from confiding in her too much. In spite of the fact that Drake intended to ask Melissa for release, I knew he hadn't hustled her from the house in the dead of night. He had told me so in his letter; however, neither did I think that she had gone away alone.

"How I hate this waiting—doing nothing," I groaned, and shoved back from the table. "What if they can't find Drake today?"

Before Rachel could reply, Jeremy burst into the room, his caped coat and tall beaver hat beaded with moisture. For the first time, I realized that fog horns were wailing in the bay. The thought of that ominous, concealing vapor swirling around Tad and his abductors somehow made everything seem more terrifying.

I started forward anxiously. "Oh, Jeremy, Tad's

been abducted! Did you know? Have you seen Drake?"

His face looked strained and haggard. "Do you mean Drake isn't here? Li Fong told me about the kidnapping. He came to The Jade Pagoda looking for Drake, but nobody had seen him at the shop all morning."

Without taking off his coat or sitting down, he poured himself a cup of coffee and stood drinking it while questions and answers flew back and forth. The only thing Jeremy hadn't heard about was the finding of the hatchet, at which he gave a start and paled. "If only we knew where Drake has gone! I looked around the City before coming here. I was afraid to go to the police after the ransom note arrived."

"What!" Rachel and I both cried out together. *"What did it say?" "Who brought it?"*

Jeremy held up a hand. "Just listen. A note came soon after Li left the shop. It was delivered by a street urchin, who vanished before he could be questioned. I took the liberty of reading it." He fished a folded paper from his pocket and read aloud: 'Ten thousand for the boy or he gets shipped to sea. Take money to cricket house today and ask to see the Dragon Master.' It was unsigned."

"That proves it," I exclaimed. "Li Fong is back of the whole thing. I saw him at the cricket house. His family works there."

Jeremy's eyes narrowed. "When was this?"

Rachel interrupted. "The important thing is, what are we going to do about this ransom demand if we can't find Drake? None of us here can raise that kind of money."

Jeremy's cup rattled in its saucer when he set it down. "Eventually Drake will return to The Jade

Pagoda. I thought he might have come back here,
but since he hasn't, I'll go back to the shop and wait
for him."

"Have you seen Conan?" I called after him as he
headed for the door.

"No, I haven't." He turned around. "He's not important. This is a family affair."

"Well, I'm not family, but I want to help," I protested. "I feel dreadful thinking about that little
helpless child . . ." I couldn't continue as tears
clogged my throat.

"We'll get him back," Jeremy assured us. "Just as
soon as we hand over the ransom money. Drake
must not hesitate a moment to meet their demands.
And whatever you do, don't summon the police. The
fewer people who know about this, the safer Tad will
be."

When he left, Rachel went upstairs, looking old
and shaken. I was surprised at how concerned she
was for Tad. She and Jeremy always had seemed
rather irritated by the little fellow and his exuberant
dog, who was now barking somewhere in the halls.
Apparently, he had come out of his drugged state.
Would Tad do likewise in some dark and awful
prison?

Oh, God! I shut my eyes and prayed he wouldn't
be too frightened or harmed in this terrible ordeal.

27

I went up to my room extremely agitated. There I paced back and forth while arguing with myself. Waiting for someone else to help little Tad went against everything I felt for both the child and his father. I knew the dangers inherent in confronting a Tong member, but I also knew the location of the cricket house and in my bureau was a bargaining tool: the yellow diamonds known as canary. First, I would look for Drake, but if I couldn't find him, I would leave a message at his shop and then seek the Dragon Master myself to show him one of the gems and promise him the rest in exchange for Tad's release. He would have to hold Tad for my return, and in that way, we might gain a little time. They knew we wouldn't bring in the police while they still had Tad.

I would tell no one in the house about my mission, not even Mai, who might decide to follow me in spite of her terror of the Six Companies. I was frightened also, but my fear for Tad's safety was greater.

Swiftly, I tied a small felt hat beneath my chin and thrust my arms through the loops of an alpaca cape. On my bureau, I placed a hastily scribbled note stating that I had gone out on an errand. Wrapping a diamond in my handkerchief, I thrust it into my reticule and hurried down the hall.

Outside, I could hear Prince barking somewhere, probably searching for his master. That makes two of us, I thought grimly.

One of the hands harnessed Lady for me and I headed for the road, but before I reached it, Prince raced toward me, leaped into my gig, and dived beneath the seat. I tried to coax him out; however, it was useless and I could tarry no longer. I told myself perhaps Prince might sniff out Tad's whereabouts. Snapping the reins, I set Lady at the swiftest pace possible down the winding road. The gig bounced and swayed, wheels clattering, while houses, trees, and gardens all flew past in a wispy, swirling fog.

When I reached the city proper, I drew back a little, but at The Jade Pagoda, I leaped out in a flash, fortunately finding a tethering place nearby. The doorman in his red and gold brocade bowed as unctuously as before, perhaps remembering me when I again greeted him in Cantonese: *"Jo sun."* I then added breathlessly in English, "Is Mr. Wynfield here?"

He bobbed respectfully, hands folded in his sleeves. "Honorable owner is not here."

I bit my lip. "What about Mr. Jeremy?"

"Not here either."

I couldn't wait. Shipping boys to sea as young as Tad was not unheard of. If the ransom was not forthcoming quickly or his abductors became alarmed, who knew what might happen?

Drawing a deep breath, I told the doorman, "When Mr. Wynfield comes, please tell him immediately that Miss Blair has gone to—to buy a singing cricket. It is urgent that he join me there as soon as possible."

He bowed gravely. "Will do, Miss Blair."

Knowing I could never take a horse through the crowded streets of Chinatown, I spun around and hurried down the street, hearing a foghorn moan its warning in the bay. I had to clamp my teeth to keep from shivering with a chill compounded of leaping nerves and worry. Soon I became aware that Prince trotted closely at my heels, but I couldn't stop to return him to the gig.

On and on I rushed and soon arrived in Chinatown. Here in the close-packed streets below the hills, I saw the usual sights of dim, dark shops with tattered banners that hung limply in the misty air. There were strings of firecrackers for sale, mounds of wicker baskets, plates of dried and pickled fish. Hordes of Chinese men and women drifted up and down, bargaining and chattering. A peddlar with a tray around his neck containing handleless cups of hot tea made my dry throat long for some, but I couldn't take the time.

Then, suddenly, I saw the red moon-door, the little cobbled courtyard, and the twisted pine tree in its bamboo tub. I swallowed hard, and for a second panic swept me. Who would be here? What would I find? Drawing a deep, unsteady breath, I stepped up to the door and banged on it with my fist, the sound echoing eerily in the strange silence that surrounded this mysterious little shop.

Finally, the door creaked open. A blank-faced

woman clad in baggy pants and black frogged tunic, gave me a cold stare. "You wish somesing?" she said, her Chinese accent hanging heavy in the air.

I pushed past her, ignoring the sudden movement to deter me. I glanced around the empty black-walled hallway. The door swung shut behind me, leaving Prince whining in the courtyard. "Is Li Fong here?" I demanded. "I wish to speak to him."

"Not here. Fong work Cliffside."

I frowned at her. "I also work at Cliffside. My name is Lesley Blair. There's been . . . big trouble. I must find Mr. Li at once."

"Is so?" She looked uneasy.

"Where is Mr. Li?" I repeated loudly.

"Not know."

"Then get me his nephew, Sammy. He helped us the other day to find the small boy, Tad Wynfield."

"Small Boy?" she whispered. "You come about Small Boy?"

My heart leaped. "Yes! Do you know where he is? Oh, for God's sake, take me to him!"

She backed away from my outflung hand, shaking her head.

It was time to make my most daring move. Thrusting out my chin, I shouted, "I demand to see the Dragon Master! I have something for him that he wants, do you hear me?"

Her face grew slack with fear and she looked about to faint. Several times she swallowed, then said hoarsely, "You stay here."

She vanished for a long time while I waited, growing more and more apprehensive with each passing minute. The shop seemed deserted. There was not a sound anywhere. I considered shouting Tad's name, but just then the woman returned, looking calmer, her bearing purposeful.

"Come," she ordered.

Could I trust this woman? It appeared I had no choice. There didn't seem to be another soul around who could lead me to the Dragon Master, so with a racing heart, I followed her to a small rear door set tightly in the wall. It opened with a key and she stepped back, giving me a swift, hard shove. "Go inside and walk. Is long way."

"Wait—it's too dark—get Sammy . . ." Stumbling, I spun around as the lock clicked shut behind me. "No—let me out!" I pounded on the door, fear almost swamping every coherent thought.

No one answered my cries; all was silent and completely dark. No, not completely. As my terrified eyes grew accustomed to the interior, I could see a far-off light, dim and flickering. *What was this place?* Was Tad held here in a secret room? Waiting in desolate fear and misery?

I leaned against the wall, breathing deeply, trying to think. When I mentioned the Dragon Master, the woman had led me into this tunnel and told me to walk "a long way." So that's what I must do. I began to move, sliding one foot after the other, my hands touching the dark walls on either side. They seemed to be covered in some padded cloth designed to absorb light and sound. The implications of evil and furtive deeds this conjured up swamped me with a fresh wave of terror so strong my teeth began to chatter.

Because I had no choice, I forced my shaking limbs to carry me farther and farther through the twisting, narrow hall lit by an occasional dim wall sconce that gave just enough light to make my shadowy progress more frightening.

At last, the way led downward in a flight of stairs without a handrail, ending somewhere in pitch darkness. I would be a fool to continue into that black void. I might be pitched into the sea. Opium dens abounded beneath the upper strata of Chinatown as well as many rooms for gamblers and prostitutes. Who knew what I might find? I determined not to take another step until I knew what lurked in the depths before me.

"Sammy, where are you?" I shouted. "I won't go any farther until someone answers me. If you don't, I'll go back to the shop and scream and pound until they let me out!"

I held my breath and listened.

Suddenly, a lantern bloomed down below the stairs. A Chinese girl in a silken cheongsam and flowing hair smiled up at me and spoke in perfect English. "My name is Lily. Do not be afraid, Miss Blair. The Dragon Master awaits you to discuss the matter now concerning Cliffside."

"Tad's here?" I choked with relief. Holding up my skirt with one hand, I stumbled down the narrow steps as fast as possible. "Take me to him at once!"

"Soon, Miss Blair. The Small Boy enjoys a little nap, quite peaceful." She waved to me with a slim, long-nailed ivory hand and moved backward. "Please follow me."

I hastened after her. The flickering light she carried showed only blank, dark walls until we reached a scarlet door of strange design. On a huge brass plaque, an elaborate scaly dragon was depicted, breathing fire, his long, fierce claws twinkling with gems. The girl made some secret signal and the door swung slowly open.

I blinked, almost blinded in the sudden radiance of flashing colors from ornaments on walls and tables. I spared no time for them. All passed in a flash before my eyes until I saw the figure seated behind a

lacquered table: an Oriental man dressed in long
silk robes of blue and gold with thin mustaches that
drooped below his chin. His gimlet eyes, black and
hard as iron, drew me like a magnet until I stood
before him. The girl vanished silently behind a
beaded curtain.

Desperately, I tried to hide my fear and held up
my head, firming my trembling mouth. Inside my
cape, I clenched on the bargaining power in my reticule. In order to save Tad, I must be extremely wary
and keep all my wits about me.

"How do you do, Miss Blair?" the mandarin whispered after a calculated, unnerving interval.

I swallowed, then thrust out my chin. "You have
the advantage of me, sir. What is—"

"My name does not matter. I control the secrets of
the most secret. They call me Dragon Master." A
yellowed hand with long, jeweled nail guards waved
me to the chair before his table. "First we take tea,
Miss Blair. Then talk."

I was thankful to sink down on the curving crim-
son-cushioned seat since my legs threatened to give
way at any moment. Only sheer willpower had kept
me upright. I knew something of the Chinese culture
and had to obey it even though my shattered nerves
protested vehemently at the delay. However, if I
gave way to screams of vituperation (as I felt inclined), such behavior would serve me ill. I would
lose face at once and maybe any hope of saving Tad
and myself.

"Perhaps you would care to look at my treasures
while we wait," he murmured, waving at the shelves
lit by pierced brass lanterns.

Impatiently, I turned my head, glancing at carved
wood, ivory statues, jeweled trees, hideous masks,
exquisite crowns, embroidered scrolls . . .

Then I saw it. *The original Jade Pagoda!*

I uttered an uncontrolled exclamation and sprang up to observe it closer. Impossible that it could be a replica. There was the patterned gold, the green jade sides, the tilted eaves from which hung pearls, amethysts, rubies, and flashing emeralds, with not a fake among them. Exactly like the picture in Drake's shop.

"How did that get here?" I cried, pointing. "It was stolen from The Jade Pagoda!"

He shrugged, unruffled. "I bought it and asked no questions except the price. The seller owed the Tongs a large sum of money and was desperate. Now he owes more and is desperate again."

"And he has kidnapped Tad!" I drew in a ragged breath. *"Who?"*

He didn't answer. It was not the time.

The tea arrived just then, carried by the silken Lily. The master muttered to her, then gestured to my chair. "Please drink your tea, Miss Blair."

He handed me a steaming, strongly flavored brew and I drank it greedily, unable to resist the need of my parched throat, where nerves and fear had dried the normal moisture.

Putting down my empty cup, I leaned forward. "Rose Wynfield came here before she died, didn't she?"

"So?"

"She wished to sell her diamonds, but she saw the Jade Pagoda in the thief's hands and ran off to tell her husband. However, before she reached him, she had a fatal accident. Or was murdered."

His only sign of irritation was the tapping of the jeweled nail guards on the lacquered desk. "What is the importance of this now, Miss Blair? You came to reach a bargain concerning Small Boy, did you not?"

"Yes, yes." I sprang up and scrabbled in my reticule. With a shaking hand, I placed one perfect yellow diamond on the clear, black shiny surface. "There are more where that came from. Many more." I sank back to my seat.

He stared down in astonishment, and for the first time, emotion swept his face and greed showed clearly. "Ahhhh, canary, the yellow prize, rarest of the rare." After a long study, he whispered, "Where are the rest? The woman said she had a chain."

"They are in a safe place."

He gave an angry hiss, quickly suppressed. "They are not all with you, then?"

"Would I be that foolish? I am the only one who knows their hiding place. I found them after the earthquake."

"And you told no one?"

"Not yet."

His eyes slitted. "We need more tea, I think." He took my cup and poured. His hand hovered over the steaming liquid, then he pushed it back to me.

I took a gulp. "Where is Li Fong? I know he is part of this plot to kidnap Tad."

"There is no such person. Li Fong died many years ago."

"That's insane." My tongue felt fuzzy. "I've seen him w-working at Cliffside ev-every . . ." I pushed up from my chair. What was happening to me?

"Miss Blair, who sent you?"

"N-no one. I came on my own. Now l-let me see Tad . . ."

From a hollow distance, I heard him hiss, "I'm afraid we must detain you for a while. Please forgive the Tea of Bitter Dreams. I think you also will be a bargaining tool when we tell Mr. Wynfield that we must have the other diamonds first of all."

"I won't—you can't . . ." The room was going around. Lily entered and supported me out into the passageway. My feet stumbled and dragged, but Lily had surprising strength. At a distant wooden door, she pushed me forward and I fell painfully to my knees on a cold stone floor.

Through blurred vision, I discerned a small room almost bare of furniture, then the drugged tea worked its power and I sank into oblivion.

28

Water rushed and gurgled at my feet, the bank I stood on held a rich carpeting of tiny plants. What was this place? A garden? The countryside? Trees, sky, clouds . . . all swam in a misty haze.

"Lesley," whispered a well-known voice and I spun around.

Conan in a casual white shirt, hands resting on his hips, stared at me with a strange, tight smile. He advanced slowly and his hands reached out to clasp my bare arms. Hadn't I just been wearing a cape? How hard it was to think . . .

He put his face down close to mine. "Lesley, you must tell me where you've hidden the diamonds, then we can leave."

"Conan, Conan . . ." I collapsed against his chest. "Where are we? What are you doing here?"

"You know, Lesley. You must have guessed. However, I can't help you or Tad unless we have the diamonds. Now tell me!" He frowned and shook me.

"I don't know what you're talking about," I whimpered. "Please, please, take me home."

"You can't go home until we have the diamonds," another voice hissed nearby. "I think you are not succeeding, Mr. Blye."

Conan flung me to one side, and when I caught my balance, I beheld the Dragon Master holding Lily by his side. To my horror, she stood shamelessly unclothed.

"You—you're a singsong girl—a prostitute," I exclaimed.

"As you soon will be, too," Lily called in her high, light voice. She turned and pressed close to the mandarin, sliding her hands in the opening of his robe.

"Lily—stop!" And Jeremy strode across the grass, jerking the girl away from her old master. "You said you'd save your favors just for me!"

She flung back her waist-long hair. "Only if you have the money, dearest Jeremy. Ask her where she's put the diamonds."

They both stared at me and then Jeremy started walking forward. "Lesley, you don't want the diamonds. They don't belong to you—so tell me where they are. I'll give most of them back to Drake, I swear."

"Conan, help me," I cried. But he had vanished. Now there was only Jeremy in the glade. Until Rachel stepped out of the trees.

"Jerry, haven't you done enough?" she cried brokenly.

He looked at her indifferently. "I'm only helping out Li Fong." His eyes focused on someone behind me. "Isn't that correct?"

Li Fong's voice murmured in my ear. "I have long sought the jewel of jewels for my collection. Miss

Blair, if you give the information, all will go un-harmed, you, Tad, Jeremy, Rachel, and Conan.''

It was the Dragon Master. No. It was Li Fong! With a high-pitched laugh, he pealed off the dan-gling mustache and threw away his robes to stand before me in starched white tunic and black trou-sers.

I screamed and stumbled back just as another form emerged from the trees! It was Drake! His eyes glowed red with anger as he strode forward and grabbed me in a clasp of iron.

"You were right about Rose. She drove me to the brink of madness, rejecting both me and the dia-monds. And you thought I killed Melissa also, didn't you? *Didn't you?*"

He shook me so violently, a scream tore from my throat. Suddenly, they all were there, Conan, Jer-emy, Rachel, and Li Fong, staring malevolently, inching toward me. I felt a wave of terror, and as darkness overwhelmed me, Prince began to bark.

My eyes opened, and suddenly I remembered ev-erything before the Tea of Bitter Dreams. I was still locked away, just where Lily had put me. I saw a cot with mounded blankets, a table and a chair. No gar-den. No people. All a fevered fantasy.

Like a clear, cold wind, awareness of my plight swept over me. What madness, what reckless action had brought me to this terrible situation? I hadn't found Tad or worked out anything with his abduc-tors; and now Drake would also have to deal with the fact that I was a hostage, too.

I pushed up from the floor, no longer dizzy. The drug's effects had vanished but not my fears. I clutched my shivering arms. Would Tad and I be killed if Drake could not be found in time? Or would we both be carried to a ship bound for a secret, foreign port? I as a white slave pawn; Tad a victim of the vicious "crimping" in which kidnapped men and boys were forced to work at sea. Anything was possible!

I crept to the table, where the only light came from a grilled opening high above. It still was daytime, but I could hear no sounds of voices or conveyances. I must be underneath a deserted alley. Even so, I might attract some help. Hauling over the chair, I climbed atop the table and gripped and shook the bars—rigid as iron. My hand could slip through, that was all.

Flinging back my head, I screamed with all my might: "Help! Help! Police!"

At once, a wet tongue licked my fingers. Prince! A sob tore through my throat. "Prince—go—go get Drake!" He whined, he barked, but he didn't move.

However, there was movement elsewhere.

The blankets on the cot became a churning mass disclosing—Tad! He rubbed his eyes then sprang toward me. "Miss Lesley—oh, you've come for me! Oh, please, let's go!" He tugged frantically at my skirt. "I kept waking up and thinking I was dreaming."

I clambered down and tightly we embraced. "Oh, Tad dear, are you all right?"

"Yes, just sleepy. How—how did I get here? What is this place? I don't like it. Let's leave." His arms were almost choking me as I knelt upon the floor.

"Listen, dearest, we must stay calm. You were kidnapped from your bed last night by an evil person—I don't know who—but they sent a note wanting money from your father, then they will let you go."

Tad's voice quavered tearfully. "My papa will give it, won't he? And then we can go home?"

"Yes, of course he will. It won't be long."

"But you—how did you get here? Were you kidnapped, too?"

I told him then about discovering the diamonds and how I had tried to make a bargain with the Dragon Master. Tad's eyes grew enormous with a little pleasurable excitement. "Oh, Miss Lesley, you're the smartest, bravest person!" Then he sobered. "What do we do now?"

"Just—just wait, I guess."

Suddenly, Prince again announced his presence with a bark and a scrabbling on the grate. Tad cried out and leaped upon the table. "Oh, Prince, good dog—go get Papa. Get Drake, go!"

The dog seemed undecided, springing back and forth and whining. Prince might be compelled to go for Drake, but how could I send a message? I had no pencil or paper, no scarf or handkerchief . . . somewhere my reticule had been lost.

But wait! The bracelet given to me by Mr. Mills dangled as always from my wrist and Drake would know it in a minute. A small chance, but we were desperate. I explained my plan to Tad and exchanged places with him on the table.

"Oh, capital!" he shouted. "Papa will recognize the bracelet and Prince will lead him here."

"I hope so." Inwardly, I worried that someone else could steal the bracelet before any of our rescuers discovered it. On the other hand, Prince might not let a stranger take it from him. At least, that's what I prayed with all my soul.

Thrusting my fingers through the grille and speaking soothingly, I locked the clasp into Prince's collar. He shook his head and pawed at it while Tad and I waved and shouted over and over: "Go get Drake —go!" Finally, Prince backed off and disappeared from sight. If he was merely sitting nearby, we couldn't tell.

After that, Tad and I sat on the cot for a long time, huddled in the blankets, speculating, pondering the mystery. I thought uneasily about my dream. How much of it was truth? How much fantasy? *Who was the villain?* It seemed I had suspected everybody.

As the shadows lengthened and the room grew colder, Tad and I became more anxious, though trying not to show it. Tad said he was thirsty, and so was I, but there was no water in the room. Surely food and drink would be provided. They wanted us in good condition . . . didn't they?

When at last a sound came from the doorway, Tad and I sprang up, our hands clutched tightly. A key turned in the lock and slowly the door creaked open.

There stood Jeremy.

Tad sprang forward with a yell and grabbed him around the legs. "Oh, Uncle Jerry, you've come for us, haven't you? Did Papa send the money? I knew he would. Let's go right now!"

I stared at Jeremy uncertainly when he made no move to get us out. His eyes looked desperate and I noticed for the first time that the handsome face had grown haggard and pale, the mouth now weakly quivering.

Was he our villain? Why wasn't I more surprised?

He saw the speculation in my eyes and sighed. "I'm sorry, Lesley. You must tell me where you've put the other diamonds. It's your only chance. Drake can't be found and"—he swallowed and rubbed his chin with a shaking hand—"the Dragon Master doesn't have much patience."

He shoved Tad's clinging arms away and came toward me. "Believe me, Lesley, it's better to tell me now than have the Tongs question you."

Suddenly Tad screamed, "It was you—I remember now! There was darkness and shadows like in here, but I saw you jump off your horse and yell at Mama, telling her to stop. When she didn't, you threw a rock and hit her horse and—and . . ." His voice grew shrill with grief and fury. "You—you killed her a-and now you want to kill us, too!" Fists clenched, he tried to fling himself on Jeremy, but I caught and held him tightly.

"Tad, stop. Don't make things worse."

I looked up. "It was you all along, wasn't it? The highwayman? The attempts on Prince—the threat in the conservatory—the poisoned cake . . ." Tad struggled and cried out in fury.

"The cake—no. An accident." He flung out his hands. "The other things—well—I needed money. Drake had plenty. I've been looking for those diamonds for over a year, but my debts to the Tongs grew and grew. The night you and Drake first heard the flute, I spoke to the man in the garden before coming in, told him I couldn't pay. They had demanded that I kidnap Tad, but the dog was always there. I tried every other way to raise the money, really I did, including the stock market, but it all failed. They warned me again with the flute. I met their man in the garden and they told me how to do it, drops in the dog food, chloroform and—and . . ." Incredibly, he caught back a sob. "I didn't want to hurt anyone. Not Rose. I tried to cause an accident so I could get away before she told what she'd seen. It's not my fault, the Tongs made me do it. Lesley, for all our sakes, *where are the other diamonds?*"

When I didn't speak, his voice grew hoarse. "*Tell me!* You don't know what you're dealing with here. The Master only gave me a few minutes with you."

I was trembling in every limb; my voice cracked. "You'll let us go now if I tell you?"

"Well . . . no. You must wait until I get back with the stones."

He had left the door unlocked. Perhaps I had a chance. I pushed Tad away and swung the chair, but Jeremy ducked it and grabbed my arms, anger flaming in his face. He slapped me and I cried out with the pain. Tad lunged, fists flying. With a snarl, Jeremy thrust him backward on the floor, then he shoved me down onto the cot and kneeled above me, looking like a stranger, red-faced, panting.

"Since you want to play rough, you'll give me something else that I've been wanting from you. After a few minutes, I think you'll tell me where the diamonds are." His voice came out thick and slurred.

"The boy . . ." I choked out, terrified at this new threat.

"If he tries to interfere, I'll knock him senseless."

His breath was on my mouth, his hands gripping, tearing, squeezing everywhere he found my flesh uncovered. I jerked my face aside and gasped out, "The stones are in the Velvet Room sewed on the dolls."

Jeremy leaped up with a wild, triumphant cry and headed for the door.

Too late. The Dragon Master stood there with Li Fong at his side. *They'd beaten us.* I cringed back on the cot, pulling up my clothes, and Tad flew to my arms.

29

I would not give way to tears and screams. I rose with Tad pressed to my side and tried to firm my shaking voice. "Li Fong, I see, hand in glove with the arch villain of the Tongs. I suspected as much. What do you intend doing with us?"

Oddly enough, Li Fong laughed. "I have always admired your courage, Miss Blair, but this time you are wrong in your assumptions."

There was something different about the way he talked. Perfect English, no hissing.

My mind was whirling, and the next minute when Drake pushed through the doorway, unchallenged, I felt that I would faint. He caught me in his arms just as I realized the strangest thing:

Li Fong had a pistol aimed at both Jeremy and the Master.

The next few hours were a blur as police, surprisingly headed by Li Fong, poured into the underground passage while Tad and I were whisked away by Drake to Cliffside. It was not until Tad had been fed and put to bed by a distraught Mai, and I had washed and changed, that Drake and I could go over everything alone. Rachel, stunned and weary, drove down the hill to be with Jeremy. If she had ever suspected him, we never knew. A message was also sent to Conan at my shop, to whom all this would be the most astonishing news.

Now Drake drew me down beside him on the parlor sofa, kissing and stroking me, wanting to be assured over and over that I was all right. Finally, he began the explanations.

"I had been worried about the theft of the Jade Pagoda and the disappearance of Rose's chain. Actually, I suspected Jeremy or Rachel and even Conan, but I had no proof. Then I heard about a skillful Oriental man named Frank Li working for the Pinkerton Detective Agency in Chicago and I contacted him several months ago. He proved to be a cousin of the dead Li Fong, who had disappeared many years ago, probably a victim of the Tongs where he'd been active. Frank used to live in Chinatown and assumed the same name as his cousin."

"That explains why the Dragon Master told me that Li Fong was dead."

"I guess he had penetrated Li's disguise but was biding his time, not sure what Li was doing. The main thing was Frank's acceptance at the House of Singing Happiness, which was the headquarters of a ring that disposed of stolen objects."

"Oh, Drake, I saw the Jade Pagoda today in the secret room."

"Yes, Rose must have seen Jeremy in there selling it and so he killed her." Pain etched Drake's face, then he sighed. "At any rate, Frank says the Jade Pagoda can be returned to my shop."

"How did Frank Li find Tad and me?"

"We met at my shop soon after you left and the doorman gave us your message. We went to Chinatown, but had to be very careful not to alert your captors before we discovered your exact location. It was the dog who led us to the alley."

"Prince! Oh, how clever of him."

"I recognized the bracelet, of course. You were pretty clever yourself. Well, Frank summoned the police he knew while I stayed at the grille, keeping Prince from barking, and I heard Jeremy's confession. For a moment, Drake's voice roughened with emotion. "God, what a terrible thing that was to hear—first he attacked Rose, then you and Tad. Even though I suspected him of stealing, the full story was a shock. I would have knocked him to the ground if I'd been near him. After that, I headed for the rear door, and when Frank arrived, he had no trouble with the lock." Drake's voice shook a little and his arms tightened. "And so my dearest ones were saved."

We sat in silence for a while, a blissful silence, until suddenly, I exclaimed, "With everything that's happened, I forgot about Melissa. Did you find her?"

"Not exactly, but a letter from her arrived today at my shop. Would you care to hear it?" Without waiting for my eager answer, he drew a paper from his pocket and began to read:

" 'Dear Drake:
By the time you read this, I shall be on the train with Tom Warren, far away from this terrifying, miserable city. We are going back home to be married. I was afraid you would try to stop me so I

sneaked out in the night with all my clothes and Tom drove me away, as previously arranged after the quake. Before that, he came to the house demanding that I run off with him, saying it was the only way to ensure a happy future for us both. I knew that he was right. I regret that I must break your heart and hope you will forgive me. Perhaps at some distant time, you will love again. Just be sure to pick someone from your own class, not an independent, saucy working girl.' "

I gave a chuckle and Drake threw me a quick grin, "Listen, saucy girl, there's more:

" 'I hope you don't mind, but I'd like to keep the diamond ring as a memento of our brief, though doomed romance. Your former love, Melissa.' "

"Only the Jewel of Jamestown could have written that masterpiece. I have to say I'm glad she had nothing to do with this mystery—and that she's gone." I laughed. "Poor thing, have you recovered from your doomed romance?"

His eyes ran over me possessively. "I recovered the moment Melissa arrived at Cliffside. The comparison was too great. You, my beauty, drove every other woman clean out of my mind."

"Tell me all about it," I purred, nestling closer in his arms.

He bent his lips to mine. "Not now. There's a time for talk and a time for this."

After a successful demonstration, I heartily agreed.

Reckless abandon. Intrigue. And spirited love. A magnificent array of tempestuous, passionate historical romances to capture your heart.

Virginia Henley

☐ 17161-X	The Raven and the Rose	$4.99
☐ 20144-6	The Hawk and the Dove	$4.99
☐ 20429-1	The Falcon and the Flower	$4.99

Joanne Redd

☐ 20825-4	Steal The Flame	$4.50
☐ 18982-9	To Love an Eagle	$4.50
☐ 20114-4	Chasing a Dream	$4.50
☐ 20224-8	Desert Bride	$3.95

Lori Copeland

☐ 10374-6	Avenging Angel	$4.99
☐ 20134-9	Passion's Captive	$4.99
☐ 20325-2	Sweet Talkin' Stranger	$4.99
☐ 20842-4	Sweet Hannah Rose	$4.99

Elaine Coffman

☐ 20529-8	Escape Not My Love	$4.99
☐ 20262-0	If My Love Could Hold You	$4.99
☐ 20198-5	My Enemy, My Love	$4.99